WATCHED

C.L. Sutton

Copyright © 2025 by C.L. Sutton.

All rights reserved.

No portion of this book may be reproduced in any form without written permission from the publisher or author, except as permitted by U.S. copyright law.

Note to reader

Just F.Y.I. — The dog lives.
(I wouldn't do that to you.)

Chapter 1

CASTING CALL

LIFE-CHANGING OPPORTUNITY

URGENT CASTING CALL Revolutionary new reality competition seeks EXTRAORDINARY individuals for groundbreaking television program.

PRIZE FUND: £1,000,000

Are you:
✓ Facing impossible choices?
✓ Fighting for someone you love?
✓ Ready to change your family's future FOREVER?

This is NOT your typical reality show. We're looking for REAL people with REAL stories who need REAL solutions.

IMMEDIATE START REQUIRED ACCOMMODATION & MEALS PROVIDED WINNER TAKES ALL

Medical emergencies? Family crises? Crushing debt? WE UNDERSTAND. This could be your answer.

Strict confidentiality required. Background checks essential.

Apply NOW - Limited spaces available Applications close in 48 hours.

APEX ENTERTAINMENT PRODUCTIONS "Where life changes forever"

Victoria

Victoria pushes open the heavy door with heart-wrenching trepidation. A blast of beige and shades of brown assaults her as she steps inside the living room. It's like an office block has birthed a residential baby in here.

Her auburn hair tumbles across her face as she surveys the space, dark-ringed green eyes flickering with wander as she takes it all in.

The room before her is large, with furniture dotted around to create a functional space. The open-plan kitchen to her left is clinical whites and silvers and appears to contain gadgetry she cannot even comprehend. She hopes one of the other housemates can cook. It'll be nice not to survive on ready-meals and takeaway pizza for a change.

Her slender fingers with nails bitten down to the quick—a habit formed during long, stressful hospital visits—grip the locket at her throat. Her pulse thunders in her ears, the roar so loud it exacerbates the crushing silence around her.

It's too quiet. She knows from T.V shows that the mirror-lined walls hide a multitude of cameras, and panic floods every nerve ending. She moves further into the vast room in a poor attempt to walk off her paranoia. Running her fingers over every surface, she hopes the tactile sensation will soothe her alarm.

The air feels different here, like it's controlled and sterile, threaded with a subtle electrical hum beneath the sound of her heavy breathing. Camera lenses track her movements with precision, mounted where the walls kiss the ceiling. They whirr in unison as she moves. She notices that every piece of furniture is bolted to the floor. No sharp corners anywhere. Everything feels just slightly off from normal proportions—chairs too wide, tables too low, everything mimicking normality but not quite achieving it.

She exhales slowly. But no more scrubbing blood from under her fingernails. No more dragging herself from shift to shift as a nurse. No more living her life beneath the fluorescent lights of her daughter's hospital room. She can breathe again—just a little.

The realisation of what she's done washes over her, and she gasps, hands flying to her heart as she looks up at the ceiling.

"Lily!" she sighs sadly, regret pulsing through her. She remembers her last words to her little girl and forces her breath to calm. "We'll get through this." She repeats those words to herself, over and over. "We'll get through this."

Bolstered by memories of Lily waving goodbye with hope-filled eyes, Victoria takes a seat on the brown sofa facing the functional kitchen to the back of the room. To her right, she looks out of the five-foot tall windows into the fading daylight.

Outside sprawls a garden. It's vast and bare; boring yet practical. More of a field than a homely space. If it weren't for the vibrant green grass, she'd describe it more as a prison yard. Metal fencing cages the perimeter, towering at least ten feet high. And what is that? Barbed wire?

Her stomach tightens with unease.

She still cannot wrap her head around all of this. Somehow, she'd survived the auditions. She must have beaten thousands of people younger than her, prettier than her, funnier than her. People who actually belong in front of the camera.

No, the Landlord had chosen her.

The house is a huge contradiction. Warm yet hollow, welcoming yet without a soul. It's disorientating. She imagines, or hopes, that once more housemates have been thrust in here, that will change. The house will feel less hungry once full.

Victoria's pulse quickens at the prospect of meeting the other housemates. To get the show on the road. She's ready to tackle everything that's thrown at her. To charm the Landlord and win his favour. To impress the crowd on the outside and be the person they root for. Because at the end of the day, it's the strangers on the outside that decide her fate. They're the ones with the power to help her daughter.

Chapter 2

From: danny@castingcreations.com

To: Marty Todd

Subject: Opportunity for Comeback - Confidential

Marty!

It's been a long time! Hope you're doing well, mate. Heard through the grapevine you've been keeping clean - good for you.

Got an unusual opportunity that might interest you. New production company called Apex Entertainment Productions has reached out. They're casting for a reality competition show. They're specifically looking for musicians who've "been through the mill" - their words, not mine.

Here's what they said in their email:
Prize: £1 million. Duration: 2-6 weeks (depending on performance)

They said they want real people with real struggles. Apparently, there's a big appetite for comeback stories right now.

The money's legit - they've already got backing from some serious investors. Could be exactly the platform you need to show everyone that you're back.

So you interested? They want to move fast - filming starts next month. Let me know ASAP if you want me to put you forward.

No pressure but thought of you when they described what they were looking for.

Cheers, Danny

Marty

Entering the Landlord's house is an enormous risk for Marty, and he knows it. But when your back is so pressed against the wall, there's little left to worry about. Fuck it, he might as well give it a go. It's the only shot he's got.

The woman in front of him beams at him, though he notices she's twisting her hands together like she's trying to wring water from air. Her mouth is moving as she approaches.

Shit. She's talking. *To him.*

He bounces on the spot; his social autopilot finally kicks in. "I'm Mart. Sorry, I didn't catch your name. I was away with the fairies."

She giggles; it's a vibrant sound that unclenches something in his chest. "Victoria. So how you feeling? You look about as terrified as I feel." He notices her glancing at his arm, and he scratches it nervously.

Marty barks out a nervous laugh. "Terrified doesn't cover it. I'm so scared I might actually drop dead before they can vote me out. This is fucking mental!"

Victoria bristles, and Marty physically recoils as if she's slapped him. "Sorry, I swear a lot. I'll try to tone it down a bit, but I can't make any promises."

"As if I give a shit about a bit of swearing." She titters, brushing off his concerns with a flick of the wrist. Her voice softens. "I just don't like talking about death." She turns away. Marty doesn't press her. It feels far too soon to be venturing down such dark and intimate paths. "It's just hitting me in waves how crazy this whole thing is."

Marty nods. Victoria is cool. He thinks he'll get along with her just fine, and the tension in his chest loosens. Just a little.

The lights flicker for a heartbeat as the door swings open behind Marty, drawing Victoria's gaze over his shoulder. He turns to see what's captured her attention. She waves and chirps a cautious "hello" to the next housemate, who wanders in like she already owns the place.

"Evangeline," the newcomer declares, lifting the feathered train of her gown like she's ascending a red carpet. It's amazing she hasn't tripped over that thing. Marty has no eye for fashion, but he recognises money when it sashays toward him.

All cameras spin as they seek Evangeline's beautiful, porcelain face, bathing her beautiful figure in the attention she so blatantly craves. She looks around them, drinking it all in.

Victoria rushes forward and gives Evangeline a welcoming hug. Next to Evangeline's magazine-perfect polish, Victoria looks unkempt with her rumpled hair and clothes askew. Marty prefers Victoria. She's keeping it real.

The women embrace with all the warmth of old friends reuniting, Evangeline touching kisses on both of Victoria's cheeks, before Evangeline pivots to face Marty. "Nice to meet you!" she says, holding a manicured hand out to him. She grimaces, and Marty imagines she's trying really hard to keep the disgust off her face when she looks at him. He's never felt so grubby and dishevelled. He figures she doesn't usually hang around with skinny, bearded men in need of a shower.

Still, he's got to hand it to her, Evangeline fights through her judgements with ease as she takes his hand in hers and gives it a gentle shake.

He's crossed paths with girls like Evangeline before—more bothered about appearances than the brutalities of life. He's watched as that's come back to bite them in the arse more times than he'd care to count. The fall's always harder when you've built your world that high off the ground.

"Marty," he says simply.

Evangeline's eyes flick to the camera mounted just above their heads before pulling Marty in for a suffocating hug. "Oh, it's such a pleasure to meet you! How exciting is this?!" her voice is loud in his ear.

"Erm, yeah." He isn't in the mood for performance.

"So—" She releases him. "Where's the bar? I could murder a drink."

Marty drifts over to the kitchen, the two women in hot pursuit, where a bottle of something bubbly is sweating in its ice-bucket, condensation sliding down its neck. He pours two glasses of Prosecco and hands one to each of the women before filling his own glass with water, popping in a couple of ice-cubes from the bucket to give it a bit more glamour.

Keep busy. Keep moving. He just needs to keep his hands occupied and then maybe his brain won't have time to catalogue all the ways this could go sideways. It's a lie he's been telling himself since he read his old agent's email.

Time slips by as more housemates enter the house.

He's been watching his housemates make polite conversation, all forced smiles and careful conversation. Their masks pressed close to their skin.

Though if they're anything like Marty, it won't be long before their pretence slips to the ground. There's only so long you can fake your smiles before either your energy is depleted or your demons rip them off.

A young, timid girl slips in quietly. She's wearing a smart trouser-suit and a nervous smile. Marty remembers her name beginning with a C. Charlotte? Charlie? Something like that. After a brief introduction, she slipped into the background, clutching a can of Sprite Victoria found in the fridge.

After her, a larger woman called Susan enters the house. She has grey roots showing through her fire-engine red hair and a friendly demeanour, her garish polka-dot dress standing out amongst the bodies starting to fill the space.

Then comes Gloria. Christ, Gloria. Seventy-two-years-old wearing a gown of purple sequins and hair coloured the same hue, holding court like she's the Queen of England. She's been talking nonstop for twelve solid minutes without taking a breath. Though watching Evangeline fight for the spotlight Gloria has hijacked almost makes the migraine worth it.

An hour in and his terror hasn't budged. It's still there, coiled in his gut, ready to unleash itself at the slightest provocation.

Marty hates this. He wants to leave.

But he has nowhere to go.

Victoria

Despite Victoria's earlier confidence at having earned a place in the house, she's already cracking under the pressure.

Former bingo caller Gloria has held her hostage for over ten minutes now, droning on about her driver taking the long route here. According to Gloria, *people of colour have no business donning a jacket and cap. They're more suited to Uber. Shared fares for safety reasons.*

Her sequins catch the hundreds of spotlights, making her look like a walking disco ball. The effect is dizzying.

The effort of forcing conversation makes Victoria's breath catch in her throat. Her fingers find the locket, gripping it until the metal edges bite into her palm, a reminder of why she's here.

She spies Marty sitting apart from the growing group. God, what she wouldn't give to sink into that silence beside him, to nurse her drink without having to fake interest in Gloria's downright bigoted opinions.

Victoria is tired. A bone-deep weariness that feeds her terror of being here. The lengths she has gone to—the risks she has taken.

What the hell has she done?

To distract her from screaming, she internally assesses the rest of the housemates; who is competition, who is dead weight, and who will be an ally? Because failure isn't an option here. She's got to win this. There's no alternative. No Plan B.

Evangeline is on her third glass of Prosecco, and it's starting to show. Her cheeks are rosy, and her voice is high-pitched. She has already casually, not so casually, mentioned her famous boyfriend and her millions of followers.

Millions. The word sits in Victoria's chest like a stone.

If she's already that popular, why has she bothered to come here? Hasn't she got everything she wants already? Attention. Popularity. A pretty face that probably launched a thousand sponsorship deals. What more could a girl like Evangeline possibly ask for?

If only Victoria's life were that straightforward.

Jealousy twists through Victoria's stomach, forcing her teeth to clench and her knuckles to whiten around the glass stem.

Gloria cackles loudly from next to the now-black windows.

Evangeline has probably never had to fight for anything that mattered. Never sat in a hospital corridor at 3am, bargaining with a God she's not sure even exists. Never felt the ground crumble beneath her feet while the world kept spinning like nothing had happened.

Victoria needs to think strategically about this. Falling at the first hurdle isn't an option. Maybe Evangeline's fame is something Victoria can work with. She can fall into Evangeline's slipstream.

She needs to be clever about this, not emotional. She can't afford emotional.

Timid Charlie presses against her arm, still clutching the same can of fizzy drink. "Don't you get a weird feeling in here? Like our fates are already sealed and we're just dancing to some else's tune?" She gestures vaguely at the cameras.

Before Victoria can conjure up a response, the door opens once again, capturing her attention.

Victoria turns to see gnarled fingers curl around the door frame. A face appears. He's smiling and has eyes the colour of forget-me-nots. He looks so friendly she knows in an instant she's found an ally, and she can breathe again.

Chapter 3

CASTING CALL

MATURE PARTICIPANTS WANTED Ages 55+ Preferred
Established production company seeks interesting individuals for innovative reality television program.

We're looking for:
- Retirement-age participants with life experience
- Sharp minds and engaging personalities
- People who aren't afraid of a challenge
- Those seeking adventure in their golden years [CS1]

What we offer:
- Substantial financial rewards (£1M prize fund)
- Luxury accommodation during filming
- Chance to show younger generation what you're made of
- All expenses paid

This is NOT a typical reality show. We value wisdom, strategy, and life experience. Age is an advantage, not a limitation.

Duration: 2-6 weeks depending on performance Location: Luxury private facility Medical support: Full medical team on-site
Interested in proving that age brings advantages? Ready to show young people a thing or two?

APEX ENTERTAINMENT PRODUCTIONS
Serious inquiries only
Call: 0121-555-APEX Email: casting@apexent.co.uk

Background checks and medical clearance required

Henry

Wearing chinos and a plaid shirt that hang loosely on his diminutive frame, Henry has perfected the 'kindly grandfather' image. His thinning silver hair is neatly combed back to cover his pink scalp, and crow's feet crinkle at the corners of his watery blue eyes when he smiles. He doesn't let his age affect him—if anything, it's a tool to use. A method of manipulation. And Henry plays the part very well indeed.

It's a shame not more people could age like Henry, poised and accepting. The overbearing lady in garish purple has clearly taken a more distasteful approach—hiding her old age behind flamboyancy and pantomime. Her makeup a poor attempt at disguising the physical changes every human is blessed to go through should they reach the great heights of their seventies like Gloria and Henry.

Henry wears his years like a well-tailored suit. Gloria treats hers like a dirty secret.

"Hello everybody," he calls out, his voice carrying that well-practised warmth of someone who has spent decades charming his clients seeking his accountancy advice. A chorus of voices calls back, voices overlapping, each clamouring to introduce themselves.

Henry doesn't catch a single name, but he brushes away the bedlam with a chuckle as he takes everything in.

His gaze snags on a quiet girl pressed against the far wall. She's staring at the floor as if it might swallow her whole; her lips are moving as if she's talking under her breath. Henry smiles to himself and grants himself ten seconds of drinking in her image.

He's missed his little Charlie.

He returns his focus to the crowd and works the room—shaking hands, accepting a glass of Prosecco, and settling himself in for the ride. Because there's nothing more fun than chaos.

When he saw the advertisement in the Guardian for the auditions, he jumped at the chance. At his age, everyday thrills are hard to come by, and this one seemed like a lot of fun.

Then when he overheard Charlie had auditioned—well, that was just the icing on the cake.

A squeal captures his attention. It's the blonde wearing the most exquisite floor-length red silk gown; she has an air about her that makes every hair on his body stand on end. She's talking to a hollow-eyed man who is scratching himself. Henry supposes he is in his late twenties and yet is someone who looks like he's had more than his fair share of hard times.

This woman though. She's magnificent. An angel in designer clothing. She knows exactly what she wants, and she'll make sure she gets it. No matter what.

Fascinating.

He fixates on her ruby-red lips.

A friendly voice cuts through his reverie. "How are you doing?"

He turns to find a plain-looking woman studying him with tired green eyes. She's clutching a locket at her throat like it'll anchor her to whatever loved one is pictured inside it. The poor thing looks like she's bitten off more than she can chew here.

"Oh, mustn't grumble," he says, letting his voice carry that gentle, self-deprecating warmth that's served him so well over the decades. "It's a bit of a shock to the system, isn't it? One minute you're sitting on your couch drinking a nice cup of tea, the next you're living with a bunch of strangers and being broadcast across the world."

"I'm Victoria," she laughs. It's a pleasant, tinkly sound, pleasant on the surface, but Henry notices the sad undertone. He sees her. He has always had a knack for sensing vulnerability.

"Henry."

"And what brings you here, Henry?"

"Oh, you know, life tends to get a little dull when you get to my age. The highlight of my day was popping to the post office!" He smiles sadly. "So I was just hoping for a little more excitement. You?"

But Victoria's shoulders slump. "I'd love a little more *dull* in my life." She sounds so tired, so dejected, like life has thrown her too many punches and she's just done with it.

He looks at her through watchful eyes. There's a deep sadness to this woman, a simmering fire that Henry cannot wait to see what will happen to the house when it starts to rage.

Gloria laughs raucously nearby, making Henry's insides shrivel up and die a little.

"You know what? I'd love a cup of tea. I've never been one for Prosecco." She abandons her half-empty glass and hiccups softly as if to prove a point.

"Well, how about you and I try to hunt down a kettle? There must be one around here somewhere. They'd never be so cruel as to deny us a proper drink." He goes to shuffle away, his new brogues digging into his feet.

The door bursts open, and suddenly it's as if the room has shrunk. A man fills the doorframe, his broad shoulders straining against his paisley designer shirt. Makeup has settled into his laughter lines, and he has a jawline that could cut glass.

"Wahey!" he bellows, demanding everyone's attention. He swaggers forward, his gold rings catching the harsh light of the spotlights overhead. He isn't just entering a room; he's claiming it.

Henry recognises that face from every checkout queue in Britain—splashed across tabloids next to headlines about sex scandals and weekend drug binges. Unless you've been living under a rock, everyone knows Jack Cowley.

Jack doesn't listen to a single housemate as introductions are made; his attention has already wandered south of Evangeline's neckline. The man's practically salivating.

Dirty boy. Henry allows himself a private smirk.

"Don't I know you?" Evangeline purrs from her perch on the kitchen counter. "Hey, you're that celebrity chef guy, aren't you? The one with the show on the telly."

"The one and only!" Jack preens, puffing out his chest.

Henry scoffs, barely disguising his cringe at Jack's brazen ego. As the youths in his office would have said—'what a knob'.

<u>Marty</u>

There's someone standing outside the entrance to the house. Marty can't explain how he knows; it's probably some sixth sense developed on the harsh streets, but he can sense it. There's definitely someone outside the door.

Everyone around him is immersed in mundane conversation, and Marty spins around hoping someone else will take the lead and see who's lurking out there.

No one does, so he drifts toward the door, weaving between extravagant theatrical gestures and Gloria's expanding personal space. His hand hovers over the door handle. Is he allowed to open the door to the entrance corridor?

Marty has read the rules. They explicitly stated that housemates are not to try exiting the house. Does this count as leaving? Because he isn't leaving, he's helping someone in.

He doesn't want to break any rules—he's done with breaking the rules. He knows what mess it can lead to.

"Jesus Christ. How long have you been standing there, mate?"

The man on the other side looks as if he's been carved from marble. His muscles are so huge he looks like he could bench press a small car. Dark hair perfectly styled to look effortless. A wonky smile that's endearing and warm. He's undeniably beautiful.

But there's something deer-in-the-headlights about his expression, like he's just realised he's wandered onto the wrong TV show.

Marty blinks. Did this guy think he was auditioning for Love Island instead?

"Sorry, just taking a minute to myself. Before... well, you know."

Marty's smile is grim but genuine. Oh, he knows all right. Before he enters the lion's den. Before he is zoomed in on by a thousand cameras. Before he's picked apart by people all over the world.

"You all right?"

The man swallows and nods. "Yeah, let's do this. I'm Gaz, by the way." He offers Marty a spectacular smile—straight, white teeth and a cheerful glow to his face. The bastard's an Adonis.

"Marty."

Gaz steels himself and straightens up, adding another three inches to his frame. Gone is the look of terror and the worried hunch of his shoulders. Gone is the uncertain man hiding behind the door. Instead stands a man radiating confidence, covered in a shroud of hopeful optimism.

It's such a contrast to the man cowering in the corridor outside.

The performance is flawless.

Marty wonders what else these people might be hiding.

Chapter 4

@DarkWatcher_2019: Finally something worth the subscription fee. These idiots have no idea what they signed up for.

@PayPerView: £500 well spent already. The nurse looks like she'll crack first.

@VIPMember_Gold: When does the real fun start? This is boring.

@Anonymous_Whale: @Producer - I paid £50k for premium access. Hope you're planning something special soon.

<u>Victoria</u>

Nine housemates sit nervously on the sofas. An odd collection of misfits and wannabes.

Victoria watches Jack with disgusted awe as he talks whilst chewing Pringles. She can't take her eyes off the beige slop working its way around his mouth.

By his side and looking impossibly small is Charlie, and Victoria wonders if she's been secretly crying in the toilet.

Sitting next to Charlie is Henry, who appears to be practically vibrating with excitement.

Then, the last in the row is Susan, who was last to enter the house just minutes ago. She's sitting quietly with her eyes closed as if meditating, though her calm composure is betrayed by her loud red polka-dotted dress and matching court shoes. Victoria likes Susan. She seems friendly and warm, someone Victoria would like to get to know.

Victoria finds herself pressed against Evangeline, who's draped across her like they're longtime friends instead of strangers who met just a couple of hours ago. Evangeline's head lolls against Victoria's shoulder. She's probably regretting the pre-entry bottle of wine she'd boasted about having in the car on the way here, especially stacked on top of the Prosecco she poured down her neck after she walked in.

Victoria holds her breath against the cloud of expensive perfume emanating from Evangeline. It sits in her throat like syrup. It's suffocating.

"I couldn't believe it!" Gloria exclaims even though no one appears to be listening anymore. "I'd paid half the price in the sale the week before. Why should I pay full price now?"

Victoria tunes her out.

To add to everyone's nerves, Marty keeps popping up and down like a jack-in-the-box, hovering for a second before shifting positions and sitting in a different seat entirely. His eyes constantly dart around the room, taking everything in. Like a caged animal thrown among the wolves.

"Chill out, mate. You're making me anxious," Gaz murmurs, now sitting beside him. His fingers brush Marty's wrist in solidarity. Victoria can see a budding friendship there. It's sweet. The public will love a bromance. Though the way Marty blushes—maybe there's something else there. Something romantic.

Victoria knows alliances are crucial to surviving this, and she gives Evangeline's hand a strategic squeeze. Evangeline looks up at her, doe-eyed, her cream skin luminescent and her atrociously long lashes brushing the tops of her cheeks. Even drunk, she's stunning.

It has been an incredibly long and emotional day, and feeling unbearably tired, Victoria smothers a yawn. Pain is tiring, and right now her heart is in agony. She longs to just go to bed and put today behind her. Saying goodbye to her daughter this morning carved something out of her chest. She would give anything for a locked door and a dark room, somewhere to let her composure slip and plan her next move.

Just as her muscles are finally relaxing, the speakers overhead burst into life with a voice that seems to come from every corner of the room. *This is the Landlord. Welcome to my house.*

He sounds authoritative and stern, the voice of someone able to seduce you into submission—or scare you into it. Victoria smiles to herself, despite everything.

Gloria gasps and practically launches herself off the sofa with excitement, still desperate to be the centre of attention. Henry chuckles and gives Charlie a conspiratorial nudge, who appears too frightened to notice. He glances sideways at her lack of response, sits upright, and bites the inside of his cheek as if chewing on his pride.

Could a housemate please collect the package from the hatch immediately?

Evangeline springs into action, tottering on high heels as she makes her way to the labelled hatch on the wall by the entrance. She tugs on a latch, and the door drops open with a clang. A stack of whiteboards slides out, and Evangeline hugs them protectively to her ample chest.

"What the fuck is that?" Jack demands, running his fingers through his suspiciously thick hair. The harsh lighting isn't doing his plugged hairline any favours.

As you know, upon entering my house, you agreed to abide by my rules. The first and most fundamental being: you must do as instructed. Failure to do so will result in punishment. Well, this is your first task. Each of you will receive a board and a pen.

Victoria's stomach clenches. Already? Did they have to throw them into the deep end so soon? As if entering the house wasn't hard enough tonight.

Evangeline compliantly hands out the boards with a flourish to each housemate. Victoria looks at the clean whiteboard with dread.

The task is simple. On your board, you're to write the name of the housemate you like the least.

Gasps and calls of shock ring out around the U-shaped seating. Victoria's eyes widen. So soon? They've barely exchanged pleasantries, let alone formed real opinions, and now they're to tell everyone who they don't like? Ouch. She scans the room, catching everyone else doing the same frantic calculation.

"Well, this is stupid. How are we supposed to decide that already?" Jack blusters, though he cannot disguise the glint in his eye. He knows exactly what name to write on his board.

Housemates, you have ten seconds.

Ten seconds. Victoria's mind races. This isn't about who she actually dislikes—it might be cruel, but it's about who poses the biggest threat, who she can sacrifice without losing potential allies. Her fingers close around the pen as if it's a weapon.

A countdown timer booms from the speakers, sending a shockwave of horror through the group.

Evangeline straightens beside her with startling clarity. Her pen moves across the board with one decisive stroke. Just like that. Her mind made up with ease.

Victoria stares at her in horrified fascination. Either Evangeline's already identified her biggest threat, or she's the kind of person who makes brutal decisions as easily as choosing what to wear.

Maybe both.

Victoria catches Marty's eye across the room. He shrugs at her, perplexed, the pen still capped in his hand. Beside him, Gaz is staring at the ceiling as if divine intervention is going to give him the answer. He finally shakes his head and writes something down, his face twisted in disgust.

One by one, boards flip face-down onto laps. Some with more confidence than others. Susan, the woman dressed in polka dots, places hers down with a theatrical flourish, pleased with herself. Victoria remembers Susan's a high-school teacher. Maybe Susan gets kicks out of abiding by the rules.

"Good grief. Well, isn't this putting a spanner in the works?" Henry's voice cuts through the tension like a blade. A few people chuckle, offering Victoria a little encouragement. She pops the cap off her pen and places the nib on the board.

The ticking timer speeds up, each beep hammering at Victoria's skull, jolting her into action. She writes a name.

Marty

The sofa feels like rock under Marty's arse, every cushion conspiring to make him more uncomfortable. He's caught between bolting for the door and diving behind the sofa to hide from these people.

Housemates.

Because that's what these people are now. The word sits strangely in his mouth, though there's something liberating about it. These people know nothing about his history—about the mistakes he's made in Liverpool. Where labels are made and hard to shrug off. Where people take pride in taking people down.

For the first time in months, he can breathe without worrying who might be lurking around the next corner. These strangers might judge him, but at least they're all starting from zero.

Marty is sick of running, playing hide and seek with his dealer. Even if he doesn't win the money to pay what he owes, at the very least he's had a much-needed reprieve from the hell his life has become.

Could Charlie stand up and show everyone the name written on your board and the reasons why this person is your least favourite housemate?

Charlie stands, her suit now wrinkled, and wobbles as if she might topple over before catching herself.

Now here's an oddball. A smile plays on Marty's lips as Charlie brushes off her embarrassment and pushes her hair out of her face. She knocks the microphone clipped to her collar and panics.

"Well, isn't this a plot twist," she mutters, still refusing to meet anyone's eyes. It's painful to watch, and Marty longs to crawl under the sofa to hide from his secondhand embarrassment.

Her voice is so quiet everyone leans in to hear her better. "I've chosen this person because there's something about them that puts me on edge." Charlie glances at Marty, and Marty fears the worst. "Sorry, no offence, but it's you, Marty. It's not that I don't like you; I just don't know you well enough yet."

Her words sting. *Something about him.* Christ. Does he really wear his sins so openly?

Marty looks up at her and nods. "No worries, we'll be friends in no time."

Why do people insist on claiming 'no offence' nanoseconds before saying something offensive? Like it's supposed to soften the blow. Like you can gut someone alive as long as you offer that disclaimer first.

It's Victoria's turn next. As she stands, the scent of fabric softener wafts through the room, and Marty is reminded of his mum. Excruciating pain twists around his heart. He misses his parents so deeply.

"This was really difficult," she says, failing to meet anyone's eye. Her fingers dance around the edge of her board. "But I'm sure you all feel that too." Evangeline grunts impatiently. "Anyway, I've voted for this person purely because we haven't gelled yet. Though I'm in no doubt that we will in time."

She looks sombre as she turns her board around. "Sorry, Gloria."

Gloria huffs and stands without being instructed. "Well, that's funny because I've picked you. I just don't like the way you look at me."

"How do I look at you?"

"Like that!" Gloria gestures at Victoria's face and looks around the room for confirmation. Silence follows, and Gloria opens her mouth to argue.

Could Susan please stand and give your vote?

One by one, they make their way around the group and, to Marty's relief, a clear pattern starts to emerge.

Finally, it's Henry's turn to cast the final vote. He stands up.

Henry

Henry is having a fabulous time. They have all revealed their votes. Tears have been shed, protestations wailed. It's simply wonderful entertainment.

The woman in the red dress—Evangeline—has just cast her vote and sealed someone's fate. They have collectively decided their least favourite housemate. Which means Henry's choice is deliciously irrelevant.

He can feel Charlie's body warmth next to him, and it bolsters his desire to have a little fun. And that's why he surreptitiously changed the name on his board.

Henry likes games; he likes to throw a spanner in the works. There's an art to chaos, and Henry considers himself something of an expert. The way people's faces twist when you introduce the unexpected—it's exquisite.

He looks at his housemates gravely. "This was no easy decision. We all have so much to learn about each other!" He sighs, glancing down at the board pressed to his chest. Ink has marked his shirt, and he has to swallow his irritation. "But, that said, there's one person in here that we all know better than anyone else. And I, for one, don't care for what the press have been saying." He pauses, savouring his moment in the spotlight. "For that reason, I have voted for..." Henry turns the board around to face the group. "Jack."

The name hangs in the air. Jack's cocky swagger deflating like a punctured balloon.

Perfect.

Henry doubts whether there's anyone in the country who has missed Jack's scandal. Jack Cowley, celebrity chef caught with his trousers down, literally, hosting orgies with prostitutes in his Manchester restaurant. Also famous for having an explosive temper that's hospitalised a few of his workers in the restaurant. And it's *that* what Henry would like to see.

Jack holds it together admirably well. Nodding gently, he looks Henry straight in the eye. "Fair enough. Though I'm here to show the real me and prove those bastard reporters got it wrong. Though I hate to break it to you, Henry, it looks like I'll live to fight another day just yet."

His words are softly spoken, but Henry spots the vein pulsing on his neck, the tense lower jaw, and the white knuckles still gripping his pen. He smiles at Jack, a full, toothy grin.

The pen snaps in two.

There it is.

Gloria, you have been voted least liked housemate.

Gloria rushes off to the garden, crying. Henry would feel bad for her, but there's nothing worse than a condescending, brash narcissist. She deserved it.

Victoria

Thank God that's over. Victoria knows that this is just the beginning. Things are only going to get harder in here. But once this task is done, she can finally go to bed, and maybe eight hours of unconsciousness will better prepare her to face what's ahead. She's survived round one. That has to count for something.

Ten minutes pass painfully slowly. The Landlord is playing with their patience, and Victoria could cry.

Could one housemate please gather the writing materials and place them back in the hatch?

No one moves. Evangeline's soft snores drift from Victoria's shoulder. Victoria shifts away and begins gathering the scattered pens and boards.

"Is that it?" polka-dot Susan pipes up. "Well, that's a bit of an anticlimax."

The room bursts into chatter. Everyone discussing the vote.

Gloria eventually returns and resumes sitting in the corner of the sofa in stunned silence. Victoria feels a stab of sympathy and hands her a box of tissues she found in the humongous pantry at the back of the kitchen. Gloria snatches the box without a word, wiping Victoria's sympathy away. There's only so much sorrow she can give to someone when her vote was cast in the same direction.

So Victoria busies herself making herself and Gaz a hot drink. Her eyes keep flitting to the light on the wall that presumably changes to green once the door to the bedroom is unlocked.

She desperately wants this day to end.

"Thank you," Gaz, the hulk, says, accepting the coffee with a dazzlingly cheeky grin.

"No worries. I don't know how you can drink coffee at this time of night. I'd be bouncing off the walls all night."

"Night owl," he tells her, taking a sip. "Though I'll still be up at the crack of dawn."

"Doesn't that make you feel like shit?"

"Probably. I've always barely slept though. It used to drive my parents crazy."

Something in his tone makes Victoria pause. There's weight behind those words, like he's carrying more than just caffeine-fuelled insomnia.

She asks him, "What made you audition?"

"The usual. Exposure, fame, money." He takes another sip, his eyes not leaving hers. "I want to be an actor. A proper one, in the movies. But you've got to start somewhere, haven't you?"

Victoria raises an eyebrow. Gaz definitely looks like he belongs on the screen—that smile alone could launch a thousand casting calls. But there's something fragile about him. Like he's been dulled down and lost his sparkle.

"Though I suppose you're not here for those reasons?" he asks, studying her with interest.

"Well..." Victoria hesitates. Not yet—it's too late to be getting into her story. "I'm just a nurse looking for a little excitement."

"A nurse?! Wow, someone with a little substance has entered the house."

Victoria's laugh dies in her throat as the lights cut out, plunging them into pure, impenetrable darkness.

Evangeline whimpers. Henry shushes her kindly. "Don't fret. Just a technical glitch. I'm sure we'll be back up and running soon." His voice drifts as if he's moving.

"Nobody move," Jack calls out. "You might trip and hurt yourself."

"Good job he's here," Gaz mutters close to Victoria's ear. "I never would've thought of that."

There's a scraping sound over by the door, which quickly gets lost amongst the nervous chatter and Evangeline's escalating sobs.

"Did you hear that?" Victoria whispers to Gaz, who has moved closer to her side, his warmth reassuring.

"Hear what? I can't make out anything over Evangeline's theatrical crying. And the Oscar goes to…"

Victoria snorts.

The lights slam back on, and everyone clasps their hands over their eyes, blinking like moles dragged into daylight.

Victoria's vision clears first.

She scans the room. Something's off. Something's missing.

The corner space on the sofa is vacant. "Where's Gloria?"

"She was just there!" Charlie gestures.

All eyes turn to the spot where Gloria should be.

Victoria steps closer. There's a spot on the floor. Three droplets not yet absorbed into the carpet.

Three small splashes of crimson red.

Blood red.

Chapter 5

<u>Victoria</u>

Evangeline's screams rip through the air behind Victoria, making her whole body violently jolt. The sound is raw and pitiful as she steps backwards, her designer gown tangling around her legs. Gaz catches her smoothly, and sets her upright, before putting some distance between himself and the hysteria.

Smart man.

Victoria's gaze finds Marty across the room. He appears to be whispering "what the fuck?" repeatedly—a prayer for answers. His face is drained of colour. "Maybe she's gone for a piss?" He calls out. But Charlie puts a stop to that theory by putting her head around the toilet door and shaking her head.

The red light is still shining above the bedroom door. It's still locked. Besides, Victoria would have felt Gloria pass by her.

"Well?!" Jack booms over Evangeline's wailing. He storms towards the camera dangling from the ceiling above the stovetop. It's facing away from the crowd. Jack jabs it with his finger. "Landlord! Care to tell us what is going on?"

The camera doesn't move. The eyes of the robot appear to be turned off.

Jack wheels around to face the group. He scans everyone with probing eyes. One by one, he counts them off with furious scrutiny. "One of you must know where she is," he says accusingly.

Victoria glances around, half expecting to find Gloria crouched behind the sofa, overcome with shock. She's nowhere to be seen. Her eyes are drawn back to the blood that has now seeped into the carpet, creating a larger blob. Did someone cut themselves earlier? Victoria can't recall.

Susan is pressed against the wall like she's trying to melt into the plaster, silently mouthing something to herself, her eyebrows raised. She closes her eyes. "I hate blood," she mutters to the surrounding air. "Can't stand it. Makes me go all funny."

Evangeline cries louder now, but Victoria catches her stealing glances at the cameras through her tears. Even in a crisis, she's checking her angles.

Henry takes a seat on the sofa, with the calm of someone sitting down to watch The Antiques Roadshow. He folds his hands neatly on his lap whilst he eyes the blood through narrowed eyes, head tilted. He's the only one who looks remotely unfazed about the situation.

Being a nurse, Victoria has seen her fair share of blood. The initial appearance may have shocked her, but she reminds herself—this cannot be real; it's just a silly prop. She can practically see the social media explosion happening right now—screenshots, theories, hashtags trending within minutes.

She approaches the sticky mess with professional detachment, reminding herself it's probably corn syrup and food colouring. This is just a sick task dreamed up by the Landlord to freak them out.

"Careful," calls Gaz, unnecessarily—Victoria wasn't exactly planning on bathing in the stuff! She waves him back.

"Well, it certainly smells real enough," she says, her heart sinking at the realisation. The copper tang is unmistakable.

Gaz drops to his knees beside her, and she is pathetically grateful for the company. Even with years of stressful A&E experience, this whole strange experience has rattled her more than she'd like to admit.

Her fingers find the locket hanging from her neck, and she squeezes it tightly, soothed by the cool, heavy metal in the palm of her clammy hand.

"Is it definitely human though?" Gaz asks, his voice cutting through her spiralling thoughts.

Now there's a thought. Victoria had been clinging to the stage prop theory until that metallic tang slammed into the back of her throat, stripping away that comfort. She's so sure that this is actual blood, but maybe Gaz might be onto something.

"You think this could be animal blood?"

"It's got to be, right? Pig? Beef?"

"Beef?" Victoria lets out a shaky laugh. "Don't you mean cow?"

"Oh yeah, sorry, my head is messed up." He rubs his face with his massive hands.

Someone appears on Victoria's other side, bringing the smell of pipe smoke and peppermint. Henry. "What's the verdict?" he asks.

He seems to be the only one unaffected by all this. Victoria studies his weathered face and wonders what his history is. She'd heard him mention being a retired accountant, but his sense of calm may come from a medical past or perhaps the military. Though he doesn't look the type. He's too unimposing.

"It's definitely blood. Has Jack got into the Confessions Room yet?"

Henry chuckles. "Not yet, can't you hear him ranting at the door?"

The Confessions Room is where housemates can speak directly to the Landlord in confidence. Victoria has wandered down the corridor and poked her head inside but is yet to take up the Landlord's offer of him being her confidante.

Victoria tunes back into her surroundings to catch Jack's furious yelling. His palms are pressed against the wooden door as if he can push it open. It's a sliding door.

"It's not real," Susan calls to him. "It can't be real. None of this makes any sense."

"It's real," Gaz confirms, taking Victoria's hand to help her stand. "It's blood. But we think it's probably animal blood."

"So we are assuming Gloria's been evicted?" Henry asks, failing to disguise the same pleasure Victoria is experiencing. The house already feels less claustrophobic without Gloria's voice filling every space and every gap in conversation.

"This wasn't part of the plan though," Susan insists, catching Victoria's eye with a look of pure panic. "The Landlord wouldn't do this. This is too messed up, even for reality TV."

Victoria can only shrug. What's she supposed to say? There's only one person who knows what's going on. She looks to the speakers as if they'll reveal the Landlord's secrets.

They don't.

Henry

Henry returns to his perch on the sofa, a picture of poise amidst the surrounding chaos.

He cannot take his eyes off the blood. "Oh my," he murmurs, adjusting his glasses as if examining a mildly interesting museum exhibit rather than a potential crime scene. "This does look rather concerning, doesn't it?"

To anyone watching casually, he's just a harmless old man trying to make sense of an upsetting situation. But if they were to look closer, they would notice how his pupils dilate slightly as he inhales deeply, savouring something about the moment.

His eyes light up when Charlie emerges from the garden looking transformed. She's now practically bouncing around with a skip to her step and a light behind her eyes that wasn't there before. She's positively chirpy.

Fascinating.

"Gloria isn't out there," she announces with startling confidence. "So, what have I missed?" Her posture has completely changed; her spine is straighter, her movements more fluid and assured. It's like watching someone shed their skin and emerge as an entirely different species.

"Absolutely nothing," Marty croaks. The poor lad is having a hard time. Sweat is running down the side of his face, and his eyes appear unfocused. He looks ready to bolt. Or collapse.

Gaz moves over to him, and Henry watches with mild interest as he places a hand on Marty's shoulder. He whispers something in his ear. A reassurance by the looks of Marty's loosening shoulders.

Henry watches with glee. Because unlike everyone else, Henry came prepared. It turns out getting information on your fellow housemates only costs a couple of hundred pounds slipped into the right person's hand.

He knows a thing or two about his housemates. Like how Marty lost his boyfriend to an overdose just over a year ago. And how Gaz might just be his type.

And as for Jack? Well... Henry turns his attention to him and is overjoyed to find that Jack has spied the tender moment between the two men. His eyes turn dark, just for a moment, before he actively removes the scowl from his face. He's playing the game well. Scrubbing away the tabloid stains and hiding who he truly is to get people to like him. Jack's got a point to prove, and Henry cannot wait to see him crumble under the pressure.

He diverts his attention to Evangeline who is crying on Susan's shoulder. Susan doesn't look best pleased about Evangeline's tears spoiling her revolting dress. Henry notices Evangeline's makeup hasn't smudged; it's either incredibly waterproof or her tears are as fake as her drawn-on eyebrows. Evangeline's a beautiful lady; there's no denying it, but from Henry's experience, beauty on the outside rarely corresponds to what is on the inside.

He catches Susan's eye, and something inside her seems to snap.

"That's enough." Susan's sharpness startles Evangeline. "I need to speak with the Landlord." She shoves Evangeline off her and stands up before marching over to the Confessions Room. "Right, let me in now, Landlord. We need to talk." Her knuckles rap against the door with schoolteacher authority.

"Let me in!" She says, louder this time. The door remains stubbornly locked, so she kicks it with enough force to rattle the frame.

"Now, now, come on," Henry says, approaching her with palms facing out. "I'm sure we'll get answers soon enough. This is probably some sort of mission."

"Task," Susan corrects him. "They're called tasks."

"Yes, of course. *Task*. Why don't I make a nice cup of tea? Nothing like a proper brew to settle everyone's nerves."

"Everyone except Gloria," Jack mutters. He's deliberately moved as far as possible from Marty and Gaz, who have claimed the stools by the breakfast bar. Marty looks noticeably less panicked than before. Gaz has done a marvellous job of soothing him.

"Well, yes, Gloria isn't here," Henry agrees, bustling into the kitchen. "But there'll be a perfectly reasonable explanation. I'm sure she was simply evicted."

Privately, he rather hopes Gloria isn't coming back in some sort of dramatic reappearance. He's rather enjoying the relative peace, even Evangeline's sobs are better than Gloria's narcissistic monologues.

"This is an awesome task," Charlie cuts in, and the entire room turns to look at her, stunned. Her eyes are lit up, arms spread wide, inviting everyone to look at her. She's come alive.

Blood does the most curious things to people.

Henry would know.

The silence that follows is deafening. No one has the courage to say anything. Or maybe they're as perplexed as he is at this sudden display of enthusiasm. He's seen this before of course, but it's still disconcerting to watch at close range.

He flicks the kettle back on.

This is the Landlord. The bedroom is now open. Goodnight housemates.

The speakers emit a strange static for a moment—almost like the house itself is drawing breath—before cutting off completely.

The Landlord's final words create a grateful buzz amongst the housemates as they look at each other with trepidation. What the hell just happened?

Isn't the Landlord going to acknowledge the massive elephant in the room? It'd be nice if the Landlord would confirm Gloria's eviction to put their minds at ease. Is this part of the game?

The situation has worked up quite an appetite in Henry, so he returns his attention to the kitchen and plucks a packet of Digestive biscuits from the cupboard.

He arranges them on a plate with careful concern, each one positioned just so, a smile playing on the corners of his mouth.

"Now then," he says, turning back to his traumatised housemates, "who would like a biscuit?"

<u>Marty</u>

Despite shivering from the adrenaline coursing through his body, Marty is hot. The kind of hot that makes you want to crawl out of your skin. The kind of hot that makes sweat bead from every pore and soak your shirt until it clings like a second skin.

Henry appears at his elbow, offering him the plate of perfectly arranged biscuits. Marty declines. Food right now would come straight back up. Though, if Charlie's transformation is anything to go by, maybe it'd help him.

She's been buzzing ever since she reappeared from the garden, pupils wide as saucers and energy crackling off her. Something he knows all too well.

"Bedtime snack?" Henry asks.

He waves Henry away. "No thanks, mate, I think I should just get some sleep."

"Of course, perfectly understandable. Get some rest. I'm sure this will all make a bit more sense in the morning."

"Sure hope so, mate." He can't bring himself to meet Henry's eyes. Something about this old man's behaviour frightens him. It's cold, yet wrapped up in friendly gestures to appear warm. Marty doesn't like it.

Henry turns to offer Victoria the plate. She picks one up and takes the tiniest nibble. "Do you think we should clean that up?" She motions at the blood stain.

"Absolutely not," Henry tells her, taking a biscuit for himself, his eyes drifting to the red smudge on the floor. "That's not our mess."

Marty couldn't agree more. He can only assume the production team put that there to mess with their heads. They can clean it up.

He wonders what reaction their Landlord was expecting from his housemates. Panic? Tears? Were they supposed to kick off? Maybe they expected someone to get excited and finger paint with it. The things people do for views these days is absolutely mental.

Marty can only hope the landlord got what he wanted from tonight's performance. He *really* doesn't want them to have to step things up a notch to make the performing monkeys dance faster to his tune. He's not sure he has the strength for that.

He cannot take any more and disappears into the bedroom. He stops dead and blows an impressed whistle through his teeth.

"Saved you a bed over here," Gaz responds from the other side of the room. He's already stripped down to his underwear and is lounging on his claimed bed.

The bedroom is painted deep purple with gold fixtures that should clash horribly but somehow work. Plush cream bedding and strategic lighting around the mirrors create an unexpectedly cosy atmosphere. A stark contrast to the living area which is devoid of personality. In fact, the bedroom reminds him of a porn set.

A door to his left reads BATHROOM, and mahogany wardrobes line the walls around it. In the centre of the room is a huge square table laden with mirrors, hairdryers, make-up brushes, and cosmetic tools Marty cannot comprehend.

Marty gravitates toward the bed Gaz indicated, grateful for the simple human kindness of someone thinking to save him a spot. After the chaos they've just endured, even small gestures feel monumental.

"Cheers, mate. Appreciate it." He sits heavily on the edge of the bed, finally allowing his shoulders to drop. The soft mattress feels like salvation after hours of tension. "Eight beds," he says.

Gaz makes a sound of agreement. "Yeah. Gloria's definitely gone then."

Marty sighs and sinks down onto the bed, the mattress giving way to his frame. It's softer than anything he's touched in months. He could weep with relief, glad to lose himself in the sanctuary of sleep.

Fuck the 'blood'. And fuck the Landlord.

"You two next to each other, yeah?" Jack appears in the doorway with his bags, looking like he's seen a ghost. Tonight has clearly affected him more than Marty realised. The man's face is completely ashen.

"Yeah. You can have that one if you want?" Marty gestures at the double bed on his other side.

"You're alright." Jack sneers and deliberately heads to the other side of the room, claiming the bed next to Susan, who's sitting rigid, shaking her head, completely lost in thought.

"That was rude," Gaz mutters. "What do you think that was about?"

Marty has a pretty good idea; he's seen homophobia in all shades and colours, but he's too exhausted to unpack Jack's obvious issues right now. He's met men like Jack a million times before; they're not worth his energy.

He shifts the conversation. "You mean the blood? No clue. But the whole thing was pretty messed up. I know that for sure. I didn't think this show would be so..." He trails off searching for the right word.

"Extreme?"

"Yeah, and dramatic, I suppose."

"Ah, well, drama I can live with. I love a bit of drama." Gaz wiggles jazz hands at him. Marty cracks a genuine smile.

"You an actor then?"

"Yeah, or at least trying to be. Can't seem to get anything better than small stage parts at the minute."

"Hey, nothing wrong with that. I'd kill to get back on those small stages where it all started."

"Actor?"

"Guitarist." The word comes out heavier than intended. "Was anyway. Used to play all kinds of venues—from local pubs to stadiums. It was a lot of fun, you know?"

"For The Bone Riders, right?" Charlie settles into the bed beside Marty, biting into a banana provocatively. Marty turns away. "I remember watching you play at the O2. You were supporting Panic! at the Disco."

"Seriously?" Marty twists back around to face her. It isn't very often that someone recognises him—and not for the wrong reasons. The frontman, Jax, yes. But not him, the disgraced guitarist who was kicked out of the band for turning up to far too many gigs wasted.

"Yeah. Didn't rate you though. I'm more of a Beyoncé fan. But Charlie wanted to go." She leaps out of bed and disappears around the corner to retrieve her bags.

Gaz blinks. "I thought *her* name was Charlie?"

Marty thought so too. "Maybe she's one of those weird people who talk about themselves in the third person?"

"Maybe. Don't like it though. It's weird."

Marty nods, but he's determined to give her a chance. Everyone has their quirks, don't they? And Charlie seems harmless enough.

Besides, she remembered his band. That counts for something.

One by one, the housemates filter into the bedroom, still discussing Gloria's absence. Henry arrives clutching yet another cup of tea, Evangeline floats in wearing silk pyjamas covered in delicate pink roses, and Susan shuffles in a long spotted nightdress. Victoria is last, and Marty wonders what she's been doing.

She potters about, unpacking clothes into pre-designated drawers and lining up photos along the shelf above her bed. Her fingers linger on the face of a child smiling from the frame.

There's something about Victoria. Something that runs deep. He can see it behind her green eyes—pain, anguish, something so intense it's as if it's burning her on the inside.

Rather than being frightened of it, he's drawn in by her. He knows what it's like to suffer, and he knows what it's like to battle through it alone, how the isolation is worse than the pain itself.

And he desperately doesn't want Victoria to feel like that too.

Sleep eludes him for hours. Jack's snores emanate from the other side of the room like a broken engine, but that's not what's keeping him awake. What's troubling him is the small bag of cocaine he found in his bag. The coke he has no memory of packing in his bags.

Someone's playing games with him, and it's a cruel joke.

He stuffed the coke deep into his sock drawer with a hammering heart, promising himself he'll flush it first thing in the morning.

But lying here in the dark, he can feel it calling to him. Just knowing it's there makes his skin itch.

When sleep finally drags him under its spell, it brings no peace. He dreams of his past, of the sweaty clubs in Liverpool where his downfall began. The disastrous tour when his self-destruction really took hold. And the black months that followed when he'd lost everything that mattered.

His dreams come thick and fast, played at double speed but pausing at the most catastrophic instances that he longs to forget.

Until Evangeline's screams rip him out of his restless slumber.

Chapter 6

<u>Henry</u>

Henry is dragged out of sleep at a startling speed. His skull immediately starts throbbing, and he takes a few moments of disorientation to remember where he is. It's only when he reaches for his wife's side of the bed to find it empty that he remembers what he's signed himself up to. His wife isn't with him. She's probably laughing at him.

The room is swathed in darkness except for the dim emergency lights along the skirting boards—just enough illumination to transform the sleeping bodies into vulnerable, shapeless mounds.

A thrill crawls up his spine.

Henry blinks until the shadows resolve into recognisable silhouettes. Some are stirring, others are sitting bolt upright. But the voice cutting through the darkness is unmistakably Evangeline's, high and panicked.

Henry's pulse quickens.

"Get away from me, you freak!"

Henry can just make out Evangeline thrashing in her bed, her long bare legs flailing as she strikes the figure hovering over her bed.

The bedroom's shadows stretch and distort against the walls like elongated fingers. Each bed is separated by just enough distance to make it impossible to reach a neighbour without getting up—each sleeper an island unto themselves.

Evangeline's foot connects with her visitor with a dull thud, sending the intruder stumbling backward.

"Huh?!" a muffled voice calls back. There's a beat of stunned silence as everyone makes sense of the situation.

"Wait, what's going on?!" It's Susan's voice that replies, clearer this time, sounding genuinely bewildered.

Caught in the act.

Henry sits up straighter, overjoyed that the entertainment has started so early. Though a little more sleep might have been welcome—he's not as young as he used to be.

"Susan, love, move away from Evangeline. You're frightening her. What were you doing anyway?" Marty's voice reverberates through the darkness. He seems like a good lad, though Henry wonders what secrets he's hiding. You don't get your life into such a mess and not have a few bodies buried somewhere.

Susan doesn't reply. She tries to turn toward Marty but loses her footing.

"She was touching my face. Weirdo!" Evangeline calls out with revulsion and fear.

"Can you turn the lights on, Landlord?" Charlie calls out from somewhere by the door, her voice muffled like she's got the covers pulled up over her mouth.

The request hangs in the air as they contemplate the vulnerability of sleep. Eight strangers unconscious in the same room, completely at each other's and the Landlord's mercy.

And with Gloria's unexplained disappearance, nerves are frayed.

Surprisingly, the Landlord obeys the command of his housemate, and lights flicker on around the room's perimeter, casting long eerie shadows along the rows of beds that somehow add to the sinister atmosphere of the situation.

Henry surveys the room with interest. Everyone is accounted for. There are no more pools of blood to contend with.

Gaz is the only other person who is out of bed. He's standing next to his bed in boxer shorts, revealing a mosaic of tattoos from head to toe. Exquisite line drawings of graphical biblical scenes. Henry's research has been thorough, so none of this surprises him, but he notices Charlie staring at him, her mouth open in wonder.

Susan moves to the centre of the room, hands in her pockets, and scratches her head, her hair dishevelled from sleep. "I'm so sorry. Erm... I don't know what happened."

"You were sleepwalking," Victoria tells her, who has moved to sit beside Henry on his bed. She smells of soap. "I watched you get up. I thought you were going to the loo, but you just pottered around the room for ages. Opened a few drawers. I only realised you were sleepwalking when you walked straight into the wall. I think you were trying to find your way back to bed when Evangeline woke up."

Evangeline sits up straighter, clutching the sheets tight over her fake breasts. Her eyes dart wildly between Susan and Victoria. "Sleepwalking?!" her voice rising hysterically. "She was standing over me, touching my face." She presses herself against the headboard, creating as much distance between herself and Susan as she can. "I don't feel safe. I need a private room."

Ignoring Evangeline's theatrics, Susan turns to Victoria. "Why didn't you wake me up?"

"I thought it might do more harm than good, and I didn't want to wake everyone. You seemed to be fine. I thought you'd just go back to bed, and that'd be the end of it."

"Well clearly not." Susan shouts. She sounds pained, like she's the victim in all this.

"Alright, calm down. This isn't my fault."

"Yeah, well, it's not mine either." Susan's face is beetroot red, her eyes still wild and unfocused. She presses both hands to the top of her head, the hem of her nightie lifting to reveal puffy knees.

"I'm going to make a complaint about this in the Confessions Room."

Though no one is listening to her, they're all slipping back down into their beds.

"How am I supposed to sleep now?" Evangeline visibly shudders as she watches Susan return to her bed.

Jack settles back down in his bed next to Evangeline's. He turns to face her with an expression that might pass as concern. "Don't worry, I'll take care of you." He reaches over as if to hold her hand, but the gesture is resolutely ignored by Evangeline as she rolls over to face away from him.

Henry can't quite tell if Jack is being sincere or opportunistic. He's guessing the latter.

"Well, now we have that all wrapped up," Henry addresses the room. "Why don't we try to get some more shut eye. I'm sure we've got a busy day ahead of us."

He sees Gaz catch Marty's eye before he climbs back in bed. They know it too; Susan is someone to watch. Whether for safety reasons or entertainment value remains to be seen, and Henry is waiting with bated breath.

No doubt sleep will be hard to come by for the housemates now, but Henry settles back into his pillow and within minutes he's sound asleep without a care in the world.

Victoria

The alarm rings obnoxiously loud, like a car horn on heat. Victoria watches from buried beneath her quilt as most of the housemates groan and roll over, fighting in vain for a few more minutes sleep. But Henry springs up, scanning the room before hobbling around, searching for his dressing gown.

Despite everything, he makes Victoria smile—the way he totters around reminds her of her dad. Though he's long gone. His heart gave out on him a long time ago.

Marty throws on yesterday's clothes and rushes straight to the huge ensuite bathroom, his face set with grim determination. It doesn't look like he's slept at all.

"Do you think it's still there?" Susan whispers from beneath a black silk sleep mask.

"What's that?"

"The blood." She looks horrified at the thought.

Evangeline appears by Victoria's side in tiny shorts and a buttoned-down shirt that leaves very little to the imagination. Victoria, feeling self-conscious, pulls her quilt higher, hiding her bobbly pyjamas that are probably older than Evangeline herself.

"It better be gone," Evangeline says, shooting a pointed look at Susan. "We're barely twelve hours in and I'm already struggling. I've got millions of followers watching. After last night's drama, I must be the laughingstock of the internet."

Victoria hopes the internet has more important things to discuss than Evangeline's nighttime visitor. Is that all this girl has to worry about? What a bunch of strangers on the internet think about her?

What a wonderfully simple life to lead. Imagine living in a world where your biggest fear is a bad camera angle or choosing the wrong filter. It is as if Evangeline has absolutely no idea what shit life can throw at you. And Victoria can't help but feel grateful for that. She wouldn't wish her pain on anyone.

"I doubt what happened between us last night was even aired," Susan scoffs, dismissing Evangeline with a wave. "It was hardly a big deal."

Evangeline opens her mouth to retort, but Victoria cuts in first before an argument can erupt. "I'm sure it's gone," she tells the women, though she doesn't feel as sure as she sounds. "The blood that is."

But she thinks the blood was put there for a reason. The Landlord wants to freak them out, yes, but there has to be something deeper at play here.

"Where do you think Gloria is now?"

Evangeline smirks. "Probably getting grilled by some tabloid reporter about her experience of being ditched. God, imagine the embarrassment of being first out!"

She leaves, claiming she's *dying* for a cup of coffee. Susan soon makes her excuses and follows her out.

But Victoria is left feeling lost in thought, thinking about what the Landlord has up his sleeve for them all. Leaving what appeared to be blood on the floor was diabolical, and now she can't help but wonder what other atrocities he's planning to unleash.

It doesn't matter. She's ready for whatever comes next. She'll see this through to the end.

She'll do anything for *her*.

Marty

Marty ventures outside for the first time, and the garden catches him off guard in the daylight. Last night it was lost to nightfall, but now he can see it properly and he's pleasantly surprised.

The garden is a large grassy space with gym equipment dotted beneath the metal fencing on the right-hand side and a hot tub dominating the centre. The Landlord is most likely hoping the housemates will get drunk and naked and jump in.

Yeah, he won't be doing that. It's been a while since he stripped and made a spectacle of himself, and he's not nearly wasted enough to start now. Those days are behind him.

He heads straight to the wooden shelter in the far corner marked 'smoking area' and lights up a cigarette. He takes a long drag whilst standing on the edge of the deck, looking back into the house.

A fishbowl. That's exactly what it is. Glass walls showcase the housemates inside, everyone performing whether they realise it or not. From out here, he can watch his housemates moving around inside. Carrying on with their day as if this is the most natural situation in the world.

He sees Henry pottering around the kitchen, filling the kettle and lining the mugs in a neat row along the counter. Marty is grateful to Henry. To be looked after again, even just a little, feels comforting. It feels like he's slipping back into childhood.

But is he actually safe here? With Gloria's disappearance, the blood, and then the coke still stashed in his drawer, he's not so sure.

He takes a deep drag of his cigarette. How the hell did that coke get into his bag? He's been clean for months. He would've remembered putting it there. Wouldn't he? Unless the drugs have scrambled his brain more than he thought.

He brings the cigarette back to his lips.

What's his next move? This morning he slipped the bag into his pocket, mindful of the cameras in every corner of the room, behind every mirror, and probably hidden in nooks and crannies.

Knowing the Landlord stops recording when the housemates are revealing themselves, he drops his trousers and sits down. The red blinking light on the camera is off.

The bag was warm to the touch; the powder inside was soft. He had every intention of flushing the contents; he really did, but he just couldn't go through with it. It's his safety net. He told himself he needs to be bolstered by its presence. But the truth is, he's just weak.

Now what? If he hands the bag over to the Landlord, he risks getting kicked out and possibly arrested for possession.

Even from out here, he can feel the drugs calling out to him from the bedroom, screaming his name over and over, making promises Marty wishes were true. Of course, drugs cannot offer him the life he longs for; they cannot repair the damage he caused.

But then how long before the voice in his head drowns out every reason he has to stay clean?

"Mind if I join you?" Charlie is back to her timid self after the excitement of last night. Her shoulders are hunched forward, eyes fixed on the deck, completely different from the animated, almost manic person who'd returned from the garden after Gloria's departure.

"Course not." He shifts over, making space in the cramped shelter as she settles onto the bench. She lights up a menthol as Gaz steps out of the house and makes his way to the gym clutching a litre bottle of water. Charlie is dressed down today, wearing skinny jeans and a simple plain black t-shirt. Her mousy hair is pulled back into a low ponytail.

Marty is stunned by the contrast with last night. It's as if someone has dimmed the light behind her eyes, reducing her to the nervous girl who'd first walked through that door. She's shy, awkward, and alone.

He feels for her. She reminds him of his younger self before The Bone Riders got their first big hit. The quiet boy who just wanted to play the guitar in the comfort of his childhood bedroom, hiding from the world in the Liverpool Football Club shrine.

"Did you sleep okay?" he ventures, studying her face carefully through the smoke. "You seemed... different last night. After you came outside."

The question hangs between them in the morning air. Charlie takes a long drag from her cigarette, the smoke curling around her like a protective barrier. Her fingers tremble slightly around the thin tube, and Marty wonders if she even remembers the confident, almost manic person she'd become.

Charlie's eyes flicker up to meet his for just a second before quickly darting away. "Did I? I don't really remember. Sometimes I get like that when I'm stressed." Her voice is barely audible, nothing like the confident, almost aggressive tone she'd used when talking about Gloria.

Marty glances over at Gaz, who is currently pressing a kettlebell above his head by the hot tub like it weighs nothing. He catches Gaz's eye and throws a subtle head-tilt toward Charlie. Gaz's eyebrows raise in silent acknowledgment—so he'd noticed the personality shift too.

"Want to talk about it? Maybe I can help."

"They cleared up the blood," Charlie says, ignoring him. She shivers in the wind's chill.

But Marty doesn't want to talk about that. The whole mess makes his skin crawl. "How can you smoke those things? Bloody awful."

Charlie blows smoke at him, a smile playing on her lips. "I like these. Amber always preferred weed, but that might be hard to get in here."

"Who's Amber?" Marty asks.

"My sister. She's dead now though." Charlie's face softens at the mention of her name. She looks away and flicks the ash off the end of her cigarette onto the ground.

Marty feels completely out of his depth. This is a conversation Victoria would probably handle better. She's a nurse. Don't they have special training in this kind of thing?

"I'm sorry to hear that." He coughs, his legs bouncing up and down. Desperate to escape the heavy turn in conversation, he grasps for something lighter. "So, what do you think about Susan's nighttime wanderings?" he says, forcing a brighter tone into his voice.

"Oh, I think she was totally faking it."

"Yeah?" He takes one last drag and stubs it out on the ashtray fixed to the wall.

"Oh yeah, for sure, me and Amber think Susan's a liar."

Marty whips around to look at Charlie, but she's looking whimsically towards the house.

"You… and Amber…"

Every instinct tells him to run, but he forces himself to stay put for a few more seconds, just in case the crazy lady beside him gets spooked and does something dangerous.

@user1995: okay, did anyone else see that? She took a lock of the hot one's hair, right?

@darkasnight: Ha! Money gets you anything you want if you pay the right price.

@user1995: you bought her hair??!

@darkasnight: fuck yeah!

Chapter 7

<u>Victoria</u>

Tears stream down Victoria's cheeks and drip onto the back of her hands. She wipes them away quickly, before someone notices. If her family is watching, she doesn't want them to think they're actual tears. To think she's struggling.

She pushes the chopping board aside. "Done!"

Jack swoops in to claim the chopped onions and throws them into the pan with a flourish. He stands so close she can feel the heat radiating from his body. His breathing seems unnaturally controlled, each inhale and exhale measured precisely, like someone working hard to contain something volatile.

As she washes her hands, Victoria's gaze is automatically drawn to the stain on the carpet. Someone came in last night and tried to clean it up, but she can still make out the outline of the dark mark, and no doubt it will be there to haunt them for the entirety of their stay.

It's remarkable how quickly people adapt to a stress situation. A defence mechanism? Maybe. Susan's convinced the lights going out and Gloria's disappearance were orchestrated by the Landlord purely to see how they'd react, to test them under pressure.

The entire event was so extreme. There was no commentary. No follow-up. No task. If it really was a production stunt, wouldn't they have milked it for all it's worth?

No, everyone else might be comfortable passing it off as a silly production experience, but Victoria feels more uneasy than ever. And the blood serves as a constant reminder that something is very wrong here. Or is missing her daughter making her paranoid?

And where on Earth is Gloria? Did their vote get her evicted? Or have they stashed her somewhere for a big reveal later?

Susan seems to think it's the latter, and Victoria hopes she's right. She needs Gloria to walk through that door with some ridiculous story about spa treatments and interview sessions, so Victoria can rest her concerns and focus on what actually matters.

She came in here with a plan—be endearing, gain popularity, win the money. Simple. Not this confusion, this stress, this fear.

As much as she wants to, she cannot go home now. She's sacrificed so much to be here. Time with Lily. To care for her, to comfort and reassure her. And has so much more at stake if she fails. Failure isn't just losing a game show—it's losing everything that matters.

She ducks into the massive pantry. The pantry is big enough for about four people to enter, and she's pleased to find it empty. It smells spicy in here, and the air feels thicker somehow. Heavier. On the shelves around her is enough food to feed an army.

She puts away the remaining onions before taking a deep, calming breath and returning to Jack in the kitchen.

"What can I do to help now?" She asks, forcing a chirpy tone into her voice. Time to activate the 'be endearing' part of her plan.

"Nothing! The Chef is in the kitchen!" Jack's catchphrase. He's already said it three times, and it's getting on Victoria's nerves, but she smiles and claps anyway, showing an excitement for world-class food she has no desire to eat.

Her appetite abandoned her months ago, along with so many other things. Now she eats purely to ensure she can fight another day.

"Ooh, what's cooking?" Gaz leans over the breakfast bar, sipping his lemonade and radiating that friendly warmth that comes so naturally to him. "Smells incredible."

Victoria glances at Jack, but he's too engrossed in the sizzling wok to answer Gaz. Though she doesn't miss the way his shoulders pull back and his jaw hardens into a tight line the second Gaz entered his personal space. The air between Jack and Gaz seems to crackle with unspoken hostility.

Does Jack not like Gaz?

Gaz steps closer to Jack as if to test him. Jack clenches his fists and presses them against the kitchen surface.

Victoria subtly shifts her weight, positioning herself where she can move quickly if this simmering tension leads to violence.

"Stir fry," Victoria answers for Jack, keeping her voice deliberately breezy as she slots the chopping board into the dishwasher.

"Ooh, great, I'm starving."

"Not surprised after all that working out in the garden." She keeps the conversation flowing, hoping to defuse whatever's building between them. The last thing any of them needs is violence erupting over lunch.

Gaz has been in and out of the garden gym all morning. First time, working out alone, then he was training Marty with significantly less weight on the bar. There was a lot of manly grunting that made Victoria blush and had to retreat indoors.

"You and Marty are getting on well. You're like old friends already."

"Yeah, he's a good guy. I reckon he's carrying some heavy stuff though, you know? I figured he could use someone in here."

Friendship. A tactic Victoria was intending to use to her advantage. She scans the room and spots Evangeline in deep conversation with Susan and Henry, waving her arms theatrically. Victoria shudders at the thought of spending time with that woman; she's not sure she's got the energy for it. But needs must, she'll sit next to her at dinner and smile at her anecdotes until her face aches.

Evangeline is a nice girl; they're just worlds apart. The universe could fill the gap between them.

Gaz reaches over to pinch a slice of red pepper from Jack's chopping board, but Jack comes down with a shocking slap that echoes through the kitchen.

"Right, get out of my kitchen. Too many people in here."

"But I'm not *in* the kitchen. I'm on the other side of the breakfast bar." Gaz throws him a cheeky wink, completely oblivious to the minefield he's dancing through.

Jack jerks away at the gesture, his top lip twisted into a sneer. "GET OUT!"

The following silence in the room sings. Every conversation in the room dies as all eyes turn to Jack, who's staring at Gaz with an intensity so cold, his jaw might just shatter.

"Alright mate. Just trying to be friendly. Relax." Gaz backs away, hands raised.

"Don't *mate* me," Jack growls, his fist tightening around a knife handle.

Victoria steps forward and tentatively places a hand on Jack's shoulder, her eyes not straying from the knife. "Jack," she says quietly. "I think dinner's burning."

With a jolt, Jack returns to the stove and flicks the wok with skilled efficiency. He closes his eyes and takes a deep breath. "It won't be long. Just give me ten minutes."

Gaz shoots Victoria a puzzled look. "Right then." And he heads back to the sofa where Marty's watching the whole scene unfold with a knowing expression.

Victoria continues observing Jack with growing unease. He's channelled all that explosive energy back into cooking, working with laser focus as if the outburst never happened. She doesn't want to talk to him. She doesn't even want to be near him, but someone needs to defuse this bomb.

"You all right?" She asks softly because keeping him calm might be the difference between a tense dinner and someone getting hurt.

Jack snaps his head in her direction. "Yeah? Why? Get some plates out, please?" His voice drips with an artificial sweetness that makes Victoria cringe.

She finds a stack of plates in the cupboard and begins laying them out on the counter, forcing her hands to remain steady.

"Want to talk about it? I mean, that was pretty intense back there. *Aggressive* actually." She knows she's being brave, pressing Jack's buttons, releasing the pressure valve.

"Don't call me aggressive," Jack breathes, plating up the steaming-hot noodles. "I've had enough of that word to last a lifetime."

"The press..."

"Liars. The lot of 'em."

"They said some pretty awful things about you. About why you lost your restaurants. The parties... A load of rubbish I bet." Victoria says this with a nonchalance, hoping to win him over. She needs his vote to survive this, regardless of what he may or may not have done.

Besides, she's far too old to be on Jack's radar anyway. He surely won't care what she has to say. Allegedly, Jack's interests run much younger.

"Of course it's all lies." Jack sets the wok down heavily and seems to deflate. "I just want to move past all that, you know? But in this country, you're guilty until proven innocent. And how do you prove you *didn't* do something? How do you show the world what you *aren't?*"

There's genuine pain in his voice now, buried underneath all that rage. Victoria almost feels sorry for him—almost. Whether he's innocent or just a skilled manipulator, she can't tell. But she recognizes the exhaustion of someone fighting a battle they can never win.

Victoria offers a sympathetic shrug. She knows there's no smoke without fire. Is that why he's here? To rebuild his reputation? Everyone is here for their own reasons, she supposes.

"Well, well, well. Doesn't this smell delicious?" Henry says enthusiastically. "Can I help? Perhaps fetch a pitcher of water for the table?"

"No no. We're almost done here."

"Please let me help. I should do *something*." Henry rummages through the cupboards with the determination of someone who won't take no for an answer, getting in Jack's way.

Victoria catches Jack's eye, and she shakes her head at him, urging him to keep his temper in check. Shouting at an aging man would be the final nail in his reputation's coffin.

Henry triumphantly brandishes a jug and swings it round with theatrical flair, colliding squarely with Jack's shoulder.

Henry

Jack is practically vibrating with fury, and it tickles Henry. To add a little more salt to the wound, he leans into Jack's personal space as he pours water from the tap, ensuring the flow is slower than it needs to be, taking his sweet time.

He nudges Jack with his elbow, purely accidentally of course. Out of the corner of his eye, he sees Jack's grip tighten around the pan's handle.

"I heard your restaurants were lovely," Henry says, positioning his face mere inches from Jack's increasingly flushed profile. "Michelin stars and everything! I was planning on taking my wife, Brenda, to the one in Birmingham for her seventieth a few years back, but then I saw the prices. Goodness me! They're steep!"

A vein pulses in Jack's temple. "Quality doesn't come cheap." He slams the cutlery down on the table.

"Now, now, let me set the table properly. A man of such high standards should know this." Henry collects the cutlery and moves to the dining table. He lays the knives and forks out with meticulous care. "Though last I heard, the Birmingham restaurant has closed now. Such a shame."

"Yeah, well, it wasn't working out. Better opportunities in London."

"Oh, I'm sure. But didn't that one in Islington close too?"

Henry turns away and spies Jack's reflection in the window. His eyes are boring into his back with undisguised hatred. "No, that one is still open."

"Oh really? I must have read that wrong." Henry's voice carries just the right note of confused innocence to disguise the lie.

"Yeah well, a lot of shit has been written about me lately." He pours himself a glass of water.

"Like the sex parties? Yes, I imagined that was a complete fabrication. Who could partake in something so sordid? It's revolting behaviour."

Jack chokes on his drink and turns away, his face burning red. Victoria slams a palm into his back. "Wrong hole," he wheezes.

"Sorry, didn't mean to startle you. That must have been tough on you, having your private life broadcast and distorted like that," Henry takes the pile of plates and places them on the table, drawing the housemates over like they've been summoned.

"So, the orgy thing wasn't true then?" Marty asks, already chewing on his food. "Because they sounded *wild*. And I've seen some pretty fucked up stuff. Though didn't they say the girls were all paid for? Instead of hors d'oeuvures, you were serving up pussy." He chuckles.

Susan whacks Marty round the head, knocking the chicken off his fork onto the table. "Don't be so crass."

"Sorry, serving up *vagina* then?"

Gaz snorts with laughter. "Sorry. That was funny," he mutters, stabbing at his food.

Henry swings around to face Jack, who is still standing frozen in the kitchen, taking in the conversation. His mouth opens as if he wants to say something but can't decide what to say.

"Rumour has it two of the girls were underage," Henry interjects. "Truly repulsive. I mean, if it were true."

The temperature in the room drops several degrees. Even Marty stops chewing, suddenly understanding he's wandered into much darker territory than crude jokes about adult entertainment.

"It's NOT true!" Jack spins, snatches the knife from the chopping board and hurls it across the room. The blade whistles past Charlie's head, missing her by mere inches before slamming into the window with a sickening crack and clattering to the floor.

"Now everyone SHUT UP! Just shut up. My life isn't to be gossiped about, you hear me?"

The silence that follows is deafening. Everyone sits frozen, forks halfway to mouths, processing how close they just came to witnessing something far worse than broken glass.

Charlie lets out a small whimper and scrambles backward, nearly toppling over her chair. Her eyes are wide with pure terror as she presses herself against the wall like she's trying to disappear into it.

"Please don't hurt us," she whispers, her voice trembling. "Please."

Evangeline rolls her eyes dramatically. "Oh my God, Charlie, he threw a knife at the window, not at your head. Stop being so melodramatic." She flips her hair over her shoulder and crosses her legs, seemingly unbothered by Jack's outburst. "Some people just have *passion*. It's what makes them brilliant at what they do." She throws Jack an admiring glance.

Henry's grin widens as he watches Evangeline's performance. The poor dear tries so hard to be liked. Daddy-issues no doubt. That would explain a lot.

Or does she have a crush on the famous chef?

Henry isn't frightened of Jack's tantrum. He knows a big baby when he sees one. And Jack is practically still in nappies. "Okay, no need to be so hotheaded," he says to Jack with infuriating calm. "You can't expect us not to talk about it. It was all over the news for weeks, and now we're thrown into a house with you!"

"Yeah, well, it stops right now. You really think I'd be here if there were an ounce of truth to any of it?"

"Well, I imagine a non-disclosure agreement or two might help with that sort of thing."

Jack's jaw drops open. A surge of vindication travels through Henry's entire body. He has no doubts that Jack plied those girls with drugs to persuade them to perform unthinkable sex acts. Then he shut them up with the complicated jargon of an NDA.

He claps his hands together. "Right, let's eat, shall we?"

Chapter 8

<u>Marty</u>

The housemates have been walking on eggshells ever since Jack's outburst. Jack himself has withdrawn from the group, and when he does speak, it's with a friendliness so forced, it's cringeworthy.

This is the Landlord. Could all housemates gather in the garden immediately?

A collective gasp of excitement ripples through the group. Fifteen minutes ago they were all requested to sit on the sofas with the blinds drawn, and they have been sitting in tense anticipation as they watched human shapes move around outside, a blur through the rigid fabric.

Now that they've got instruction, they're giddy with action. Except Marty.

Marty's anxiety, which has been building since finding the bag of cocaine, has reached breaking point. His hands shake slightly as he stands, and he can feel sweat beading on his forehead despite the cool air. The stress of being trapped in this house, surrounded by cameras and volatile personalities, is wearing him down faster than he'd expected.

The stashed bag has been calling out to him from his sock drawer, fighting for his attention, begging for it, singing a tune so loud.

His eyes keep drifting to every surface where he can line up the pure white powder. He can practically feel the rush.

So far he's resisted. But for how much longer?

As they file outside into the afternoon sun, Marty takes a deep breath, drawing in the scent of the forest outside the colossal walls.

When his car picked him up outside Euston Station, he was blindfolded. He soon sensed they'd reached the M25, but he had no idea what direction they had taken. Hours later, the scent of damp wood and moss filtered into the car, and he knew they'd entered deep into the countryside.

Now he gets a deep sense of space, and he breathes it in deeply. Whatever is happening now is at least a distraction from the claustrophobic atmosphere inside the house.

He stops short, confused. The garden now contains a neat row of podiums, each topped with a square black box about ten centimetres tall and with a hole in the top.

"What's all this then?" Henry asks, approaching the box furthest away from the house. They all claim a podium and stand behind them, like obedient soldiers awaiting orders.

Marty eyes his box warily. The hole in the top looks just large enough to fit a hand through—which immediately makes him not want to put his hand anywhere near it.

Evangeline chatters away whilst they wait for further instruction. "You know, this reminds me of my boyfriend, Peters. God, I really miss him," she whines.

Gaz rolls his eyes. "How does a box on a stand remind you of your boyfriend?" he drawls, fed up with Evangeline's constant ploy to draw the conversation back to her fella outside.

Gaz's lack of tact amuses Marty, and he can't help but smile. What you see is what you get with him. Though if the name Peters comes out of Evangeline's mouth one more time, he thinks he might lose it. What kind of shit name is that anyway?

Evangeline has been telling anyone who'll listen that she's dating some radio presenter from a station called Radio Juice. She'd been genuinely shocked to discover that none of them had heard of him.

She glares at Gaz. "He's a famous radio DJ, actually. This black box—well, it reminds me of the equipment in his studio."

"Right. Whatever." Gaz's dismissal is perfectly timed to cut her off, and Marty has to fight back another grin.

Marty turns his attention back to his box. There's nothing distinctive about it, just a plain black cube bolted to the podium. Even when he presses his eye to the hole in the top, the interior is painted so dark he can't make out anything inside.

This is the Landlord. The rules for this task are simple. Each housemate is to place their hand in the box and keep it in there. I will time you individually, and if your combined total hits my predetermined target, you will win a party tonight.

If you fail, you will be punished.

The housemates erupt into a chorus of protests, Susan loudest of all.

Marty stares at the innocent-looking hole with growing unease. Last time they were given a task, one of them disappeared.

He glances around at his fellow housemates, catching the same wariness reflected on their faces. Whatever's waiting inside these boxes, it will not be pleasant.

The speakers cut out with an abrupt click.

"Do we start now?" Jack asks.

A claxon sounds, startling everyone into action.

Jack plunges his hand into the box first. "It's empty," he shrugs, looking almost disappointed.

Charlie's fingers dance over the opening of her box. She's retreated into her shell and barely spoken a word since the drama with Jack yesterday.

Yesterday she clung to Evangeline's side, probably finding safety in being Evangeline's shadow. She spent most of this morning on her own, staring wistfully out the window.

Now she grits her teeth, casts one last glance at Jack before placing her hand inside her box.

"Empty," she confirms.

Marty has tried to avoid Charlie since their strange conversation in the smoking area. Though now seeing her so withdrawn, he misses the more vibrant side of her personality that emerged that first night after Gloria's disappearance.

At least she had brought some colour into the group. This subdued version comes with an intensity that makes him feel on edge.

Victoria is next to brave the box, and Susan follows soon after with a theatrical squeal.

Now only Marty and Evangeline still have their hands hovering over their boxes.

"Come on, we're going to fail because of you two," Jack barks at them. "It's empty. Just get on with it."

Evangeline bats her long lashes at him. "What if there's something nasty in here? Like a spider or something? I bet you'd feel bad then."

"They're all empty. Right everyone?"

The sounds of agreement rise from the group, and Evangeline throws a glance at Marty. "What's holding you back?"

What is holding him back? Fear of the unknown? Probably. Feeling powerless? Likely. But then he signed up for this. What did he expect? Garden parties and polite conversation?

His fear drew him here. The fear of losing his life to his crazy dealer.

But it's time to stop being a coward.

He drops his hand into the box and rests it against the base, preparing himself for whatever this test turns out to be. "It's empty," he confirms to Evangeline, who hesitantly follows suit.

"Well, this is fun," Susan says dryly. "How long do you think we need to stand here like idiots to pass this thing?"

"Until I need a wee," Gaz says. "And that won't be long; I must've drunk a gallon of water today. I should've gone before I came out."

Marty chuckles. Now that Gaz mentions it, he might need a piss too. He won't let them down though.

Evangeline squeals, capturing everyone's attention. "Ooh, it's tingling."

Marty knows what she means, though he's struggling to describe the odd sensation. The box is definitely empty; he's certain of that. But it feels like the box itself is somehow alive, pulsing with a strange energy that sends gentle vibrations through his palms and fingers.

"Well, this is dull," Susan repeats. She's been in a foul mood all morning, snapping at everyone who crosses her path. She spins to face Henry on her left. "So, still glad you came on the show? Exciting enough for you?"

Everyone's eyes shift to Henry, who flushes slightly under the scrutiny. "Why yes, of course. I mean, this might not be the most riveting experience, but it's nice to be involved all the same."

"Why *are* you here anyway?" Jack asks him. "You're not the most obvious choice for reality TV." He's still smarting from Henry's teasing yesterday. Because, despite Henry's silly old man routine, his words are calculating and taunting. Marty has noticed Henry winding Jack up.

"Good question. I suppose I just wanted a bit of adventure, you know? My wife always said I'm a silly old fart trying to recapture my youth, so I thought, why not?! You only live once after all."

Jack grunts dismissively and returns his attention to his box. "It's really buzzing in there now."

Everyone shifts uncomfortably. The vibrations aren't unpleasant, just deeply unsettling. Marty's hand is getting incredibly warm, like it's pressed against a radiator.

"Mine's buzzing too," Victoria says, her voice tight with concern. "How long are we supposed to keep doing this?"

The sensation is spreading up Marty's arm—a strange tingling that makes every nerve ending hypersensitive. He glances around at the others, noting the mix of confusion and growing unease on their faces.

Whatever's happening in these boxes, it's escalating.

Victoria

Evangeline has been chewing the inside of her cheek for the last twenty minutes. The box is vibrating so aggressively now, it's actually causing pain, and Evangeline looks like she's about to cry.

"You don't have to do this, you know," Victoria whispers pointlessly—everyone can hear her. "You've got nothing to prove."

"No. I can't let my followers down," she says, tears pooling in her eyes. "I can do this." She tries to project confidence in her voice, but the tear that slides down her cheek gives her away.

Victoria has reached her limit. It's not just the steadily growing pain in her hand; it's her aching legs from standing motionless. It's the incessant bullshit chatter from the rest of the housemates.

Victoria has had enough. She's too tired. Tired of being away from home. Tired of living with a bunch of strangers who know nothing about her real life. Tired of pretending to be some bubbly, game-for-anything contestant when all she wants is to go home and hold her daughter.

But she can't. Home isn't an option until she wins this nightmare.

"I'll quit if you do," Gaz tells Evangeline. "We can be failures together."

Evangeline shakes her head stubbornly.

Gaz sighs. "Not everything's about strangers on the internet, you know. You're allowed to put yourself first sometimes."

"Then why did you do it?" Henry asks. His mouth immediately clamps shut like he's accidentally said too much.

"Did what?" Gaz asks guardedly.

Henry hesitates, glancing around for someone to save him. No one does. No one appears to have a clue what's going on.

He sighs, looking pained. "The porn movies."

Gaz's eyes widen. "Shush!" he snaps, his voice sharp enough to make everyone forget their discomfort. "Just shut your mouth!" His casual charm evaporates as he yanks his hand from the box and steps back.

The group freezes in stunned silence. None of them have seen Gaz's cheerful demeanour crack like this. His chest heaves as he stands there, fists clenched at his sides, eyes wide with fury.

"Gaz—" Victoria says softly.

He catches her eye, and shame floods his face. "I'm… I'm sorry," he stammers, visibly fighting to pull himself together. "I didn't mean to have a go."

He stops, swallows hard, and turns to Marty with something like desperation in his eyes—a silent plea for understanding, for help from his friend. He looks utterly ashamed.

Marty gives him a small nod of solidarity, but the damage is already done. Gaz's secret is out for everyone to see.

"Oh, fuck this. I need a wee." Gaz marches into the house, his whole body radiating humiliation and rage.

"Sorry!" Henry calls out after him. "I didn't know it'd upset him. How was I to know it was a big secret?"

The door slams with enough force to rattle the windows.

Henry moans quietly under his breath and turns away, but not before Victoria catches the grin spreading across his face. Why is this amusing to him? Victoria would have thought Henry would be horrified to be sharing a house with a porn star.

How did he know Gaz's secret past anyway? Maybe he's more worldly than Victoria gave him credit for.

It's Jack who breaks the awkward silence. He whistles low and long. "He did porn? Well, who would've seen that coming? Dirty bastard." He tries to sound scandalised, but there's unmistakable glee in his voice—probably relieved he isn't the only one in the group with a questionable past.

Victoria feels sick watching them feast on Gaz's humiliation like vultures. The man had been nothing but kind since arriving, and now they're treating his private shame like entertainment.

"I think we should give him some space," Marty says, unusually firm. "Whatever he did before coming here is his business."

Jack scoffs. "Oh please. Can't do me the same courtesy, no?"

"That's different," Marty snaps.

"How is it?"

"I'm guessing the people Gaz slept with consented to it."

That shuts Jack up. He returns his focus back to his box, grumbling something about speculation and lies under his breath.

Victoria is genuinely surprised by Henry's revelation. Gaz seems like such a well-rounded, cheerful guy. Decent. The type of man who lightens the atmosphere in any room. She struggles to reconcile that warmth with an industry built on the exploitation of women.

She thinks of her daughter. To that sweet, angelic face and of her pure innocence. The idea of what darkness might be waiting out there in the world makes Victoria feel sick.

She sighs and glances up at the sky. Storm clouds are gathering overhead, casting everything in an ominous grey light that matches the mood.

"You're out!" Susan shouts at her.

Victoria looks down in confusion, surprised to find her hand resting on top of the box instead of inside it. The strange buzzing sensation is still working up her wrist.

"Oh! I didn't mean..."

"You were miles away. Pulled it out to touch your necklace."

"I'm so sorry everyone." Victoria is mortified. She wanted to win this, to be the hero.

Susan just shrugs. "I guess it's down to us now."

"Yeah well, count me out too," Evangeline announces, withdrawing her hand and cupping both hands together against her chest, puppy-dog eyes shooting meaningful looks to the cameras.

Victoria steps back from her podium, sad to have let everyone down. Her mind had wandered to her daughter again—it always does when she touches the locket. But now her distraction might have cost them their reward.

With five players still in the game and an unknown target to reach, Victoria can only hope that as a house, they can do enough to win the prize. A party would be fantastic. Dancing and a little alcohol will be a nice way to get to know one another better.

Charlie suddenly yelps and whips her hand out. "It stung me!" she cries, cradling her palm in her other hand. "It was like…" She makes a buzzing sound. "And it hurt." She holds up her hand for Victoria to examine, but all Victoria can see is some slight redness that could easily just be from the pressure of being pressed against the bottom of the box.

"You'll be fine," Victoria reassures her with a gentle smile. But Henry crying out behind her draws her attention away.

Henry still has his hand in the box, but his face is ashen, and his jaw is clenched tight. Jack wears a similar expression as Henry lets out a low groan.

Only Susan seems completely unfazed by whatever's happening inside the boxes. She must have nerves of steel.

"I think it's electrocuting me," Henry says, his voice strained.

"Take your hand out then," Victoria urges him. "You're hurting. You don't have to do this."

"But the prize..."

Marty drops out of the game. "No. This is stupid. Henry, take your hand out now before you get really hurt."

Henry's eyes dart around the remaining players, clearly torn between the agony and his determination not to be the one who sabotages the task.

"Come on, Henry! That's enough!" Victoria shouts. "Take it out!"

The old man's face is becoming alarmingly pale; sweat is beading on his forehead as whatever's happening in that box intensifies. Victoria takes a step toward him, ready to physically intervene if necessary.

This has gone far beyond any reasonable challenge—it's becoming genuinely dangerous.

<u>Henry</u>

The pain shooting through Henry's hand feels like lightning bolts running straight up his arm on a collision course for his heart. Every rational thought screams at him to withdraw, but his stubborn streak is getting in the way.

"Take your hand out, old man, I've got this," Jack grunts through clenched teeth.

Though Henry would rather endure a painful palm than give Jack the satisfaction of playing the hero. There are plenty of things he'd like to do to that arrogant man, and none of them involve adding to his inflated ego. He digs in deeper.

Susan closes her eyes, a look of slight discomfort on her lined face. So the Landlord has finally allowed her to join in the game then? Interesting that she'd been spared the worst of it until now.

Because Henry is well aware that Susan isn't playing by the same rules as everyone else. The Landlord has been giving her special treatment from day one, and Henry would like to know why. She has spent more time in the Confessions Room than anyone else. He's seen her always watching, always waiting for something to happen.

And unlike his oblivious housemates, Henry hasn't missed the way Susan talks to herself when she thinks no one's listening. Quiet little conversations with someone who isn't there, responding to questions nobody asked.

The woman's hiding something significant, and Henry's beginning to suspect it goes far deeper than sleepwalking incidents. Susan's got secrets that could change everything about this twisted game they're all trapped in.

Henry's vision blurs slightly around the edges, but he holds fast. Jack will break before he does. He's certain of it.

Jack roars.

"Take your hand out of the fucking box!" Marty yells at the two men.

Susan looks almost overjoyed to be the strongest player in the game, though the bead of sweat trailing down her temple suggests her level of comfort is cracking.

Henry's arm feels like it's made of lead. His vision tunnels, the world spinning dangerously as his head rolls back and his legs turn to jelly.

"Jesus Christ!"

Is the last thing he hears before the buzzing stops and then there's nothing at all.

Marty

Marty rushes forward as Henry slumps to the ground. He grabs the old man's wrist and yanks his hand free from the box before Henry's fall causes his wrist to snap against the box opening. Henry's deadweight is heavier than Marty expected, and he staggers under the burden.

Gaz bursts outside, his eyes wide in terror. "What the hell happened?"

"The box. It got too much for him," Marty explains breathlessly. "Here, take him. Victoria, go and help."

Marty watches as Victoria and Gaz carefully guide Henry into the house, Gaz calling out to the cameras for medical assistance. Henry is regaining consciousness, and his legs tread forward, wobbly and unstable, but at least supporting some of his weight.

He'll be looked after—the Landlord cannot possibly ignore this. Marty turns his attention back to Jack and Susan. The last two standing.

"It's time to stop," Marty tells them firmly.

Charlie is perched on the edge of the hot tub. Marty does a double-take. The glint behind her eyes is back, and she's looking positively euphoric at the turn of events.

"But shit just got interesting," she says with disturbing brightness.

Evangeline, seated nearby, looks at Charlie with alarm. "What's *wrong* with you? Are you okay, hun?"

The question hangs in the air like a challenge. Because whatever's happening to Charlie, it's becoming harder to dismiss as simple stress.

"Nothing. What's wrong with *you*?"

Not wanting to get dragged into a catfight, Marty turns away. He focuses on Jack, who is slumped forward against the podium, his free hand gripping the edge of the box. "Take your hand out," Marty shouts at him. "Don't be a stubborn bellend."

"I can't," Jack grunts, his voice strained with pain. "It's stuck." He tries to tug out his arm, but it won't budge; his breathing is becoming rapid and shallow with panic.

Marty rushes forward and pushes into Jack, trying to dislodge him. But Jack doesn't move, and the impact sends a shock through his trapped arm. He roars to the darkening sky above.

"Shit, shit," Marty mutters. Whatever's in that box has Jack's hand properly trapped, and the man looks genuinely terrified.

"I told you I can't get it out, Marty!" Jack cries. "You think I'm doing this for fun?!" He yanks at his arm, but it doesn't move. The opening in the box has somehow closed, pinching the skin around his forearm. Jack sobs. "I can't get it out," he whimpers.

Holy shit.

Marty grabs Jack's lower arm and pulls with everything he's got, but nothing happens. The box has devoured Jack's arm.

A horrifying sizzling sound fills the air—like meat hitting a scalding pan. Jack's screams change into something inhuman, something primal and animalistic. The veins in his neck bulge as he throws his head back in agony.

Evangeline ventures closer, her face pale. "Susan, you should take your arm out!"

"Why? I'm fine." But Susan sounds unsure. Either her pain threshold is through the roof, or something very different is happening inside her box.

"Take your hand out," Marty urges her.

"I can't," she stutters. "I want to win."

"There is no winner! Take your hand out, and all this can be over. The game stops when there's one left standing." It's a complete bullshit guess, but maybe guilt will force her to stop.

"You don't know that."

"And if I'm right? Susan, you might be the one to stop this."

"No, you don't understand—"

"Take your fucking hand out!"

She hesitates and looks to Jack, who's grey-faced and drenched with sweat, still trapped and writhing in agony. She glances directly at the camera mounted on the house, nods, then pulls her hand free of her box. What is she looking for?

"Okay, I'm out," she says glumly.

The moment her hand clears the box, there's an audible mechanical click from Jack's podium.

Jack drops to the floor, gasping for air and making an awful keening sound as he rolls onto his back. Marty drops next to him, his stomach lurching.

Jack's hand is an angry mess. The skin on his palm has bubbled and blackened in sections; raw, weeping tissue underneath. The burns are worst at his fingertips—the nails partially melted into the flesh. Where the box had gripped his wrist, a perfect ring of charred flesh has formed, branded into his skin like a signature.

The injuries look severe—far beyond anything that should happen during a reality TV challenge. Anger courses through Marty, but he pushes it aside. He needs to focus on what's important: getting help.

The smell of burnt flesh hits Marty's nose, and he must fight back bile. "We need to get you inside. As ambulance will be coming." Shouldn't it? The Landlord can't possibly ignore this.

He carefully helps Jack to his feet and guides him to the house, Jack shaking violently .

"What's going on?" Jack sobs. "This isn't right."

"Couldn't agree more, mate. Must be some sort of technical glitch. A problem with the electrics or something."

But Jack doesn't respond. He's cradling his burnt hand to his chest, a grim look on his face that speaks the words Marty can't say out loud. Can this really be a glitch? With Gloria's disappearance and the blood staining the carpet, who can be sure of anything anymore?

No, he's being paranoid. Gloria was voted out. And this wasn't meant to happen.

One thing he knows for sure though—he doesn't like any of this. He doesn't like any of this at all.

@SadistPrime: The chef's hand is cooking nicely! Can we get a close-up camera angle?

@MedicalFetish: As a doctor, those burns are third-degree minimum. Infection will set in soon. Delicious.

@PayToWatch: This is what I'm here for! Real consequences, real pain. The nurse trying to help is adorable.

@TorturePorn_King: Request: Can you make the next task even more physically demanding? I want to see bones break.

Chapter 9

<u>Victoria</u>

Gaz has been hammering on the Confessions Room door for what feels like hours now. With no clocks in the house, time has become abstract, a guessing game where the object of guesswork can stretch and contract depending on the contestant's emotional state.

Sweat darkens the back of Gaz's shirt as he continues his futile effort on the door, his breathing becoming increasingly laboured.

"They're not coming," Charlie observes. "We don't think they're listening?"

Gaz finally gives up and stomps away.

"We? Who's *we*?" Victoria asks, grateful for any distraction.

Victoria has been tending dutifully to her two patients. Henry bounced back quickly and is now resting with a cup of tea in bed. Jack, meanwhile, lies bandaged and medicated with the painkillers from the medicine cabinet. He's in the next bed over, trying unsuccessfully to sleep through Henry's relentless chatter.

She's given Jack as many painkillers as she can, but Victoria is deeply concerned about infection. Jack needs to see a doctor, and fast. Yet the Landlord has been resolutely absent since the start of the task.

Victoria settles back with a glass of water, glad for any conversation that might keep her spiralling thoughts at bay. If she lets her mind wander, the anxiety will consume her completely.

"Me and Amber," Charlie says, looking puzzled by the question.

Victoria casts her mind back to a previous conversation with Marty. "Your sister? The one who..." She trails off, not wanting to say 'died' out loud in case it upsets Charlie. She knows it's cruel, but she isn't in the mood to soothe Charlie's grief after the day she's had.

Charlie nods absently and nibbles her slice of toast. Victoria has heard of strong sibling bonds before, how they can communicate with each other in unusual, telepathic ways, but does it work like this? With one sister living and one who's not.

"Do you talk to her often?"

From across the room, Marty catches her attention, his eyes wide. He looks visibly shaken by the conversation.

Victoria knows Charlie freaks him out, but she's harmless enough. Right?

"Oh yeah, all the time. She likes to come and visit me."

A shiver runs down Victoria's spine, raising goosebumps along her arms. The casual mention of her dead sister visiting her is deeply disturbing. The temperature around Charlie seems to drop by several degrees, creating a pocket of cold air around them.

"Right, well, I should check on Jack," she says quickly, making her escape before this conversation can get any stranger.

She leaves Marty looking pale and shaken on the sofa, clearly as unsettled by Charlie's words as she is.

Jack is still lying on his bed, facing the wall. Henry appears to be napping.

"Jack? You awake?" she whispers.

He glances over his shoulder briefly before turning away again. "They didn't send help," he says, his voice heartbreakingly sad. "They don't care."

"Not yet," Victoria encourages, but there's no conviction in her words.

Jack suddenly sits up with determination. A new, darker energy radiating off him. "No, they won't come. Don't you get it? They don't give a damn about us." His face contorts as rage takes hold, the hot, fiery emotion spreading through him like poison. "They did this to me on purpose!"

Victoria takes an instinctive step back. She's seen Jack's temper before, but this feels different—more dangerous. The combination of agonising pain and betrayal is creating something volatile.

"Jack, you need to stay calm. Getting worked up won't help."

He thrusts his bandaged hand at Victoria and pushes himself off the bed. The mattress springs creak in protest as his weight suddenly lifts. He storms over to the mirrored wall and slams his good hand against the glass with enough force to rattle the entire panel.

"I know you're watching!" Spittle sprays over the surface, leaving a speckled display of thick fluid. "You need to send help. You hear me? You can't do this to me; it's barbaric." His frustration builds into a roar that echoes through the bedroom.

"Jack, stop!"

But Jack doesn't hear Victoria's pleas. He turns around and grabs a vanity stool, hoisting it above his head despite his injured hand trembling with the effort. He's fuelled by pure adrenaline. Adrenaline and rage.

"Fuck you!" The stool crashes down with the force of a sledgehammer. The sound reverberates through the room like a gunshot, making Victoria flinch.

But the mirror doesn't even crack. The stool bounces back and hits Jack in the chest, sending him staggering back. The impact knocks the wind out of him with an audible whoosh, and his face pales for a split second before flushing an even deeper shade of red.

The unbreakable glass does nothing to dissipate his fury. He pulls at his bandage, tearing at the gauze that comes off with a sickening ripping sound as it pulls off his damaged skin.

"See this?" He holds up his mangled hand toward the mirror. "YOU did this! All for the sake of views. You're sick! Do people actually enjoy watching this shit?"

Victoria realizes the mirrors aren't just one-way glass—they're reinforced, unbreakable. Like everything else in this house, they're designed to contain rather than protect.

Marty and Gaz rush into the room, taking in the scene with wide eyes as Jack continues his assault on the mirror. Marty throws Victoria a glance as Jack slams his palms against his reflection, bursting a blister and leaving a yellowish-red smear across the surface. He screams, though Victoria doesn't know if it's in pain or anguish.

Jack grabs a bag at random and launches it at the wall, lost to his rage, then he brings up his knee and kicks at Susan's bed, his foot connecting with a thud.

Both Marty and Gaz stand by Victoria's side, frozen in shock. Gaz is tugging at his shirt.

"Help him!" Victoria cries at them, snapping at their paralysis.

To her relief, they spring into action and restrain Jack's flailing arms. Marty pins his arms behind his back to stop him from striking out, while Gaz positions himself in front, speaking in low, calming tones. Jack doesn't hear them. He twists out of Marty's grasp to yell at him.

Victoria gasps as Marty slaps Jack across the face. The crack of his palm against Jack's cheek fills the room and immediately cuts off Jack's yells.

"What? What did you do that for?" All anger drains from his voice, and he visibly deflates, now held up by Gaz's muscular arms.

"You need to get control of yourself, mate. Before you do yourself even more harm."

Jack's eyes sweep the room, taking in all the housemates now crowded in the doorway, staring at him like he's a dangerous animal broken free from his cage. His jaw clenches.

"So you all think this is normal, do you? Not even three days in this hellhole and they've got rid of that old hag on the first night, left a random blood stain, and now burnt my hand to a crisp. Don't you get it? We have no idea what's going to happen. Or to who."

The words hang in the air like a death sentence.

Susan drops to her knees and frantically starts gathering her scattered belongings. She shoves everything into her bag like she's terrified the mess will provoke the Landlord.

A weight settles in Victoria's stomach. Deep down, she knows Jack is right. Nothing about this feels normal. It's time to leave.

But then another part of her mind fights back, desperate to rationalise everything away. Everything can be so easily explained. Technical problems with the electrical systems. The fake blood was set up purely to frighten them. Gloria is out there somewhere, perfectly safe, watching the show and laughing at them all.

It's a war between two terrors—fear of what might happen next in this house, and fear of what's waiting for her outside if she leaves.

No, she must stay. And pray her excuses are true.

Henry

Susan slips her hand into Henry's and gives a little squeeze as they watch Gaz and Marty work to calm Jack down. Henry has been expecting this outburst since they arrived, and it's truly glorious. Honestly, he would have preferred to see him lose control over something trivial, like someone over-seasoning his cooking, perhaps, but this will do. There's something deeply satisfying about watching the alpha male reduced to a snivelling child.

The box incident was unfortunate, certainly. But there's no need to act like this. A few red spots on one's hand is hardly something to throw a tantrum over.

Henry feels perfectly fine. The box didn't bother him; he'd simply grown tired of standing in the garden like a fool. Giving up didn't seem like the most sensible approach for keeping his place in the house, so he played the 'old man' card. A card he likes to play often.

Truthfully, Henry is probably stronger than all three men combined. His hobbies make peak physical performance paramount to his success. No, Henry is in fantastic shape, and now he's even better having avoided whatever Jack had to endure.

He feels Susan's clammy hand give his another squeeze and he pulls away, refusing to meet her eye. If she's looking for comfort, she'll have to find it elsewhere. Physical contact isn't something he can offer her; it's too intimate. Too *tempting*.

He turns away from Susan and studies Evangeline, who's silently weeping into her sleeve. For once, she appears to have forgotten the cameras. Black mascara streaks her blotchy cheeks, and her eyes are puffy from crying since she came out of the Confessions Room.

He approaches her cautiously. "Are you alright, my dear?" Henry asks her kindly.

She bursts into fresh tears, covering her face with her hands before leaning against him, resting her forehead on his chest. He stiffens momentarily before awkwardly patting her on the back. He runs his hands a few inches downwards, feeling her spine, jutting out with each sob. Each vertebra feels fragile under his fingers.

"There there," he whispers. "It'll all work out, young lady, you'll see."

Her perfume is cloying in the close air, but he drinks it in all the same.

"Why don't you sit down? I'll make you a cup of tea."

There's nothing like a crisis to remind people how much they need someone stable and caring in their corner.

Evangeline pulls back to look at him through tear-clumped lashes. Her lower lip quivers visibly as she struggles to find the right words.

"Is it though? Henry, I want to go home, but Susan already asked in the Confessions Room, and the Landlord said we can't. Some sort of contractual obligation. We're trapped here."

"Why on earth would you want to leave? We've barely gotten started."

"You really want to stay now? Henry, this isn't what I signed up for. I thought this would be my big break, my chance to really show my audience my true self, and instead I'm an absolute *mess*." Her voice cracks. "This isn't any good for my brand. And I miss my boyfriend."

Ah, Peters. The radio presenter with a tendency to piss people off for ratings. Henry's extensive research into Evangeline had led him down a rabbit hole. There's only one word Henry has for Peters, and it's not one he'd dare utter aloud—*gobshite*. A word he heard Marty say and one that made him chuckle. It fits Peters perfectly.

It seems Evangeline is attracted to arrogance. Arrogance and fake tan. According to his research, Peters isn't exactly known for his fidelity either. According to the internet, Peters is sleeping with every Z-list celebrity who'd dare go near him. Which, confusingly, is many.

He presses his hands on Evangeline's shoulders and pulls back to get a better look at her.

"First, don't let a couple of minor incidents put you off."

"*Minor*? Henry, someone might be dead, and they tortured Jack. Hardly minor."

Henry cuts her off with a cocked head. "Speculation and exaggeration, my dear. A few unfortunate incidents doesn't define the entire experience. And you mentioned your brand—don't you think resilience and strength are exactly the qualities you want to showcase? Show your followers what you're capable of. Let your light shine through in the darkest of situations, and they'll lift you to the heavens."

"I guess you're right," Evangeline finally manages after taking an embarrassingly long time to process Henry's words. She pulls away, leaving Henry feeling cold.

She smiles wanly. "Thanks, Henry, you're a kind man. Every woman needs a man like you in their life." She stands as Victoria re-wraps Jack's hand behind her, Jack crying pitifully. His whimpers turn the corners of Henry's mouth upwards.

"Keep your chin up. And if it gets too bad?" He grins at her warmly. "I'll help you break out of here."

"Ha! Really? I don't see you as a 'break the rules' kind of guy."

"No? I'll scale that fence like a squirrel if I have to. You just watch me."

She actually giggles at that, the sound lifting some of the oppressive atmosphere in the room. Henry finds himself genuinely pleased with her response. He likes Evangeline.

Not in the same way as Charlie of course, but she's still pleasing to be around and entertaining to watch.

"What do we do now?" she asks. She already sounds stronger, and he notices how she's now holding herself differently, her head higher and her shoulders back. His little pep talk worked.

"Now, now we have a cup of tea."

Susan's Confessional

"This isn't what I signed up for, and you know it. I would like to leave now."

Susan sits in tense silence, waiting impatiently for a response. Her foot taps a rapid rhythm against the floor—the only outward sign of her growing panic. Finally, she snaps.

"Landlord. Talk to me. I know someone's listening. There's always someone there. You assured me of that in our pre-production meetings."

The silence stretches on. Only the red light on the camera blinks back at her, unfeeling and mechanical.

Susan's hands twist in her lap, nails digging half-moons into her palms.

"Please! Talk to me! Tell me what's going on. You said nothing about harming people. I want no part of that. I kept my hand in that box only because I thought that chef-guy was acting. I didn't think for one second you were hurting him."

Her eyes fill up with tears as she looks directly into the camera lens, pupils dilated with fear.

She folds her arms and slumps back. The leather chair protests as she shifts, the sound unnaturally loud in the suffocating silence. It feels like it's devouring her.

"Well, I'm not going back in that house."

Nothing. The temperature in the room seems to drop several degrees.

"If you don't talk to me right now, I'll scream. I'll tell them everything I know."

The silence drags on until finally, a dull tone crackles through the speakers on either side of Susan's head, making her jump.

"Susan, the Landlord appreciates your concerns, but we would like to remind you that you signed a contract before entering the Landlord's house. You're obligated to stay."

Susan's face drains of colour. "No, that's not right. I had my solicitor go through it all. She said I was free to leave at any time. She said you couldn't hold me here against my will." *Her voice rises in pitch, the first notes of hysteria creeping in.* "It said that all requests to leave prematurely just have to be made directly to you in the Confessions Room. Well, here I am."

"Susan, the Landlord cannot keep you here."

"Exactly! So what do I need to do next? Where's the door?"

"Shall we talk things over first?"

The Landlord's voice is soft, so kind, it pulls Susan out of her frustrations. "I guess we can talk for a little while."

"The Landlord is so grateful for your part in creating the show. You have done an exceptional job. Your acting skills when you cut Evangeline's hair were exceptional. Bravo!"

Susan can't help the proud smile that tugs on her lips. "Thank you. That was... difficult."

"I bet. Though it was so impressive, we've had the producers of Coronation Street reach out to us."

That stops Susan. Her eyes widen, and she lurches forward. "Really?!"

"Oh yes. They said they very much enjoyed watching you. There might just be a career waiting for you when all this is over. Just see this as one long audition."

Susan blinks once. Twice. Then, she shakes her head.

"What happens if I stay?" *she asks, her head hanging low.* "You're not going to hurt me, are you?"

"The Landlord has no intention of harming his tenants."

Susan breathes a shaky sigh of relief.

"Providing the tenants follow the house rules."

The conditional threat hits her like ice water. She shivers and pulls her arms around her torso protectively. She thinks of Coronation Street and the rules she has no intention of breaking. "I'll stay."

"In the hatch to your left, you will find what you need for tonight. Enjoy your party, Susan, and thank you for helping the Landlord. Your service is noted."

Chapter 10

Jack's Confessional

"Hello Jack. Care to tell the Landlord why you're so angry? Damaging the Landlord's property is deeply frowned upon."

"What you going to do? Punish me?"

"No."

Jack winces as the pain from his hand pulses up his arm, his blood-stained shirt sticking to his chest. "I need help," he grimaces.

"The Landlord is sourcing antibiotics."

"That isn't good enough! I need professional medical care."

"Certainly. The Landlord can see you've got yourself into rather a pickle."

"Me?!" Jack stops his feet on the floor. "I didn't do this, you did! How dare you sit there and say I'm to blame?"

The pain is getting too much. It's draining every drop of Jack's energy. He closes his eyes and breathes deeply, focusing on staying conscious. "What happened out there?"

"The Landlord is investigating. From initial enquiries, we think there may have been a technical glitch with your box."

Jack laughs now. This whole situation is beyond ridiculous. "I need out."

"The Landlord is making arrangements for your exit. Give us time."

Stunned at the Landlord's compliance, Jack nods. "Thank you."

"Though I must admit, it'll be a shame to see you go now."

"Yeah? Why's that?"

"Well, according to the latest polls, you're coming out on top!"

"Really?" Jack doesn't know what to say. This is the last thing he expected. He knew coming here would be difficult after the orgy scandals, but he knew he had few other options. It was this or drifting into obscurity. And Jack was born to be successful, not to hide in the shadows.

"Yes. Just last night, in fact. The consensus seemed to be that you're a man of the people. Not afraid to live your truth."

Something swells inside him. "Well, they've got that right."

"So you'll be free to go in an hour. Transport is on its way."

Jack ponders this, his eyes flicking occasionally to his damaged hand. "Did you say you've got antibiotics coming?"

"Yes. We can give them to you when you leave."

"Am I allowed them inside the house?"

Silence follows. Jack shifts to the front of the seat.

"If you were to stay, you would have adequate medication."

"Then I'd like to stay."

Marty

The housemates sit around glumly whilst the house has switched to party-mode. Apparently, that means music being played too loud and a depressing spread of supermarket snacks arranged on a disposable platter.

Marty sits beside Victoria at the kitchen counter, both of them watching Gaz attempt to teach Charlie some TikTok dance routine whilst Henry looks on from the other side of the room.

"How are you getting on?" he asks her. Her inherent sadness seems to be sharper tonight. As if she has something unbearable on her mind that she cannot shake off.

"Oh, just grand," she says, laughing at her joke. "Between Gloria vanishing, leaving blood behind, and Susan's night-time wanderings, what more could I ask for?"

Marty chuckles. "You know you're not alone in here, right?"

Her eyes meet his; hope and desperation stare back at him. "That's just it. I'm always alone."

He knows that feeling all too well, and it hurts to see her in identical pain. How can someone so good be experiencing the same anguish he has to endure on a daily basis? "I'm promising you now, I've got your back in here. We need an alliance to get through this. Well, consider me yours."

Tears shine in her eyes.

"Deal?" Marty presses.

"Deal."

Susan is moving through the kitchen with practiced efficiency, preparing fruit punch in a large glass pitcher. She hums quietly to herself, the picture of domestic tranquillity. When she happens to glance up, their eyes meet across the breakfast bar.

Her humming stops.

She swallows and quickly looks away. "I've made more fruit punch!" she announces to the room with forced cheer. "It's a mocktail!"

Victoria turns around. "I'll have some, thanks. Not really in a drinking mood tonight after what happened today."

"Don't blame you, lovey. Plus, that wine is dreadful. A cheap supermarket brand probably." Susan reaches for a tall glass from the cupboard above her head. "You get a big one. You deserve it after taking care of our patient today."

Jack's guffaws from the sofa draw their attention. Marty has been watching him with growing unease. He appears to be drinking to numb his pain. But the more red wine Jack drinks, the bolder he's becoming around Evangeline. His entire demeanour has changed as the evening has drawn on. Gone is the hunched, wounded figure clutching his bandaged hand. Now his shoulders are squared, chest out, eyes tracking Evangeline's every movement around the room.

There's something unsettling about the way he watches her.

Marty rises from his stool at the breakfast bar to settle on the sofa opposite Jack and Evangeline, propping his feet up on the coffee table.

He might as well be invisible for all the attention Jack and Evangeline pay him. And he watches them through narrowed eyes. Given Jack's rumoured past, he doesn't like what he's seeing.

Jack has positioned himself uncomfortably close to Evangeline, one arm draped across the back of the sofa behind her. His fingers keep 'accidentally' grazing her bare shoulder, and each time they make contact, his mouth curves in a self-satisfied smirk.

"You're even more stunning in person than on Instagram," Jack's voice carries across the room during a lull between songs. "I've been following you for months."

Evangeline giggles, swaying slightly. Her finger traces the edge of her nearly empty glass containing the last dregs of whatever fruity concoction Susan has put together. "Have you really? That's so sweet." Her words slur together. "I have three million followers, you know. Maybe even more now."

Her eyes close for a moment as if she's falling asleep. How did she get so wasted?

Jack shifts closer, his good hand drifting to her waist and his fingers splaying possessively across her hip. "I bet not one of them sees your potential like I do though," he says, his voice dropping to a growl. "I know talent when I see it." He reaches up to brush a strand of hair from her face, lingering too long against her cheek. "What do you say we find somewhere a bit more... private? I could tell you all about my restaurants. The things that happened there." Something dark flickers across his features. "The things that could happen in here."

Marty leans forward, trying to catch Evangeline's attention. "Hey, Evangeline, maybe you should slow down on the drinks," he says gently, reaching for her empty glass. "How about some water?"

Jack's arm tightens around Evangeline, pulling her closer. "She's fine with me," he says, his eyes narrowing. "Aren't you, gorgeous?"

Evangeline looks up at Marty through glassy, unfocused eyes. "Go away, Marty," she slurs, attempting to wave him off. Her fingers just jut out as if confused by the instruction. "Jack and I are having a... a professional conversation about my career."

"I really don't think—" Marty starts.

"I said go away!" Evangeline's voice turns shrill, loud enough to draw stares from everyone. She pushes at Marty's chest with surprising force. "Stop being so controlling! Jack *knows* people. Important people who can make me famous." She leans heavily against Jack's side, looking up at him with exaggerated admiration.

"I just think we should take a break. We have plenty of time to discuss this. We're not going anywhere."

"Oh, piss off Marty."

Jack smirks at Marty over Evangeline's head, his hand sliding lower on her hip in a deliberate show of possession. "Run along now, boy. The grown-ups are talking."

Marty hesitates, torn between intervening further and respecting Evangeline's wishes, however impaired her judgement might be.

When Jack leans in close to whisper something in Evangeline's ear that makes her giggle and blush, Marty reluctantly backs away.

The guilt hits him immediately, crushing him. But what can he do if she's actively forcing him away?

He catches Victoria's eye, and she gestures for him to come to her.

"How's it going?" he asks, glad to be away from the car crash on the sofa.

Victoria sighs deeply. "I feel like I'm babysitting a house full of people who have lost their minds."

"You not feeling the party then?"

She shakes her head. "My party days are long behind me. I've barely drunk anything since my daughter was born. The glass of wine I had earlier has gone straight to my head." Victoria turns away as if her words have stung her.

"You miss your daughter," Marty observes. "You don't talk about her much."

"That's because I'm scared that if I do, I'll completely fall apart. Honestly, I don't know how much longer I can be here. Missing her is killing me." She pauses, as if she wants to say something else, but something prevents her from opening up.

Susan appears beside them with her jug of juice. "More fruit punch?" she asks brightly. Without waiting for a reply, she fills Victoria's empty glass.

Marty declines—he'll stick to water and plan for an early night—but Victoria accepts hers gratefully. As Victoria drinks, Marty spots something fleeting in Susan's expression. Was that guilt? Maybe she's having a harder time in here than she's letting on.

It's hardly surprising given everything that's happened. Marty knows they all have their own reasons for staying put.

And they can only hope now that the Landlord has his so-called technical problems under control.

<u>Henry</u>

The crowd in the kitchen is getting rowdy, and Henry wanders over with keen interest, throwing Charlie one last glance as he leaves her behind. Victoria leans heavily against the breakfast bar, a glass of juice in hand. She's gesticulating wildly, sloshing the liquid around in the air as she talks theatrically with Susan and Marty.

Her movements are loose and theatrical—nothing like the controlled, careful woman he's observed all week.

Susan keeps glancing at the mirror behind Victoria—looking checking her own reflection or trying to catch sight of the camera beyond, Henry cannot tell. Marty looks frightened, his eyes never leaving Victoria for a second. He's suspicious.

Smart lad. He's picked up on what others have missed.

"So, this is where the party's at?" Henry calls as he approaches, raising his glass of sherry at them. Three pairs of eyes turn to him.

"Yeah," Victoria barks at him, followed by a hiccup. "Wouldn't call this a party though—some Gangnam Style and a glass of juice is hardly a *party*." She spits out the 'p' in 'party', spraying Henry with juice.

He wipes his cheek with his sleeve. "I think Evangeline and Jack might disagree with you."

The group turns in unison to watch the other housemates. Evangeline is now sitting on Jack's lap, successfully distracting him from the pain in his hand. Though the fistful of pills he's taken may be helping somewhat. He whispers something in her ear that makes her giggle.

Gaz and Charlie sit nearby, deep in conversation. Henry's never seen Charlie so animated. What version of Charlie have they got tonight, Henry wonders? The timid, shrinking version, or the brash one that keeps fighting through? Judging by the upright posture and roaming hands, he imagines it's the latter.

Something tugs at Henry's memories, but he pushes it aside. This isn't the time.

Gaz catches his eye and gives him a little wave. It's nice Gaz has already forgiven Henry for his little mishap earlier. Though why Gaz got so upset is beyond him. Being a porn star in today's world is hardly a shock. Even his single-mum neighbour funds her 'Hello Kitty' addiction with OnlyFans. Or at least that's what Gabby at the post office told him.

He supposed it's the finer details that frightened Gaz. And Henry can't quite decide whether to reveal those darker details himself or let them surface naturally. Secrets have a tendency to claw their way out eventually.

"That Jack guy is a *disgrace*," Victoria slurs next to him, her voice carrying far across the room.

Jack looks up at her, eyebrows raised in surprise.

"Yeah, that's right, *you*, you're a disgrace," she calls over to him, swaying slightly.

Marty steps closer, his eyebrows pressed together. "Alright, that's enough of that. We should get you some water."

"What are you on about? I've had hardly anything to drink." She motions to the juice.

"It's just orange and mango," Susan blurts out.

"You sure about that?" Marty pulls the pitcher closer and gives it a deep sniff. Satisfied the juice is non-alcoholic, he frowns. "She must have had something else."

"Sneaky sneaky," Henry chortles. "Though with today's events, it's no wonder she's felt the need to have a stiff drink. Steady her nerves."

"I am right here, you know. Stop talking about me like I'm invisible." Victoria hiccups so loudly it sounds like she's about to vomit. "I remember when I could drink every guy in the bar under the table. And now I'm just a lightweight." She sounds so pitiful about her diminished ability to drink. She burps, then her face crumples as she looks like she's about to burst into tears. "I don't feel right."

To everyone's horror, sobs burst out of her. "I want to see Lily. I miss her so much." She reaches for the locket around her neck, misses and scratches the delicate skin around her throat, leaving an angry red line.

Marty wraps an arm around her.

She fights him off. "Get off me! Don't pretend you understand. None of you do." Her eyes dance wildly around. "I need to get to Lily."

She jumps off her stool and rushes to the nearest mirror, pounding her fists against the glass. "Let me out, you Landlord prick!"

There's no response.

Henry approaches cautiously, hands raised. "Come here, my dear. Let's sit you down." He pulls out a dining chair and guides her towards it. "Lily's your daughter? Why don't you tell me about her?"

He takes her hand gently and helps her into the chair, which she flops down into heavily. Tears drip onto the table as Victoria pulls at her hair, distraught. Her head lolls to one side.

"Something's very wrong," Marty says quietly, his eyes fixed on Susan with undisguised suspicion.

"Look," Victoria pleads, thrusting the tiny locket to Henry's face. "Just look at her. She's so beautiful, isn't she? So perfect."

Henry opens the delicate clasp. The image inside shows a small, painfully thin child with Victoria's eyes. She's smiling bravely at the camera despite the tubes running out of her. Victoria traces the image with her fingertip, leaving a smudge across the protective plastic.

"She doesn't even cry when they put the needles in anymore. Four years old and already stronger than I'll ever be." Her voice breaks on a sob. "Her shit-excuse-of-a-father couldn't handle it. Walked away a few months after she was born—took one look at all that hospital equipment and decided he didn't sign up for this. Said he wanted a 'normal' family."

You could slice through the silence in the room with a blunt blade.

Victoria's voice breaks on a bitter laugh. "Left me with a two-week-old baby fighting for her life. Then, because I had to drop my hours at work to take care of her, I was drowning in bills." Her face flashes with rage for just a moment before it slips away, crumpling back into grief. "Do you know what she asked me before I left? She wanted to know if I was going away because she cost too much to keep. But I had to make a hard choice, you know? I'm the only one providing for her."

The confession hangs in the air. Even Henry's practiced composure falters at the devastation in her voice.

"Oh, Victoria," he says softly. "I'm so sorry. I'm sure she'll be doing just fine at home."

Victoria pushes him away angrily. "Or she might be really sick! What if she's dying?!"

Everyone freezes in horrified silence.

"Now, that's a little dramatic, Victoria. Don't you think?" Susan eventually says, her tone completely misjudging the moment. Henry fights off the urge to laugh at Susan's disgraceful lack of tact.

But Victoria shakes her head, too distraught to care. "Dramatic? That poor girl has spent most of her life fighting. It's a battle I'm here to fight, but you know what?"

No one answers.

"I don't know how much fight I've got left in me anymore. I came here for the money. To pay for treatments that might save her life. Unlike you lot, I don't *want* to win; I *have* to."

Marty pulls her closer. "Oh, Victoria. I had no idea."

Henry likes Victoria. She's strong-willed and feisty—nothing like his ordinary girls, who hide behind image and pretence. "What's wrong with her? Your daughter, I mean."

"Lily. Her name is Lily."

"Sorry, Lily. A very pretty name it is too."

"She has Spinal Muscular Atrophy."

Victoria is met with blank stares. Everyone exchanges uncertain glances, clearly out of their depth. Marty gives her shoulder an awkward pat while Susan takes a nervous sip of her drink.

"What's that then?" Henry asks.

"A genetic disorder," Victoria hiccups through her tears. "The short version is that her muscles are slowly failing as her motor neurons degenerate. She doesn't have long left before she loses sensation in her lower body. Soon she won't be able to walk."

"Oh, darling, I'm so sorry," Susan murmurs, with Marty and Henry offering quiet sounds of sympathy. "Is there anything the doctors can do?"

"Oh yeah, there's something they can do all right. They just won't. There's this experimental stem-cell treatment over in Boston. The thing is, it costs a fortune, and we're running out of time. The doctors think she's only got about six months before her condition becomes irreversible. I *need* to win this, or all this sacrifice is for nothing."

Her heart seems to crack in two as she crouches down, burying her head in her hands. Her sobs take her breath away, and her body convulses with the effort.

Susan drops to her knees beside Victoria, tears streaming over her cheeks as she wraps her arms around Victoria's shuddering shoulders.

"Perhaps you should take her to bed," Henry suggests to Susan. "She needs to sleep this off."

The men watch in solemn silence as Susan gently coaxes Victoria away. Victoria follows docilely, drained by the emotional outpouring.

<u>Marty</u>

"Poor woman," Marty says, shaking his head.

Henry nods. "So many people are carrying such tremendous burdens, and we're none the wiser."

Marty stares wistfully into the darkened garden, processing everything. "What I don't get is how she got so wasted. Can one glass really do that to someone? Unless she's got a bottle stashed somewhere. But then why would she do that? No one is judging here."

"Perhaps she's judging herself?"

Marty can only sigh. He knows what that kind of condemnation feels like. He also knows what suspicion looks like, and it's currently tapping at his gut for attention.

Henry looks Marty in the eye. "One thing I know for sure though—if by some miracle I actually win this thing, I won't be keeping the prize money."

"Henry, you're an honourable man." Marty claps him on the back and heads to the toilet, guilt pushing down on his chest. He'd give Victoria every penny he had if he could. If he were free to make that choice.

But the brutal truth is he owes serious money to a lot of dangerous people. If he doesn't win the money, he'll lose his life.

Though the way things are going at the minute, that doesn't seem so bad.

If he gave the money to Victoria, at least he'll die doing something honourable. Maybe his parents could finally feel an ounce of pride in their only child.

The speakers crackle into life as he's shaking himself off.

This is the Landlord. Could all housemates please gather in the living area immediately? It's time for nominations.

Chapter 11

<u>Henry</u>

Three days of polite smiles and surface-level chats is hardly long enough for deciding who gets the boot. But Henry knows rules exist for a good reason. And one mustn't break them if you want to stay here. And Henry truly wants to stay.

The atmosphere in the room feels charged with tension as housemates arrange themselves on the sofas. Fingers fidget with clothing, tap against thighs, twist hair into anxious knots.

Evangeline sits slumped beside Jack, who casually works his unbandaged hand up her thigh, booze coursing through his system, his co-ordination shot.

To Henry's surprise, Evangeline opens her legs ever so slightly, an invitation. Dirty girl. Such a shame.

Henry cannot get to grips with Evangeline, and he knows from experience that they're the ones to watch. Brimming with confidence on the outside masks insecurities buried so deep they make her vulnerable and confused. Those kinds of mixed signals inevitably lead to unpredictable behaviours. And that never ends well.

Just ask his last girl.

Charlie sits opposite him, looking around the room as if looking for something. He wonders if she's missing that older man she's been seeing. The one she likes to meet at Costa Coffee on a Friday afternoon after her classes.

"Where did Victoria slip off to?" Gaz asks. He's been subdued all afternoon; the confident energy he showed when he first walked in is fading. Henry highly suspects that his revelation regarding his career choices has shaken him more than he's letting on. Though there's something deeper troubling Gaz that Henry can't put his finger on.

Being thorough, Henry took the time to watch Gaz's starring roles—purely research, of course. He's not easily shocked by many things. He's open-minded and open-hearted, but Gaz's videos were quite surprising. Henry can still picture the perfect 'o' his lips made at the peak of an orgasm.

"I put her to bed," Susan replies. "She was in no fit state to nominate."

Susan, could you please bring Victoria to the living room?

The Landlord, ever watchful when *not* required.

Susan's eyes widen. "I don't think she *can* come, Landlord. She's pretty out of it in there."

"I don't think we have a choice in the matter," Jack mutters, visibly miffed to be sitting here with everyone and not tucked away in a corner with an intoxicated Evangeline.

Could Susan bring Victoria to the living room immediately, or all housemates will face consequences?

Still Susan hesitates, wringing her hands together. Charlie stands up, taking the lead. "Here, I'll help you, Susan." Susan avoids eye contact and wobbles off to the bedroom with Charlie by her side.

It takes what feels like an eternity for them to fetch Victoria. When they finally appear, her make-up is smeared down her face and her lips are curled. Henry knows that face and rushes to the kitchen to fetch a bowl. If Victoria is sick, it'll be easier to clear up if she can catch at least some of it.

"Thanks Henry," Susan whispers, her face ghostly pale. Her eyes keep darting around the room as if she's worried someone is going to call her out on spiking the juice.

Henry finds her behaviour fascinating. Most people wouldn't have noticed the subtle way Susan had been controlling who got which drinks tonight, but Henry makes it his business to observe everything. The way she'd carefully prepared different glasses, her insistence on serving everyone personally—it all painted a very interesting picture.

He'll save that little nugget of information for future use.

Victoria immediately falls asleep against Susan's shoulder, snoring softly.

Jack, could you please stand up and tell everyone who you'd like to evict and explain why you'd like them to be evicted?

Jack has to practically peel himself away from Evangeline, who falls forward into the space he has vacated. She steadies herself with a comical flick of her hair, all grace and elegance gone.

Jack scratches his head and scowls at the ceiling. "Some sort of warning would be nice, Landlord. Fuck me." He sighs and looks back down at the floor. "Well, I don't really have an issue with anyone," he shrugs.

Gaz lets out a derisive snort.

"Got something to say there, Gaz?"

"No, nothing at all."

The look Jack shoots Gaz could strip paint. Charlie pulls her knees to her chest and hides behind them, frightened.

"Okay, well if I *have* to nominate someone, I guess it has to be you, Gaz."

Susan gasps. Charlie peeks over her knees with startled eyes. Henry disguises his laugh with a clearing of his throat. If Jack came here to clear his name, he's doing a spectacularly shitty job—his homophobia is more prominent than his arrogance.

Jack smirks at Gaz. "Sorry mate, I just don't think you and I can ever get along. We're too *different*."

Gaz laughs. "No hard feelings. Whatever." Though there's no hint of truth in his nonchalance. He looks furious.

Henry cannot fathom why. Gaz doesn't need approval from someone like Jack. No one does.

Jack sits back down, but with a little distance between him and Evangeline now. The spell is broken.

Next up is Evangeline. "I'd like to nominate Charlie," she slurs. "I like her well enough, but she proper scares me." She giggles and sits back down without a trace of remorse.

"Well, that's not fair," Gaz protests, but Marty silences him with a hand on his shoulder. It's not a fight worth having when everyone is already walking on eggshells. Besides, Charlie looks genuinely relieved by the nomination.

Unsurprisingly, Marty votes for Jack, citing concerns that the house environment isn't right for Jack. Gaz follows Marty's lead, at which Jack laughs bitterly. "Trust you two gays to stick together," he sneers.

The silence that follows is fuelled with suspense wound so tight you could snap it with your fingers. Everyone freezes, unsure where to look. Except Henry, who watches the drama unfold with fascination. He expects Gaz to explode, but instead the young man just smiles slightly and shakes his head.

Most interesting of all is the Landlord's complete silence. Apparently, both torture and homophobia are permitted in his house. How enlightening.

"Gaz isn't gay, you moron," Victoria suddenly shouts, making everyone jump. "He's as straight as they come." She throws him a flirtatious smile. "Marty however..."

All eyes turn to Marty, who meets their stares with quiet dignity. "My sexuality is none of your business," he declares.

Susan votes for Jack on the grounds that he's too aggressive, and Victoria slurs the same sentiment.

Henry knows that one more for Jack will seal the man's fate. But Jack is an obvious choice, and Henry is far from predictable.

"I'm terribly sorry to do this, but I'm voting for Susan. She's been harbouring many secrets, and I don't believe she can be trusted."

No one says a word. Everyone appears to be lost in thought, processing the unexpected twist. Henry is delighted; he enjoys watching people squirm.

Now could Charlie please stand up and tell everyone who you would like to nominate for eviction?

But Charlie doesn't move. She has untwisted her body and now sits rigidly upright, her spine unnaturally straight as if pulled up by invisible string. Her eyes have gained an unsettling brightness, locking onto Henry's with laser focus. Her lips curl into a sinister smile.

"Charlie," Gaz nudges her. "Your turn."

"Oh, that's me!" Charlie springs up, laughing. "I forgot who I was then." Her voice carries a deeper, more assured tone. She's back.

"Well, Charlie wanted to vote for Susan—she said she cannot trust her. But I'm voting for Jack, because he's a bit of a knob."

She drops back down with a smile.

"Who you calling a knob?!" Jack snarls.

"You. I'm calling you a knob, Jack."

Jack's mouth works silently, like a fish out of water, clearly at a loss for words.

"May I ask you something?" Henry asks. Charlie nods at him.

"If Charlie wanted to vote for Susan, then who wanted to vote for Jack? Who are you?"

"Amber. I'm Amber. Though I'm sure that comes as no surprise to *you*."

Curiouser and curiouser. The pieces are starting to fall into place for Henry, though he isn't yet sure how it all works.

"Well, hello Amber," Henry says, his tone deliberately light. "How lovely to see you. I wonder though, do you and Charlie have different opinions about all of us, or just about Jack and Susan?"

Amber tilts her head, studying Henry with an unnervingly direct gaze. Her smile widens slowly, like a predator who's just spotted weakness. "Oh, we have different opinions about everyone," she says, her voice taking on a sing-song quality. "Especially you, Henry. But that conversation can wait."

The room grows still. Even Jack's anger seems momentarily forgotten as all attention shifts to this unexpected confrontation unfolding before them.

"Me?" Henry's expression remains pleasantly bemused, but something sharp flickers behind his eyes. "How interesting. And what opinions might those be?"

Amber leans forward, resting her elbows on her knees. "Charlie thinks you're a sweet old man," she says. "Harmless. Grandfatherly." She drags out this last word, making it sound almost obscene. "But I recognise you."

Henry's smile never falters. "Is that so?" His voice remains even, but his fingers have gone very still in his lap.

Adding Charlie to his collection has always been part of the plan. He never expected Amber to get involved. He feels sick with worry. What is going on here?

Charlie's body suddenly jerks, cutting off Amber's next words. Her eyes squeeze shut, her hands fly to her temples as if struck by sudden pain. When she opens them again, they're filled with confusion and embarrassment.

"I—I'm sorry," she stammers, Charlie's timid voice and nervous mannerisms firmly back in place. "I don't know what just happened. Did Amber say something bad?" She looks around anxiously at the stunned faces.

Henry's pleasant smile slides back into place, though it doesn't quite reach his eyes. "Not at all, dear. Just a bit of party banter. Nothing important." But his gaze remains fixed on Charlie long after the voting continues.

Chapter 12

<u>Victoria</u>

The next day drifts by in a haze. Victoria has spent most of it in bed, only getting out when the Landlord demands her presence—which is happening more frequently and always frustratingly pointless. She's convinced he is toying with her, playing with her hangover for entertainment value.

Well, the joke's on him. At midday, she threw up all over his fancy bathroom.

Her head throbs with every heartbeat. She cannot piece together most of last night, but she's absolutely certain she couldn't have got *that* drunk. She'd had one small glass of wine and that fruit juice Susan kept pushing on everyone, and there definitely wasn't any booze in it—she'd taste it on her breath now if there had been.

So how did she get so wasted? There's only one explanation, and it frightens her. Someone in the house spiked her drink, and seeing as Susan made the drinks all night, she's the screamingly obvious choice.

Victoria's instincts about Susan are conflicted. She seems so nice, so sweet, but there's something *off* about her. Something artificial. Something Victoria hasn't got the energy to either tease out or pretend it doesn't exist.

Telling everyone about Lily wasn't part of the plan. She didn't want to use Lily to invoke sympathy. The thought of her housemates and the public feeling sorry for her makes her queasy.

Lily deserves better than being reduced to a sob story for reality TV. Victoria's here to win the money they need so she can care for her daughter properly, not to turn her child's suffering into entertainment for strangers.

"You were right to share." Henry keeps reassuring her, his meaning clear—if she wants to win this for Lily, she needs to share her story and earn the public's sympathy vote. To use her.

She sees the logic in telling people about Lily's illness. It's an argument she's been having with herself ever since she applied to come on the show. But when it came down to it, speaking about Lily just felt *icky*. Exploitative and painful.

Now that the house knows about her daughter, it's as if Lily has entered the house with her. Victoria keeps expecting to hear her little voice calling for Mummy.

Only she isn't. She's hundreds of miles away in the north of England with Victoria's mother, sick and afraid. And wondering where her mummy has gone.

And once again, the tears come.

Marty

Marty has had other things on his mind. He'd assumed Jack would be gone by now, but he's still here, one-handedly dominating the kitchen with a grin plastered on his face.

Jack and Evangeline had stayed up long after everyone else went to bed last night. Marty had realised too late that he was the only one left in the living area with them—Jack pressed up against her, breathing her in. Evangeline making little moaning noises in her throat.

The memory of that scene still sits heavy in his stomach. He'd wanted to intervene, but Evangeline had made it clear earlier that she didn't want his help. The guilt of walking away when someone might have needed protection gnaws at him.

He keeps watching Jack now, looking for signs of what really happened after he'd retreated to the bedroom. The man's acting like nothing's wrong, but there's something in his posture—a satisfied smugness that makes Marty feel sick.

He fights through his guilt by telling himself Evangeline wasn't truly alone. There's an entire production team watching through those cameras. No matter how fucked up things have been already, they wouldn't allow *that*. Would they? They wouldn't let Jack take advantage of a drunk young woman. They can't blame that on a technical hitch.

Besides, Evangeline is a savvy girl. She wouldn't have done anything stupid.

He needs to talk to someone and looks for his friend, but Gaz has been avoiding him all day. Every time Marty has tried to engage him in conversation, Gaz finds an excuse to walk away, feigning interest in someone else's conversation.

Marty assumes it's Jack's comments during nominations that have made Gaz uncomfortable. He knows Gaz isn't gay; Marty's gaydar is well intact. But is being called gay *that* offensive to him? Is he now ashamed to hang around with the gay housemate in case he gets accused of being the same? The thought that his sexuality might be driving away the one genuine friendship he'd found in this place hurts.

Marty has always been relaxed about his sexuality. Growing up with supportive parents meant he never had to hide or pretend to be someone else. Although it's an attitude that has got him in trouble more times than he'd like to count, sadly some people feel compelled to kick the shit out of people for something that doesn't impact them—but he's proud of his honesty. He's proud of being that man.

Though he isn't proud of the way he's behaved. Now that he's sober, he can reflect on the last few years with agonising shame. The things he did for the high. The people he stole from. The loved ones he hurt.

He's been going barefoot constantly since arriving, his feet perpetually cold against the hard floors. It's his way of avoiding his sock drawer entirely—and the coke hidden there. But knowing it exists is eating him alive.

The temptation grows stronger every day, especially with the stress of this place, the paranoia, the isolation from everything familiar. He'd thought he was stronger than this, thought he'd put that part of his life behind him. But the house seems determined to strip away whatever progress he'd made.

Cocaine is where it all started. It started innocently enough. After-show parties with the band. Then late nights searching the clubs for connection that might fill the emptiness inside. Just harmless fun, he'd told himself.

Until it wasn't.

The parties became more frequent, the drugs harder, and Marty just slipped past the point of no return without a care in the world. He thought he was living his best life, but in reality, the fun was stripped away long before the parties stopped.

The band kicked him out after an incident with a fan during a live show. In his drugged-up state, Marty was giving the performance of his life. At least he thought he was. When they showed him the video afterward, he was horrified to see himself wielding his guitar like a weapon, lashing out at the fans pressed against the barrier.

He's lucky no charges were filed. It seems you can get away with a lot when you're the one in the spotlight. But the shame of what he'd become—the realisation that he'd endangered innocent people who'd just come to enjoy the music—that was punishment enough.

But he lost everything anyway. The tour, his career, his friends. Soon after, his childhood home too. Stealing all the electronics to pay for your habit will do that.

Living on the streets made him more desperate, more stupid. Bad decisions were made, so many lives were ruined.

His dealer, Carl, has been hunting for him ever since. He thought moving to London would save him, but Carl has friends tucked away in all corners, so Marty has been constantly running. Until he came here.

Now he's dragging himself back, trying to save himself and those he loves the most. He's got just under a month to get the money together to pay Carl or he'll make good on his threat to burn his family home down—with his parents inside.

Like Victoria, winning this is life or death.

Charlie steps outside. It's definitely her—Charlie is the more sombre of the two, shy and sweet. Amber commands space, the more fun one.

Marty doesn't know which one he prefers. The Ambers of the world, though more entertaining, are usually more dangerous.

"Hey," Charlie says, sitting down beside him on the bench. She lights a cigarette and takes a long drag. "How's things?"

"Pretty shit."

She laughs, the sudden intake of air making her cough. "I know the feeling."

Marty has been longing to learn more about Charlie. Not out of judgement, everyone has their quirks—but because it'll take his mind off the blow in the bedroom. "So, how's Amber doing today?"

Her initial alarm at the direct question quickly melts into a look of relief. "She's fuming because I won't let her out to play."

Goosebumps erupt all over Marty's skin, and he immediately regrets asking, but his curiosity won't let him drop it. "She's your sister, right?"

"Yeah, older."

"And she died?"

"Kind of. She went missing. Presumed dead."

Her lack of emotion unnerves Marty, but then maybe when someone you've lost continues to exist in you, the grief is diluted.

"And now she's..." he presses.

"She stuck around. Said it wasn't her time to go yet, and since we shared a womb, we could share a body."

Marty swallows. "And you don't mind?"

"Most of the time. Sometimes she pisses me off, you know? But that's what sisters do." Charlie's voice softens. "I've been trying to find her body in the hope she can rest easy then, but the private investigator I hired is crap. I'm hoping to win the money to get a better one."

This is the Landlord. Could Gaz change the mic packs? New ones are in the hatch.

Gaz enters the garden with a basket of fresh mic packs. Battery changes happen twice daily like clockwork. He moves through the routine efficiently, his posture stooped.

"Thanks, boss," Marty says to him. When Gaz doesn't acknowledge him, he tries again. "You okay, yeah?"

Gaz ignores his question and turns to Charlie. "Where's Amber today?"

Charlie smiles at him. "Scared of her?"

"No. Just don't know if I have the energy."

"Fair one. I doubled the dosage of my meds today. Though she'll be pissed when she's allowed back."

Gaz just stares at her dumbfounded.

"How's Jack today?" Marty asks, mainly to change the subject. Watching Jack crumble with the weight of his impending eviction has been oddly satisfying, and Marty can't wait to wave goodbye to the homophobic arsehole.

"Nervous as hell. Ever since the nominations, he's been more miserable than ever, and apparently, he's running out of painkillers. Let's hope he's gone before then."

Miserable is better than angry, Marty thinks. Jack's rage is frightening, like a ticking bomb with a faulty timer, waiting to explode any second and not caring about who he takes with it.

"He's refusing to wear a mic," Gaz says. "Thinks he's *sticking it to the man.*"

"Ah shit, does that mean he's going to be punished?"

"Or we'll all be punished together. Let's face it, Jack was nominated, what more can they throw at him?"

Jack is a man teetering on the edge of a breakdown. This show was supposed to be his redemption, his chance to win back public favour; he's royally fucked it. He's got nothing left, and instead of lashing out, he's collapsing inwards.

Charlie watches him with an unnervingly perceptive stare. "I reckon he's not raging because he already took his frustrations out on Evangeline."

Both men whip around to face her. "What is that supposed to mean?" Gaz demands.

But Charlie mimes zipping her lips shut. "I promised her I'd keep quiet. And I'm not my sister, I can keep secrets."

@monstermuncher: the chef guy is losing it. LOL

@subscriber996: met that Jack at an awards show once. He was a knob. Deserves to suffer that one.

@bodycount_27: so when is the fun going to start?

Evangeline's Confessional

"Good afternoon, Evangeline. What brings you here today?"

Evangeline wipes a tear from the corner of her eye. "This conversation isn't being broadcast, right?"

A long pause stretches through the tiny room.

"How can the Landlord assist you today, Evangeline?"

"You need to guarantee this stays private."

The silence is excruciating. Evangeline is horribly aware that the Landlord is calling her bluff. She desperately needs help, and the Landlord knows she must talk to get what she needs.

What other option does she have? She knows that her reputation is now in ruins. Any hope of future sponsorship deals or brand partnerships will have already evaporated. What choice does she have? If she's already lost everything she's worked so hard for, what's the point in keeping quiet?

She takes a shaky breath and wipes away another tear before it can fall. She won't give them the satisfaction—refusing to make this more entertaining than it already is.

"I need to know exactly what happened last night."

The pause that follows is painful.

"With me and Jack."

"The Landlord does not know what you're referring to, Evangeline. Please be more specific."

Something inside her snaps. "You know what I'm talking about. Just tell me, did Jack wear a condom?"

More silence. It's as if the camera itself is laughing at her, and she turns away, disgusted with herself.

"Get me the morning-after pill. Just in case."

Because the alternative is abhorrent. The mere possibility of carrying Jack's baby activates her gag reflex. She dry-retches violently before swallowing and forcing herself to take deep breaths to ease the nausea.

She's still within the window for the pill to work, right? She has to be. Take the pill, wait for Jack to get kicked out of the house, and she'll never have to see him again. She'll slip into obscurity and get a job at Burger King or something.

She presses a tissue to her eyes, no longer able to wipe them away quickly enough.

"And why do you need the morning-after pill, Evangeline?"

"You damn well know why! Don't mess with me."

"I cannot supply what you want until I have understood your reasons for wanting it."

Evangeline can't bring herself to say it out loud. She doesn't want to even think it. But fragments of memory keep playing over and over. Jack pushing her down onto her stomach, her ass waving in the air. The way she arched her back, gladly bucking backwards into him so he could take her for the entire world to see.

She doubles over, dry heaving again, her body rejecting the memory as violently as her mind does.

How many people saw what she did? Just a handful of production staff? An entire team? Surely it wasn't streamed online like the rest of the show. They couldn't air something like that, could they? That has got to be breaking some kind of law.

"You know what I did," she whispers. When she doesn't receive a response, she says. "Okay, I slept with him. All right? That disgusting old man out there. I don't even know why. I—I was absolutely wasted."

Her words trail off.

"So, you think you might be pregnant, Evangeline?"

Amongst other things. But she'll deal with those fears when she's out of the house. Right now, she needs to stay put. The thought of facing her family makes her chest tighten. They're going to be so disappointed in her. And she genuinely thinks her mum might just kill her for dragging their name through the mud, for ending the career she's ruthlessly built.

And Peters! She can kiss that relationship goodbye. There's no way he'll stand by her after this. Despite his multiple affairs.

Neither of them has ever been faithful, but then neither party seemed to mind. But then Peters is concerned about just one thing—his image. And being cheated on television with the tabloid laughingstock might just be a humiliation too far.

All men in her life let her down eventually. Why should Peters be any different?

It was a farce anyway, a mutually beneficial ploy to get more publicity. The exposure he bought her really helped her really launch her career as an influencer.

"The Landlord will provide you with what you need."

"Soon, yes? The longer I wait, the less effective it will be."

"I'll be in touch in due course."

"Please, it needs *to be soon."*

"Have a nice day, Evangeline."

Chapter 13

Henry

Most of the housemates are talking in the garden when Susan shuffles out of the Confessions Room looking immensely guilty. Henry watches as she retreats to the kitchen, where she attacks the simple task of making a sandwich with barely controlled violence. She slams cupboards and rattles drawers, throwing the butter knife onto the counter with a loud clatter.

She's blinking furiously, fighting off tears that threaten to spill from her lower eyelids.

He watches her hands tremble as she spreads butter on the bread, missing the edges and leaving greasy smears across the counter. Twice she nearly drops the knife, her coordination compromised by what appears to be significant distress.

When Victoria glides past to check on Evangeline, Susan recoils as if struck and turns away.

Henry approaches her carefully. "Susan, is everything okay? You look rather shaken."

She forces a smile onto her face, but it looks dismally false. Her lips quiver with the effort of maintaining the expression, and her eyes remain dull.

"Talk to me. It might help. What happened in the Confessions Room just now?"

Henry steps closer as he speaks, making Susan instinctively step back until she bumps into the counter. Henry continues forward, closing the distance between them. He leans in, enjoying the panic on her breath.

Susan's eyes dart to the camera in the corner, then back to his face. "Oh, you know. The normal wobble. Want to leave but can't quite summon the courage to do so. It's all so very confusing."

Henry nods thoughtfully then tilts his head to study her with uncomfortable intensity. He's sympathetic toward Susan's plight. When you do awful things like spiking someone's drink, it's only right that she feels like this. Remorse makes it hard to live with yourself; it helps you to rectify and grow. To change.

It's exactly why Henry has never bothered himself with such an inconvenient emotion. He doesn't need to change. You make your decisions and then you stand by them.

"You want to leave? That's such a pity."

But Susan shakes her head, catching him off guard. "Oh no, I don't want to go at all. I just feel like I *have to*. You know? Like all this is too much for me, and I'm not sure I can handle it all. I'm frightened, Henry. Really scared."

"I don't understand. Frightened of what?"

But before Susan can even open her mouth to respond, he presses on, catching her off guard. "I've been watching you, Susan. Very carefully." He squints at her, his expression cold.

"What?" Her voice trembles. "What are you talking about?"

Henry steps back and runs his tongue along his lower lip; his icy demeanour evaporates as quickly as it appeared. "Why look so panicked? I only meant that your time here hasn't been particularly difficult. Not like Victoria and Jack. You and I—we're the lucky ones. There's absolutely no need to leave, silly billy."

Susan sighs shakily, her relief palpable as she pushes her sandwich-laden plate at Henry. "Here, you can eat this. I'm not hungry."

He glances at the sandwich, and his stomach grumbles in response. "Why make it then? You couldn't have made this just for little old me."

"I like to cook when I'm stressed." She manages a watery smile. "Maybe that's why I'm struggling. Jack has made it crystal clear that the kitchen is his domain, and I don't want to upset him. So, I kept well away from the one thing that relaxes me."

"Ah, so you've been denied your coping mechanism?" Henry knows how that feels. Though his own methods of stress relief would hardly be suitable television content. The thought makes him smile all the same.

Susan nods. "Eat. Please."

"There's nothing in this, is there? You haven't *spiked* it with something?"

Susan's eyes widen; her mouth falls open. Henry hides his laughter by coughing into his hand. This is a rather fun game.

"Just ham and cheese. Why would you—?"

"Oh, no particular reason." Henry takes a generous bite and thanks her warmly. He hadn't realised how hungry he was. "Well, maybe when Jack is gone, things'll get easier in here for you. Don't leave just yet."

"You really think he's leaving?"

"He was nominated, wasn't he? A majority vote means you're out—those are the rules, aren't they?"

Susan leans in closer, dropping her voice to a whisper. "Then why is he still here?"

Henry just shrugs. "No idea. You'll have to ask our gracious host."

"I tried. He said housemates are not privy to Landlord decisions until he wishes to divulge. Basically told me to piss off."

"Ha! Well, I suppose we're at his mercy then, aren't we?"

Susan grunts. "Hey, did you hear about Evangeline?"

This is the Landlord. Could all housemates gather on the sofas immediately?

"Perhaps this is it?!" Henry tells Susan, polishing off the sandwich. He pats her on the hand, and they dutifully head over to the sofas.

Victoria

The atmosphere in the house has changed since the night of the party. Tension crackles through every room in the house; it seeps into every conversation. If you could graph the stress levels, the line would have spiked that night and flatlined at breaking point ever since.

Victoria is praying for things to settle, but she fears that as long as Jack lives under this roof, the cortisol level in this house will remain sky high.

Amid all the chaos, though, she feels an unexpected lightness. Now that her secret is out, she can talk openly about Lily, easing the pressure that was building inside of her.

Now that she can finally see clearly through her grief at missing Lily, she can look at this from a more competitive angle. Maybe Lily's story will resonate with the viewers at home, earning her some sympathy votes and pushing her into first place in the polls. Maybe at the end, she will be voted winner.

She came here for her daughter's future—why shouldn't she use everything at her disposal to secure it?

All of this is for Lily. Every humiliation, the unknowing, the sleep deprivation—it's all leading to that prize money and the media deals that follow. She'll book the first flight to Boston when she gets out of here and get her girl the help she needs. The thought of all this makes her feel like she's floating through the air, powered by hope.

But as she settles on the sofa, she cannot shift the sense of dread that comes over her as soon as her bottom hits the chair. The Landlord thrives on their stress, and things have been relatively quiet since the party. He'll have something up his sleeve for sure.

Time to throw a fox among the chickens.

Jack slouches across from her, his posture rigid and his eyebrows furrowed. He's still refusing to wear a microphone. Though now his agitation is palpable. Victoria has watched him give Evangeline a wide berth since the party, like they've fallen out. Maybe the girl finally showed some backbone and told him exactly where he could shove his wandering hands.

Marty catches her eye and jerks his head towards Jack, smiling slightly. He's convinced Jack's about to be served his eviction notice. Victoria hopes he's right; one less housemate is one step closer to the end. To winning. But she's not stupid. The Landlord has few morals, and keeping a predator in the house of sheep is far too entertaining to end.

On Sunday evening, you cast your nominations. As you know, Jack received the majority of the nominations.

Every eye turns to Jack, who looks like he wants to disappear down the back of the sofa.

However, because of public poll positioning, Jack has been granted immunity from tonight's eviction.

Evangeline makes no effort to disguise her groan of disgust. Around the room, faces fall in disappointment—everyone except Henry, who remains utterly composed. If anything, there's a flicker of satisfaction in his expression.

Jack manages a smile, but it's short-lived. He looks utterly drained as he cradles his bandaged hand to his chest.

Victoria cannot fathom why he came here. She'd assumed he was attempting to rehabilitate his image after the tabloids crucified them for his habit of shagging, and allegedly abusing, sex workers in his restaurants.

But putting yourself under 24/7 surveillance only to treat another housemate like a piece of meat. Is he really that stupid? Apparently so.

As such, all nominations are rendered void.

"Looks like you're stuck with us '*gays*' then, mate," Marty says. "Lucky you!"

Jack's lip curls as he turns away. "I have nothing against you people. Just what you do."

"Oh Jack, you're such a twat."

Jack just shrugs, jaw tightening as he swallows whatever venom was rising in his throat. Victoria doesn't care which way Marty swings, but she does know he's comically skilled at cutting straight to the bone with the truth. Jack *is* a twat.

Charlie laughs, the glint in her eye signalling that Amber has come out to play. Victoria straightens. She vastly prefers Charlie. She feels safer around Charlie's timidity to whatever darkness Amber brings with her.

Now, could Charlie please come to the hatch?

Amber skips to the small door beside the Confessions Room. She pulls it open and frowns at the contents. "What's this?" She pulls out a small box and holds it up for inspection. Her eyes widen when she reads the description, and her mouth drops open.

Could Charlie please hand the box to Evangeline?

Understanding floods Amber's face, and she actually blushes with excitement. "Holy shit! It's the morning-after pill!"

Evangeline turns frighteningly pale, and Victoria tenses. Her lips tremble as she watches Evangeline's humiliation.

Victoria has been here before. She remembers with vivid clarity the confusion, the crushing shame, the uncertainty about what you consented to.

The difference is Evangeline has witnesses. Cameras. Proof of what Jack did or didn't do. Victoria had nothing but her own fragmented memories and a man who insisted she'd begged for it.

Amber hands the box over with a smirk. "Charlie told me what you did, you naughty girl. But seriously, you didn't use protection? Rookie error."

Evangeline snatches the box and bolts, disappearing into the bedroom.

"Is she allowed to just walk away like that?" Amber spins around, addressing the room. "We haven't been dismissed."

"What's the Landlord going to do? Storm in here and drag her back in?" Gaz asks. He's looking at Jack as if he wants to murder him.

"Oh, screw this." Victoria pushes to her feet and follows Evangeline's footsteps.

Marty

"You'll be punished!" Susan calls after Victoria, looking around desperately for support that never comes. "What now?"

Amber giggles. "I guess her boyfriend isn't going to be thrilled. Watch out, Jack, *Peters* is coming for you."

But Jack just snorts and rolls his shoulders. "That ponce? He doesn't scare me. I met him at some awards thing once. Complete bellend."

Rage floods through Marty—sudden, and white-hot. He crosses the room in three quick strides, bringing him face-to-face with the bastard.

"You absolute piece of shit," he hisses, towering over Jack. His fists shake at his sides, every muscle tense. "Evangeline was completely wasted that night. Everyone could see it. How can you just sit there and not give a single fuck about what you did?!"

Jack tilts his head back with maddening indifference. "Didn't hear her complaining, mate. Quite the opposite, actually." His injured hand waves him away. "Quite vocal about how much she was enjoying it actually—"

Marty's hand shoots out, grabbing Jack's shirt and hauling him half off the sofa. "I don't give a fuck what you think you heard. She's going through hell, and you're acting like it's all a big joke."

Jack's smirk falters as he realises the genuine threat in Marty's rage. Gasps ripple through the room. Susan half-rises from her seat, uncertain whether to intervene or run away.

"I was drunk too," Jack protests, his voice losing some of its confidence. "We both were. I don't see you accusing *her* of —"

"Of what?" Marty's knuckles whiten. "What are you trying to say, Jack?" He drops Jack back onto the sofa. "She's twenty years old, Jack. Twenty! And you're what? Nearly fifty?"

"Forty-seven," Jack mutters, attempting to straighten his rumpled shirt with as much dignity as he can muster.

"Is this how you treat all women? Is this what you did to those girls at your restaurant?" Marty's voice climbs higher, months of pent-up self-loathing finally finding a target. "Because from where I'm standing, you're exactly the monster the papers said you were."

Jack pushes to his feet, but Gaz materialises between them, a solid presence between them. "That's enough," he says firmly. "This isn't helping anyone. Victoria's with Evangeline fixing what you did. There's no need to be such a massive tool about it. She's a nice girl."

Marty steps back, chest still heaving. "If you go near her again—if you so much as breathe in her direction—I will end you." He turns away but catches Henry's expression: a strange blend of approval and calculation.

Henry nods thoughtfully and turns to Jack. "You ought to watch yourself, Jack. Your reputation is hanging by a thin thread already." He folds his hands in his lap. "And isn't that why you're here? To rehabilitate your image?"

Jack's laugh is harsh, a deep bark that makes Amber jump and spill her tea across her lap. "You heard the Landlord. I got immunity. My reputation is doing just fine, thank you."

Henry cocks his head to the side. "Well, I suppose that makes sense, logically. Morally, however—"

Marty takes all this in, his emotions all over the place. Though guilt dominates everything. It suffocates him for not having intervened that night. Then comes disgust at the Landlord's cruelty, letting Jack take advantage of Evangeline for the sake of views and likes. His heart aches for her. She's so young and confused. Exploited.

Right now, he wants to know how Evangeline is doing. The poor girl must be terrified. The thought of potentially carrying Jack's baby... Christ, what a nightmare!

She finds her curled up into a tight ball on her bed, face buried in her pillow, her words lost in broken sobs that shake her slim frame.

Victoria sits on the edge of her bed, gently stroking Evangeline's hair. When she spots Marty by the door, she gives him a helpless shrug.

Marty silently asks Victoria for permission to approach. She just stares back, wide-eyed and lost. No one knows what to do for the best.

"You alright, Evangeline?" he eventually asks.

Her crying intensifies, becoming louder and unrestrained. "I'm such an idiot!" she wails. "I can't believe this is happening." She lets out a bitter, choked laugh. "I mean, I've done some stupid stuff in my life, but this is on a whole new level."

"For what it's worth, no one out there is judging you for any of this."

Evangeline laughs a snotty, wet laugh. "No offence, Mart, but it's not you guys I'm worried about. It's them out there." She jabs a finger at the window. "What must they be thinking? I can already see the headlines: *Slaggy influencer bangs Z-list celebrity with tiny dick.*"

Marty hides his grin behind his hand, but Victoria catches his eye, and they share silent amusement. She discreetly wiggles her pinky finger at him.

"Maybe everyone out there is just talking about Jack's little penis then? Maybe they're not talking about you at all."

Evangeline's sobs reach new volumes.

"Shit, sorry," Marty backpedals. "I mean, I'm sure they're talking about you too. All positive stuff." He flounders, not knowing what the right words are here. He should have just left this to Victoria.

Evangeline hiccoughs violently. "Do you think the Landlord showed us actually having sex? What if he did? Mum is going to kill me!"

"Right, stop spiralling," Victoria cuts in sharply, taking control. "First thing's first. Have you taken that pill?"

Evangeline sits up and shakes her head. Her face is splotchy and swollen; her eyes bloodshot. Victoria reaches for the bottle of water on the bedside table and hands it to her.

"Take it right away."

Evangeline fumbles with the packaging, her hands shaking as she complies. "This will work, right?"

Victoria's eyes flick to Marty for a fraction of a second before turning back to Evangeline. "I'm sure it'll be just fine, darling."

Evangeline swallows the tablet and visibly relaxes. With the pregnancy scare handled, she can now focus on other problems created during her drunken recklessness. She takes a shaky breath, but the tears continue to flow, and there's still that wildness behind her eyes that makes Marty worry she's going to start wailing again.

"Right, you wanna know what I think?" he says, though not entirely sure what he thinks yet. He just cannot bear more squealing. Both women turn to him—Evangeline with desperate optimism, Victoria with amusement.

"I think right now you're stuck in here. You're in the bubble. Whatever shitstorm is going on outside, it's unknown. It's invisible so you can't see it, can't control it, can't change it. So you know what?"

"What?" Evangeline breathes, hanging onto his every word.

"Fuck it."

"Fuck it?"

"Exactly! Okay, maybe poor choice of words there. But what I mean is, literally anything could be happening out there—good, bad, the ugly. So let's just assume the best-case scenario and deal with the reality when we have to. There's no point in torturing yourself in here over things you can't change."

Marty is rambling, but Evangeline is nodding along like he's dispensing profound wisdom.

"You're right," she says finally, her voice sounding steady. "What's the point of stressing over the unknown? Falling apart isn't going to fix anything. I need to work on damage control." She stares at her shaking hands and presses them together, willing them to be still. "I'm not the first woman on Earth to have got drunk and slept with the wrong person, am I? Maybe I can be a voice for all the women who've made the same mistake. Show them we can hold our heads high."

"Exactly," Marty tells her, genuinely impressed by her resilience.

"Marty, you're the best. I'm rooting for you and Gaz—you'll make such a lovely couple."

Victoria laughs. "God, yes. I'd pay good money to see you two together."

Marty stands up and takes a step back. "Well, I hate to break it to you, but Gaz doesn't swing that way."

"Really?" Evangeline tilts her head, studying him. "Are you sure about that? I've heard otherwise."

"Does it matter?" Marty snaps. "Does is actually matter? Anyway, even if he was gay, that doesn't mean we'll automatically hook up."

Evangeline's eyes narrow. "The truth always matters, Marty. Don't you think the truth should matter above anything else?"

Chapter 14

<u>Henry</u>

This is the Landlord. Can all housemates please gather in the garden immediately?

"Nope!" Jack announces, slapping his good hand against his thigh. "I'd rather chop my bollocks off."

"Maybe you should. Save a lot of women a world of trouble," Evangeline quips, provoking a laugh from Charlie, the real Charlie today.

"Quiet you. What happened wasn't all my fault, and you bloody well know it. I distinctly remember it was your arse in the air, inviting me to eat it."

Evangeline yelps and rushes out to the garden, leaving Jack's cruel laughter echoing behind her. He swivels to Marty. "I bet you like eating ass, don't you?"

"Shut the fuck up."

"Ooh, touched a nerve, did I, big man? You wanna watch that temper of yours."

"Careful Jack, you have absolutely no idea what I'm capable of."

"Is that a threat? Hey, Landlord!" Jack calls out, waving his arms theatrically. "Marty is threatening me. What you going to do about it?"

Henry saunters over. "Likely nothing. He didn't seem particularly bothered when your hand was cooking. I doubt that a few harsh words will ruffle his feathers."

Jack wrinkles his nose at him, and steps aside to let him pass. He peers anxiously into the garden, scanning for the black boxes from their last task. Seeing the garden empty, he follows Henry outside, his eyes flitting left to right and his cheeks devoid of colour.

The housemates gather in a tight circle as if trying to protect themselves from whatever torment awaits.

For this task, the housemates will be presented with various adjectives. You must rank yourselves from least to most for each given trait.

"Oh, this should be fun," Henry murmurs, already savouring the inevitable carnage. He can see the outcome already. Everyone clamouring to present themselves favourably to the public, regardless of the truth.

You'll score points for every ranking that matches the public vote conducted earlier today.

Henry laughs a tinkly laugh. This task just became exponentially more interesting. Not only must the housemates brutally assess themselves, but they have to second-guess what millions of strangers think of them too.

This could be very telling indeed.

Your first adjective is: funny. Who is the funniest housemate, and who is the least? For every person placed correctly, you win a point.

The group freezes, exchanging uncertain glances, no one daring to make the first move.

Henry takes action.

"Well, I'm clearly the least funny, so I'm going to put myself at the bottom." He positions himself by the hot tub, facing the house, encouraging his housemates to play along.

"Rubbish, you're a funny guy," Susan protests. "I should go at the bottom."

"She's right, you know," Gaz pipes up. "You come out with some blinders. The funniest people have no idea how funny they are."

"Yep, shift over and let me in the bottom spot." Victoria gently nudges Henry and slips in between him and the hot tub. She gives his elbow a gentle squeeze of reassurance.

Things move swiftly then, and before Henry can process what's happening, he's found himself shuffled further up the pack. Victoria, Susan, Marty, Gaz, and Charlie have all claimed spaces below him, while Jack has brazenly crowned himself the funniest housemate. Evangeline hovers uncertainly between Jack and Henry.

Henry isn't sure what delusion makes Evangeline feel she's the second funniest here. Though he suspects it's more about screen time than actual comedic talent.

The speakers emit two loud beeps, indicating that two people are correctly placed—Susan and Henry. That's two points awarded. The Landlord has given no clue of what they might win, and no one seems bothered. They're more concerned about the psychological chess match of playing the game than the consequences that might follow.

That's the problem with the younger generation—they get so lost in the immediate details they fail to see the bigger picture. Then they wonder why they always end up getting stuck.

The housemates next rank themselves on physical attractiveness. Henry isn't remotely surprised to find himself at the bottom of the list while Evangeline claims the top spot. Though he would have positioned Victoria considerably higher—her beauty is understated, muted by layers of grief, but it's there, bolstered by an unimaginable strength.

Susan stands next to Henry, grumbling something about how true beauty is kept on the inside. Henry doesn't engage.

Three more points awarded.

Housemate most likely to win the million-pound prize.

Now that's an interesting question.

The housemates shift awkwardly, probably calculating how best to play this. Position yourself too high and you appear delusionally arrogant; too low and you're essentially admitting to being boring on television. No, this requires finesse.

Henry can practically see the gears turning in their heads as they weigh public perception against personal ambition.

"Well, I'm going here." Henry places himself at the bottom. The truth is, he couldn't care less about winning. He isn't here for fame or riches. No, he's here for the thrill. His life has become so insufferably tedious lately. Conversations with his wife dried up long ago, and he's been starving for genuine excitement. Excitement and Charlie, that is.

Following her in was a risk. Would she recognise him? Would she be just too tempting? But at the end of the day, Henry couldn't resist.

Having Charlie in close proximity has been hard on him. He's so used to keeping in the shadows, he's felt horribly exposed. He's had to constantly remember that it's okay. That *he's* okay.

Though the thought of what's coming makes the effort worth it.

"No mate, you need to give yourself more credit. You're way closer to the top." Ah, Marty, playing the humble, kind-hearted hero card.

Henry shakes his head dismissively. "I'm happy here. You can fight for the remaining spots. I don't have the energy for it."

"Henry, this isn't about how to see yourself; it's about public perception," Susan insists. "Marty is right; you should be higher. I bet the people out there love you."

Henry narrows his eyes at her. "Who do you think should be at the bottom then? Who's the biggest loser, Susan?"

Susan squeezes her eyes shut, looking pained. It's almost as if she's receiving instructions from an invisible earpiece. Henry smiles. He's more convinced than ever that Susan is a mole. Her constant visits to the Confessions Room, the strange behaviour at the party. Then her personality changes so rapidly, so violently—she's clearly under stress.

The Landlord has to be directing her; Henry would bet his entire pension on it.

"Right, let's get this over with. I'm bored," Jack says. "Henry, if you're happy in the gutter, stay there."

"Oh no, I'd like to hear Susan's thoughts."

Susan rocks from one foot to the other, her eyes darting to Jack for a mere nanosecond—it's barely a flicker, but Henry catches it. Henry widens his eyes innocently, practically salivating at the prospect of watching Susan hang herself.

"Well, actually." She looks frightened, and rightfully so. Ever since Jack's injury and then his sordid encounter with Evangeline, he's been operating with nothing left to lose. He's a walking powder keg, just waiting for the right spark.

That's probably why the Landlord is playing with him, dangling medication in front of him, making him beg.

After the initial supply of painkillers and antibiotics, the drug train stopped, sending Jack into a frenzy of panic. It's been glorious.

"Yes, Susan?" Henry prompts, his voice silky.

"Actually, I think Jack should be at the bottom. You know, after..."

Jack's eyes widen, and his cheeks turn scarlet. "So you think I'm completely fucked then? You reckon I've got less chance than a couple of faggots and an old fart?"

Gaz rolls his eyes, but Henry sees Marty clench his fists behind Jack.

"I... I just think you've got a little bit of work to do, that's all."

Jack lurches forward, invading Susan's personal space. "I don't need judgement from trash like you. Who the hell do you think you are? Well, I'll fucking tell you, shall I? You're a *nobody*. A fat, middle-aged bitch."

"That's enough!" Marty pushes Jack back, away from a cowering Susan. He steps between them. "You think you're a big man, yeah? Squaring up to a woman just because she bruised your delicate ego?"

"Don't you *dare* touch me."

"What, in case I infect you with my sexuality? Oh, get a grip, Jack."

The punch comes without warning—a blur of movement culminating in the sickening crack of knuckles meeting bone. Jack's fist slams into Marty's jaw. The impact whips Marty's head sideways as blood and saliva spray across the garden in a crimson arc.

Gaz launches himself forward then, tackling Jack to the ground. Jack's fist misses its mark as it cuts through empty air.

"That's enough!" Victoria screams.

"It's not though, is it? That twat needs a good hiding." Jack spits, livid.

Gaz pins a thrashing Jack down; his forearm pressed firmly against Jack's throat with just enough pressure to restrain him. Jack's legs kick uselessly against the grass. "Nah, mate, that's you. You've been acting like a Grade A prick since you got here."

Henry watches the chaos unfold with barely concealed delight, noting how quickly civilized behaviour crumbles when the right pressure is applied. Now *this* is the level of entertainment he signed up for.

Victoria

The atmosphere is so thick Victoria is afraid she might choke. She tears her gaze away from Gaz and Jack, who look like they're about to kill each other. Gaz, the charming joker who has only ever been so gentle and sweet, has transformed into a completely different person.

Strong. Commanding. Dangerous.

Jack, usually so bloated with narcissism, now looks pitiful beneath Gaz's considerable bulk. For the first time since entering the house, he resembles what he actually is—a broken, aging man with nothing left to lose.

"Where's security when you need them?" Evangeline mutters to Victoria's left. "I didn't sign up for this macho shit."

Victoria suspects everyone is thinking the same thing. This was supposed to be fun. Friendships made. Money in the bank. And so far, it's just been one big mess. Still, the viewings must be through the roof. That must count for something.

This is the Landlord.

Oh, thank God, it's about time someone stepped in to take better care of the housemates.

Could housemates rank yourselves in order of who is most likely to win the prize, from most to least likely? Failure to do so will result in consequences.

Thanks for nothing.

The intervention seems to work though. Gaz releases Jack with a final shove and springs to his feet, checking on Marty, who blinks back, his nose dripping blood.

Victoria goes to Marty instinctively. "Let me take a look at you," she says, gently nudging his chin so she can assess the damage.

"It's nothing," Marty mumbles, flinching away from her touch.

"I'll get you cleaned up after this circus is over."

She hears muttering behind her, and when she turns around, she's surprised to see all eyes on her.

"Come on then, step forward," Charlie says, her cheeks flushed by the chilly air. Victoria doesn't move. "Well, it's obvious who's going to win, isn't it?"

"Is it?"

"You silly. Get up there."

Victoria stays rooted to the spot.

"Come on, gal. You're tops," Susan encourages. "Let's just get this over with before we all freeze to death."

Victoria reluctantly steps forward, exhaling heavily. "Fine. But for the record, I don't think I'm the favourite. I'm hardly entertaining." She stands in first position anyway. Susan's right; this charade needs to end. It's just another silly way to drive a wedge between the already fragile relationships in here.

The rest of the housemates seem to just shuffle into random positions then, clearly over the entire exercise.

They win two points.

The categories keep coming with little drama: best and worst dressed. Most and least intelligent, athletic, emotional. The housemates shuffle into position with little discussion.

The task drags on for another hour. Marty's nose still spattering the grass beneath his feet. Jack maintains his perpetual scowl as if he's at war with the entire world. Charlie looks like she's close to tears.

And finally: who is the biggest liar?

The garden falls into absolute silence.

Chapter 15

<u>Marty</u>

"Presumably, the people watching out there." Henry motions to the enclosing walls. "Know things about us we haven't shared with our fellow housemates. Things the producers are divulging after researching us a little more. That's likely what the public will base their votes on."

"Or maybe it's just based on perception. Who they *think* is lying," Gaz counters. "Let's not make more drama, eh? There have been enough punches thrown today."

Henry shrugs and turns away, but Marty thinks he has a point. What if they are being judged on the things they've kept back? Things that have been dug up on the outside?

Marty shudders at the thought.

He notices Victoria staring into space. "You okay? You look shattered."

"Yeah, yeah, all good. So how are we doing this then?"

"Well, Jack's already stuck himself at the bottom, says he's got nothing left to hide—the whole world knows his secrets. And honestly, I think he has a point."

"That's bullshit," Evangeline suddenly interjects, her voice tight with anger. She pokes at Jack. "You're a liar."

The garden goes dead silent, stunned by the vehemence in her voice.

Jack's eyebrows shoot upward. "Excuse me?"

"You told me you used protection." Evangeline's voice wobbles but carries clearly across the garden. Her cheeks burn crimson with humiliation, but her gaze remains steady on Jack. "That night. You told me you had it covered. *The Landlord* corrected that lie when he gave me the morning-after pill. Do you have any idea how embarrassing that was?"

An uncomfortable silence descends. Victoria sucks in a sharp breath. Henry's eyes practically glitter with delight at this unexpected gift. Jack's face darkens.

"That doesn't make me a liar. I thought I did." He shrugs with infuriating casualness. "I was drunk, you were drunk—I didn't lie, I was just wrong. Everything is blurry."

"Oh, this just keeps getting better and better," Marty cuts in, his words slightly muffled through his swollen lips.

"Oh, fuck off, you sanctimonious prick. Nobody asked you." Jack advances menacingly toward Marty, who doesn't flinch despite his injuries. Gaz immediately moves closer to Marty, creating a human shield between him and Jack.

"Did you lie about the girls at your restaurant too?" Charlie asks suddenly, her voice different—Amber is speaking now. "The ones who accused you of drugging them? Pressuring them? The same girls you called liars while privately paying them hush money?"

Jack's face pales. "You don't know what you're talking about."

"Really?" Amber tilts her head, smiling coldly. "Because the way you treated Evangeline doesn't inspire confidence."

Marty steps forward. "Fuck this. This isn't getting us anywhere. Henry, just stand next to Jack," he orders. He places a reassuring hand on Evangeline's shoulder, and she cups her hand over his as a thank you.

Henry flashes him a cheeky grin. "Bold of you to assume I have nothing surprising up my sleeve." But he moves to Jack's side, nevertheless. Jack gives him a brief nod of acknowledgement.

"Victoria, you're next to Henry," Gaz tells her.

"Oh, I'm not sure about that."

"You got something juicy you're not sharing with the class?" Gaz banters. "Any dirty little secret?" He winks at her.

"Well..."

"Sorry, just joking. Let's face it, we're all basically strangers. I bet we all have a thousand things we've kept buried."

Victoria swallows and goes to stand beside Henry.

"Right then, Susan ..." Marty begins.

"No, not Susan," Henry cuts in smoothly. "She's not next in line." All heads turn to face him. "I simply think there's more to Susan than she's letting on." He looks at Susan. "Am I wrong?"

Susan's face drains of colour. "Yes, you absolutely are wrong, actually. I'm an open book."

"Is that so?" Henry's tone remains gentle, almost kind. Absolutely terrifying, "Well, I have a keen eye for details others tend to overlook."

Marty's attention ping-pongs between them, wishing the ground would swallow him whole. He's never felt so uncomfortable. Secretly though, he's relieved Henry has brought this up. There's been something about Susan that's been bugging him for a while. Something he hasn't been able to put his finger on.

She's a game-player, for sure; Marty just can't decipher the rules she's playing by.

Susan bristles, her eyes landing briefly on a camera behind Marty. "Whatever. I don't care. You're wrong, but I couldn't care less."

Henry chuckles with amusement. Susan looks like she's about to snap, and Henry seems hellbent on winding her up until she does. Gone is the nice guy; the wind-up merchant has come out to play. Marty can't help but feel amused.

"Gaz, why don't you go next?" Victoria suggests. "Or Charlie. I think you're an honest girl."

Amber waves an arm dismissively and steps forward. "I'll go next, then Gaz after me." They both shuffle into position, with Henry and Susan stepping in line behind them.

"But Marty shouldn't be at the top. He's not a liar. Nor Evangeline," says Victoria, scanning the line.

Evangeline has gone unnaturally incredibly quiet, the skin on her neck mottled. "I don't care anymore. Really. I'll be the biggest liar if it ends this nightmare."

"Yeah? You hiding some dark secrets then?" Marty whispers in her ear, a poor attempt at a joke.

But Evangeline just looks at him, her eyes wet. "Can we just get this over with?" Her plea is meant for him alone. She looks so tired and young. So heartbroken.

"You feeling okay?"

"Please. I just want this over with."

Marty takes her by the hand, and they walk to claim their positions. He places her next to Gaz, and he takes the top spot at the biggest liar. Still clasping Evangeline's hand, he looks down at her and throws her an encouraging smile.

A klaxon sounds.

The task is now over. Housemates failed to score the required number of points. The housemates have therefore failed this task.

"Oh, you're kidding me?!" Jack explodes. "All that for nothing." He stomps away. "Burgers for dinner. If you don't like it, you can just fuck off." He disappears inside.

Housemates, please note that due to disappointing the Landlord, all luxuries have been removed from the house. You must earn them back.

Henry

All housemates stampede inside, impatient to assess the damage. Henry lingers by the back door, absorbing the chaos with interest.

The cushions have been removed from the sofas, leaving uncomfortable wooden boards to sit on. Jack is bellowing from inside the empty pantry. Evangeline's hysteria echoes from the bathroom—something about her makeup and products being confiscated.

Victoria emerges from the bedroom, catches Henry's eye and shrugs. "They've taken my deodorant. Looks like I'm going to smell for the foreseeable." She takes a seat at the dining table. "Aw, they've taken the salt and pepper too."

Now that is a shame. Jack takes great offence whenever someone dares 'improve' his precious cooking with extra seasoning, and Henry rather enjoyed adding surplus salt to his plate purely to wind him up.

"I've still got *this* though," Victoria says, tugging at the locket around her neck. "There's no way the bastards are touching this."

Henry seriously doubts that. Now that she's drawn attention to it, she's practically painted a target on her most treasured possession. He keeps that thought to himself though; he doesn't want to cause a panic.

Gaz ambles over. "Henry, mate, your pillow's done a runner. They left both of mine though, so I put one on your bed."

"Thank you, Gaz, very thoughtful."

"No big deal."

Charlie comes in then, pale and tearful. "They took my meds," she says, her voice cracking.

The group stares at her blankly.

"I have to take pills to keep things under control."

"Amber?" Victoria asks carefully.

Charlie nods, tears falling. "Amber visits me sometimes."

Silence. That is hardly big news.

"And I like it when she does, you know? Because I miss her. But sometimes she's a bit much. A bit demanding."

Henry scratches his chin. "So the medication helps you regulate when she... appears?"

"I don't *need* to; I *have* to. Amber can be a little bitter about being dead. And sometimes she can get really angry about it. And that anger makes her dangerous."

"Right..." Gaz says uncertainly.

Victoria leaps into action. "Well, they wouldn't just take your pills. They're a medical necessity, not a luxury. Maybe you just misplaced them?" She takes Charlie by the hand. "Come on, I'll help you look."

Victoria looks to Gaz and Henry. She clearly doesn't want to be alone with this girl. Charlie might be tiny and timid, but there's a darkness to her that is almost pulsing beneath the surface, fighting to break free.

Henry is fascinated by Charlie. He does not believe she's channelling her dead sister; that's absurd. But there's no denying there's some undeniable truth to her personality shifts. Either she's extraordinarily skilled at manipulation, or something genuinely unstable lurks within her.

Henry and Gaz follow Victoria and Charlie into the main bathroom.

"I always keep them in here," Charlie says, lifting a small pink cosmetic bag with a chunky, gold zipper. She pulls out a plastic pill organiser with compartments labelled for each day of the week. "They should be in here."

"Well, if you still have that, chances are you haven't misplaced your tablets," Henry says, almost too brightly. He thinks this is amusing; however, it might be best he kept that to himself lest his housemates think him heartless.

"No shit," Charlie snaps. "Listen, you're not grasping the severity of this. I absolutely *need* my meds. Amber cannot take control. I'm scared she won't let me back in." Her hands shake violently as she dumps the bag and begins frantically going through everyone else's toiletries.

Victoria helps her with terror in her eyes while Gaz stands around awkwardly, out of his depth. "I'll ask the Landlord," he eventually says. "Make it clear how important they are."

They continue their desperate search, throwing toothpaste and moisturisers across the bathroom surfaces.

Finding nothing, Charlie drops to her knees. "Where is it?!" she cries through Victoria's increasingly frantic attempts to calm her.

When Gaz comes back in, shaking his head and muttering apologies, Henry makes an excuse and leaves them to it. He'll just wait to see how this pans out.

In the kitchen, Jack continues his tantrum about the lack of ingredients. Apparently, even a Michelin star chef would struggle with the meagre provisions left behind. Henry turns the kettle on and reaches for the jar of tea-bags. He unscrews the lid.

It's empty.

Henry slams the jar back down, earning raised eyebrows from Jack. "Those bastards took the tea!"

Chapter 16

<u>*Jack's Confessional*</u>

"Hello Jack, how can I help you today?"

Jack swallows hard, his jaw clenched so tight his teeth make cracking sounds. "I need this to stop."

"And what might that be?"

"You know what. My hand is fucking killing me! Make the pain go away."

"There is paracetamol in the medicine cabinet."

"Oh, fuck you. You confiscated the stronger stuff, and paracetamol is shite. I need something that actually works."

"You will be given the opportunity to earn luxuries in due course."

"Luxuries! Oh, fuck you and fuck this. I'm out."

"Care to explain what you mean?"

"I'm going home. This is my formal notice."

"But the viewer polls..."

"Fuck the polls!"

The hissing sound emanating from the speaks stops, dumping Jack into a silent void.

"Landlord?"

"Yes, Jack?"

"I'm leaving today. Make the arrangements."

The landlord's silence makes his pulse hammer against his temples. "Come on! You can't leave me here like this. You won't let me go home, so you should at least help me with the pain."

...

"Answer me, you sadistic fuck! You did this to me! Do you not care at all?"

"Why don't you try talking through your problems? Maybe that will provide some relief?"

Jack's eyes bulge and his mouth gapes, but nothing comes out. Instead, he just crumples in the chair like a punctured balloon. Tears spring to his eyes, and he presses the palms of his hands to his face to hide them.

"I shouldn't have come here," he eventually whimpers. "This was a stupid idea, and as soon as I'm out of here, I'm firing that PR bitch who told me to do this."

"You don't like my house, Jack?"

"This nightmare?" he laughs. "You've got to be kidding. I didn't sign up for this shit."

"Are you upset, Jack?"

"Of course I am! I'm in constant agony and I don't know what's worse—staying in this house where we're controlled by a useless

fuck, or being outside where the public want me hung, strung, and quartered."

"You're most welcome in the Landlord's house, Jack. You're a valued housemate here."

Jack's laugh comes out as a loud bark. His hand claws at his scalp. Whereas the injured hand hovers in the air, trembling uncontrollably. "Is this some sort of twisted punishment?"

"The Landlord doesn't know what you mean, Jack. Please explain."

Jack sobs. "What happened with Evangeline. You're blaming me for that, aren't you? You're just like everyone else. Is that what this is? Are you punishing me for sleeping with her? Because you saw it! She wanted to! She was a dog in heat."

He drags his hands down his face and immediately cries out, jerking his damaged hand away to stare at it in horror. "Christ, this is unbearable."

"Why would you assume the Landlord wishes to punish you, Jack?"

"Oh please. Who doesn't want to see me suffer? All that carnage on social media. Calling me a pervert. A paedophile, saying I should rot in hell or be sent to prison to be raped. But I'm not those things. I'm not!"

"Maybe talking things over with the Landlord will help you ease your pain, Jack."

Jack barks another bitter laugh. "Nice try. You can't change the subject. I'm here to talk about my hand, not ancient history." He looks to the heavens and sighs shakily. "What happened at my restaurants was my private business. No one else's. No real harm was done. Everyone took part willingly, despite what they're saying about me. All were of legal age."

"There were no minors involved?"

"What kind of monster do you think I am?! I checked, all right? All girls said they were over sixteen. How was I to know the I.D was fake?"

His heart pounds in his chest. He knows how that sounds, but the law is the law, and he didn't break any. Not knowingly.

"The Landlord understands, Jack. What's a little party between friends? It's no one else's business."

"Exactly!"

"So what did you do with your guests?"

Jack shakes his head, trying hard to suppress his knowing grin. "We played games."

"Go on…"

"You can't judge me. I bet you got off on watching me and Evangeline. Everyone's a pervert, just in different ways."

The Landlord doesn't respond.

"I'm partial to a bit of bondage myself." He runs his tongue across his top lip.

"And children."

"FUCK YOU!" Jack explodes to his feet, slamming both hands on the chair. He screams, a high-pitched wail, and his cries pour out of him like those of a tiny child. "Please, Landlord. I'm begging you. Help me."

He forces himself to take a deep breath and whispers a desperate prayer.

"The Landlord is here to serve you. Pain medication will be issued upon completion of the next task."

"Wait, seriously?"

The static fades to nothing.

"Let me out! I'm not doing any task."

The silence worms its way through him, making his heart pound and his blood pump fast through his infected hand.

"Fine. When is the task?" Jack shouts. "When will I get the drugs?"

But the Landlord is gone.

Victoria

Victoria wakes to the angry protest of her empty stomach. It gnaws at her insides as if consuming her from within. Every muscle aches from shivering all night. The house is devoid of heat. In fact, Victoria could swear the production team has ramped up the air conditioning. Another punishment for failing the ranking task.

The bedroom has transformed—somehow it feels bigger in its coldness, and more brutal without pillows or proper bedding. A prison cell. Around her, the other housemates stir from their foetal positions on their stripped mattresses, their bodies curled tight against the chill, faces miserable with hunger and poor sleep.

The housemates no longer have access to comforts like hot water, warm blankets, cushions, and good food. They're to live on rations until further notice, and it's creating a terrible atmosphere in the house. Relationships are frayed.

Three days ago, such discomfort would have been inconceivable. Now, after blood and burns and humiliation, it's merely just another twist of the knife. Another demonstration of the Landlord's total control.

These past three days have been mercifully dull compared to the rollercoaster of the first week. Jack has withdrawn, spending most of his time in bed nursing both his hand and his wounded pride. He continues to demand that the Landlord either let him out or give details on the next task, but it's to no avail. The Landlord has gone quiet.

The rest of the housemates move like they're walking through a minefield. They're cold, hungry, dirty from the lack of water. Gaz has been working out, squealing in the cold shower afterwards. Evangeline has been filling the bath with boiled water only for it to have cooled before she's even slightly filled the tub.

Susan has been breaking out into tears, claiming her hunger is unbearable yet refusing the meagre portions of porridge served at breakfast, lunch, and dinner.

It's been hell.

Victoria tries to sit up, but the effort—whether from the lack of food or the psychological drain—feels insurmountable. She falls back down to bury herself under the thin sheet covering her.

A sound drifts across the room that makes Victoria's skin crawl—a soft, unsettling giggle. She watches Charlie sit upright on her mattress, head cocked at an unnatural angle, eyes locked on some invisible point in the corner. Her spine protrudes sharply through thin, pale skin.

Victoria's blood turns to ice. Because Charlie—no, Amber—is staring directly at Henry with an expression of pure, predatory satisfaction. It's as if she's seen him for the first time and doesn't like what she sees. Not one bit.

Without her medication, Charlie's grip over Amber has slipped dramatically, revealing more of Amber's potentially violent impulses.

Victoria, unwilling to share space with Amber any longer than necessary, rises and begins her morning routine.

"Has anyone seen my hairbrush?" Victoria asks, her voice small and uncertain. She wants to draw Amber's attention to the present, help her escape whatever chaos she's concocting this morning.

Charlie glances up from her spot in the corner. "The Landlord probably took it," she answers, her voice normal. "Things keep going randomly missing."

"Brilliant," Evangeline sighs. "Mine's gone too." She struggles to detangle her hair with her fingers. Victoria shudders at the thought of someone wandering around the house undetected. Her hairbrush was here last night, so someone must have taken it whilst they slept.

But who? Sleep has been so restless lately, surely someone would have noticed an intruder entering the bedroom.

"Morning sickness will start soon," Amber tells Evangeline, lips curling into an unnaturally wide smile. "Then you'll soon start showing."

Evangeline freezes, all colour draining from her face. "Charlie, that's not funny. I'm not pregnant."

"Call me Amber," Amber replies, throwing off her thin sheet to reveal her completely naked form. She rises to her feet. "Charlie won't be back for a while." She sashays her pert backside as she walks away. Victoria watches with fascinated jealousy.

Jack sits bolt upright, ears pricked like a dog, his tongue tracing a path across his lower lip. Despite looking frail and ghost-like, he's still revolting.

Victoria shoots him a withering look. "Behave you."

But Jack ignores her, refocusing on Amber's lean frame. "Aren't you cold, Amber? I can keep you warm." He pats his mattress beside him.

The sight of him, this aging predator salivating over what he perceives as fresh meat, sends rage surging through Victoria's veins. 'Don't you dare,' she hisses, injecting as much venom into her voice as possible.

"Oh, come on. I'm suffering here. Can't you grant me a little distraction?"

"Piss off, Jack. Girls aren't a *distraction*."

But Amber remains silent, simply grinning as she glides from the room, her nakedness a mockery of Victoria's fury.

Jack groans with pleasure.

"Classy Jack," Victoria calls out, but Jack just shrugs her off.

"Can't blame me. Look at her! Henry, you get it, don't you?"

Henry pretends Jack hasn't said anything, and busies himself with his dressing gown. His cheeks pink.

Victoria doesn't know where to place herself. "Women aren't meat, Jack. You can't treat them like that."

"Like what? You can't have a go at me for giving her the attention she's obviously asking for. I'm being nice!"

"Oh, fuck off, Jack," she snarls.

Thankfully, he complies and slips out of the bedroom, pushing past Gaz in the doorway. Victoria collapses back onto her bed, drained.

The tension in the house is escalating. There's a pressure surrounding them all, as if the house itself is about to implode, and Victoria questions how much more she can endure.

She crosses her arms and rolls onto her side. What's the point? What's the point of any of this?

"We need to get rid of that sick bastard," Gaz says, settling on the edge of Victoria's bed. He's wearing tiny red Calvin Klein boxers that Victoria can't help but appreciate. She looks away, ashamed by the hypocrisy.

He slides closer, near enough that Victoria can feel the warmth radiating from his tattooed skin. His proximity sends electricity through her nervous system—a reminder that beneath all the grief, she's still a woman. Though unlike Jack, she keeps her eyes averted.

She hasn't felt this kind of physical awareness since before Lily's father. Her body responds with embarrassing immediacy: her pulse quickens, skin flushes, and her breath catches in her throat. His scent—yesterday's deodorant mixed with masculine sweat and something distinctly him—makes her want to lean closer, to inhale him properly.

'You alright?' Gaz asks, and there's something knowing in his voice, an acknowledgement of the electricity sparking between them. His eyes drop briefly to her lips before meeting her gaze again, and Victoria realises he feels it too, whatever this is.

Victoria coughs. "Yes!" she squeaks. "Yes. Jack... totally agree." She sits up and throws her legs off the bed, turning her back to him completely to hide her flushed cheeks. "But what can we do about him?"

"The Landlord wants him here, or he'd have granted Jack's request to leave. Nah, we need to flush him out. Make him want to leave."

Intrigued, Victoria's voice drops to a whisper. "And how do we do that?"

"That's the problem. I've been looking and there's no way of getting out of here without the Landlord's say so."

Something terrifying shifts in Victoria's stomach. They all know Jack's request to leave has been denied. She knows Susan wants to leave too and wasn't able to. Victoria isn't ready to go, not yet. The prize money far outweighs the discomfort, but she hates the thought of being trapped here. Would the Landlord refuse her exit too?

"How is he getting away with this?" she whispers.

"I don't know. But he can't get away with it for long." He takes her hand in his.

"So you're telling me you don't know how we get Jack out?"

"No clue," Gaz laughs. "I was hoping you did. You're cleverer than me." He moves closer to her, and she resists the impulse to move away.

"I'll have a think," she says. "I'll have a word with Marty too. He might have a few ideas. He hates the guy; I bet he's thought of nothing else."

Gaz lets go of her hand; his fingers trace her arm as he stands back up. He makes his excuses and leaves her alone.

She's handling this wrong. Being a scheming bitch won't earn her any votes from the outside, and she *really* needs to win or the whole ordeal is a complete waste of time. Time she could have spent with Lily.

Yet living here with Jack much longer might force her out. And if she walks away now, she won't get a penny.

Lily.

Her sole motivation to keep going. All of this is for her. She can get Jack out and turn this situation to her advantage. For her. Everything's for her.

Henry

Henry's fingers trace lazy circles around the rim of his glass of water as he observes Gaz and Victoria huddle together like conspirators. The glass grows slick beneath his touch.

What scheme are they hatching over there? Their whispered plotting amuses him. Such transparent little creatures, thinking they're being discreet. They keep stealing glances at Jack—hardly MI5 material. Their amateur surveillance makes Henry's chest constrict with suppressed laughter.

They're likely contemplating the same thing he's been thinking about: how can they get Jack out?

They needn't worry though; Henry has a plan.

Over the past couple of days, an alliance has been forged. Victoria, Gaz, and Marty have formed a tight-knit group. An amusing one, given the dynamics. Both Victoria and Marty are attracted to Gaz, and he knows it. Yet the only person Gaz is attracted to is himself.

Henry harbours no ill will toward Gaz. He's a likable lad, but Henry wishes he'd spill the beans about his past. He's rather looking forward to the fallout. Especially Jack's reaction.

Which explains why Henry is delaying getting rid of Jack; he wants to see him blow up before his departure. And for that, his timing needs to be perfect.

Henry drains his drink, excuses himself to go to the bathroom, and brushes his teeth before returning to the bedroom to dress. Susan approaches, her hands wrapped around a steaming mug. She's good at making tea, the perfect strength and with a good milk to water ratio. Though Henry gives it a sniff with crushing disappointment.

"Sorry, it's peppermint. It's all we have. Sorry," she says warily. Her hands shake as she passes him the mug.

Ah yes, the task failure. Henry's stomach rumbles as a reminder.

"Thank you, Susan. How are you managing today?"

"Oh, you know, coping." She refuses to meet his eyes.

Coping. That seems to be everyone's current state. "I wonder what the Landlord has in store for us today."

Susan blushes and turns away. "How would I know?" she giggles. "He's full of surprises, that one."

"Aren't we all?" Henry grins over his mug, his eyes crinkling.

She continues to watch him. As the days have passed, their relationship has taken on extra strain. A delightful game where Henry knows her secrets and Susan knows he knows. Yet she hasn't said anything, just in case. She's been a nervous wreck in his presence, so naturally Henry has been spending more time seeking out her company.

Susan takes a deep breath and edges closer to Henry's face. He can see the veins threading through her eyeballs. "Henry, I know you know."

"I haven't the faintest notion what you mean."

"Please, Henry, you can't blow my cover."

"Cover?"

Susan presses nearer to Henry, knocking his drink. He pulls back before the hot water can splash him. "Stop messing with me. You *must* keep my secret from the other housemates."

"That almost sounds like a threat."

Susan looks alarmed but doesn't back off. "Not a threat, no. More of a …"

"A plea?"

She nods. "Yes, I suppose."

"How about an arrangement?"

"What do you mean?"

"I'll keep your little secret, Susan. But loyalty is a two-way street." Henry's smile doesn't touch his eyes.

Susan frowns and moves away. "Okay. What do you need?"

"I don't know yet."

"Then how can I agree to that?"

"Do you promise you'll be here for me when I need you? Just like I'm here for you by keeping your secret?"

She surveys the room, but it's empty now; everyone has migrated to the dining table, trying to force down watery porridge.

"Fine."

Henry extends his hand, and she shakes it tentatively. Her hand feels delicate in his grip, like bird bones wrapped in ham. He moistens his lips, an unconscious gesture that reveals far too much.

When he finally releases her hand, Susan stumbles backward, rubbing her palm against her thigh as if trying to scrub away his touch. Henry watches her retreat with great satisfaction. The game has begun in earnest now, and he's already several moves ahead.

Marty

Marty's hands shake as he scrubs the same bowl for the third time, his fingers cramping around the sponge. The tremor isn't from hunger—though his stomach gnaws at him—it's from the invisible weight pressing down on his chest, the constant whisper from his sock drawer.

The ceramic slips from his grip, clattering against the metal sink, making him wince.

"Careful," Victoria tells him from beside him, taking the bowl to dry it. "I doubt they'll replace broken crockery, and I refuse to eat off the floor."

This is the Landlord. Please could Victoria come to the Confessions Room?

She dumps the towel on the side with an exasperated sigh and marches away, grumbling to herself.

You've got this, Vic!' Marty calls after her. She groans and flips him the bird, making him chuckle as she disappears through the sliding door.

The second the door clicks shut behind her, the Landlord calls through the speakers: *This is the Landlord.* The tone is different today, more subdued. All housemates robotically gather in the living room, hollow-eyed and tense. Only Jack looks hopeful.

I hope you've had time to reflect on the failure of the ranking task. Luxury items will be returned following successful completion of today's task.

"What is it this time?" Jack demands, his voice gravelly with pain. The wounds on his hand have become deeply infected, and with no painkillers remaining in the house, his mood is insufferable. Marty can only pray the pain gets so bad Jack has no choice but to break out of here.

Now there's an idea. Marty makes a mental note to speak to Gaz.

Jack grimaces and shifts in his seat. "We have to swear to do whatever he says. No matter what."

"I'm not swearing to anything," Amber declares, crossing her arms. "I'm not being tortured like you."

"Me neither," Henry declares.

Amber slowly turns to face Henry. "Did I say you could talk to me? Weirdo."

Henry recoils, looking appalled. "Please leave me alone."

But Amber just laughs and leans back, her eyes still fixed on Henry.

For the next ten minutes, you're going to remain where you are. If anyone leaves the seating area, you will lose the task.

"Sounds easy enough," Gaz says, though he looks as uneasy as Marty feels.

Something is wrong. It can't be that easy to win their stuff back, surely.

"Right," Jack addresses the room. "Everyone sit your asses down. We've got this."

"Will you tell us when the ten minutes are up, Landlord?" Susan asks, looking upward as if the man himself is floating over them.

The Landlord doesn't respond.

"Apparently not," Evangeline says. "Great. I've lost all concept of time in here."

Thirty seconds later, the screaming begins.

Chapter 17

<u>Victoria</u>

There's something strange about the Landlord today. His voice is different. More intense and grave. "How are you today, Victoria?"

"What do you want, Landlord?" The room feels smaller somehow. It's as if the camera positioned before her is dissecting her every movement. Every breath.

"The Landlord just wanted to check in with you."

"Right. What's this really about?" She's not in the mood for this shit. Not when she's desperately craving a generous bowl of carbonara and an ice-cold glass of Pepsi.

"Just a casual conversation." The speakers fluctuate in volume—rising then plummeting—the effect is disconcerting.

"I've been thinking," Victoria says. "As part of the agreement, you promised to let me know if anything happened to Lily whilst I'm in here. But I think I need to check on her myself. I need to speak to her." Because she cannot trust the Landlord to fulfil his promises. He's already failed them in so many ways.

"That can be arranged."

Victoria's eyebrows shoot upwards. "Really?!"

"Yes. The Landlord aims to please."

Her heart skips a beat before reality crashes down on her. "Right. Of course. What's the price?" She asks the question, but she knows it doesn't matter what the answer is—she'll do anything.

"I don't understand, Victoria."

"Well, you're not just going to grant me a phone call without taking something from me. So what do you want? My soul?"

"Not at all. Please be patient, and I will make the arrangements."

"What, right now?!"

"Do you have a different time in mind?"

"No, no, not at all. Now is perfect."

The crackle of the speakers dies away, leaving Victoria's skull feeling strangely empty. She sits on her hands and kicks her legs out. This cannot be happening. Can it? She feels sick. From anticipation or anxiety, she doesn't know.

What if Lily is deteriorating? What if speaking to her triggers strong emotions in her little girl that push her over the edge and, as a result, make her even sicker? She won't even know; the Landlord surely won't be generous enough to permit another check-in.

Is this a good idea?

There's pounding at the door, though it sounds muffled, as if they're hammering through multiple layers of wood. She didn't know the door was so thick.

"Victoria, you need to get out. Now!" It's Gaz. He sounds panicked. No, he sounds petrified.

"Gaz? What's wrong?" She rises and reaches for the door before hesitating. If she opens this door, the Landlord might cancel the call with Lily.

"Vic! Get out of there!" Marty this time. Victoria has never heard him sound so frightened.

Heat floods her. Her armpits dampen, and sweat beads above her lip. She whirls around, trying to make sense of it all.

"Landlord? Do you have Lily? Can I talk to her?"

"Fire!" Someone shrieks from outside the Confessions Room—a woman's voice. Evangeline.

The screaming erupts then. Susan loudest of all, her wail a screech of pure terror. There's banging from the other side of the door as her fellow housemates explode into panic.

"Gaz?!"

But he doesn't respond. He's gone. He's abandoned her.

She lunges for the door handle, forsaking all hope of speaking to Lily. There's no point in talking to Lily if Victoria's going to die as a result.

The door won't move. It's locked. Adrenaline floods through her as she wrenches at the door, again and again.

"Let me out!" she squeals. But there's no response. "Landlord, please open the door."

As the temperature in the cramped room soars, the door handle becomes scalding to touch. Her breath burns in her lungs. Sweat streams from every pore, running over her raw skin.

She can hear the unmistakable roar of flames beyond the door, and she pivots, searching for another exit. There isn't one. There's no escape.

The screams ring louder through the door. She pounds it with both fists relentlessly until her knuckles burn and swell. "What's going on out there?!" The scent of charred wood reaches her nostrils and makes her cough. There's something else there too. Something she recognises from her days as a nurse. Burning flesh and singed hair.

She can smell her housemates dying.

She spins to confront the camera. "Let me out of here!" Her eyes are feral and saturated with raw panic.

The lights go out, plunging her into absolute darkness, broken only by the incessant blink of the camera's red light.

Victoria's scream is so piercing her chest burns with the effort.

<u>Henry</u>

"We can't just leave her in there!" Marty cries.

"Don't you dare stand up," Jack growls, still pinning him down. "She can do ten minutes."

"She might be in pain!"

Jack's expression flickers for just a second. Guilt maybe? Though by the way he's examining his hand, he's more likely thinking of himself as usual. Screw Victoria's pain, what about *his*? "Yeah well, she'll be okay. She's a woman. The Landlord wouldn't hurt one of the fairer sex."

"What kind of stupid statement is that?" Marty tries to rise again, but Jack has him crushed beneath his full weight, compressing his chest, making him wheeze.

"Don't you dare stand up," Jack hisses, his breath hot and putrid against Marty's face. Marty can see the madness dancing behind Jack's bloodshot eyes. "You heard the Landlord, we move and we fail the task."

"It's fake," Gaz says, horribly pale. He's sporting a black eye, having already encountered Jack's wrath. "The screams can't be real. They're playing a recording or something." He turns to each person in turn. "Right?"

But no one can answer him. Everyone is too shocked to speak. The screams certainly sound authentic. But what if they're not and they fail this task? The hunger might take them if Jack's fist doesn't kill them first.

"That's not the sound of someone being tortured. I don't think she's in pain," Amber declares.

Susan regards her with a frown, most likely thinking what everyone else is. How does Amber know what torture sounds like? "Though there's more than one type of torture," she says ominously.

Evangeline whimpers from the corner of the sofa. She hasn't uttered a word since they sat down. Her entire body is twitching.

Henry watches everything unfold with escalating anxiety. Victoria's screams are making his heart race, in more ways than one. He's concerned about her; her anguish physically pains him. It also stirs memories in him that get his pulse thundering.

"How long has it been?" Amber asks.

"How the fuck should we know?" Gaz asks, perched so precariously on his sofa's edge he might topple off. "Five minutes? Forty? Does anyone have any idea of the time in this place?!" He sits bolt upright, his butt not quite leaving the bare boards.

"Careful, Gaz, stand up and I'll crush the life out of you," Jack snarls.

"Who you threatening, big man?"

"Not a threat. A promise."

"That's enough!" Susan screams, her hands clamped over her ears like a child blocking out the booms of a firework display. "Isn't this hard enough already without you all attacking each other?"

"Do you know what's happening in there, Susan?" Henry asks, his voice steadier than he feels.

Susan's eyes dart to him. "No? Why would I?"

"Oh, just wondering. You have a knack for knowing what's going on in this house."

That shuts everyone up.

Victoria's screams persist behind the door. Or at least what sounds like Victoria's screams. Surely it's not real. What could possibly make her scream like that? The Landlord can't have anything that powerful in his arsenal of tricks.

"What's going on between you two?" Marty asks, still held down by Jack. "You're being weird."

"Oh, nothing, nothing at all. Just checking in with Susan. She's a highly perceptive woman, that's all. I thought she might have insight into what we should do."

Susan scowls at Henry. "Yes. Well, I don't know."

Henry shrugs. "Fair enough."

The screams stop. Everyone turns to the Confessions Room door.

"Have we done it?" Evangeline asks.

They all avert their gaze.

They see smoke bleeding out from underneath the door.

<u>Victoria</u>

Her ears ring with an incessant buzz beneath the roar of flames outside the door. She's drenched in sweat; the droplets feel like her flesh is melting. She keeps touching her skin regularly to check it's not blood—the pain and torment are so excruciating she must be bleeding. Right?

Apparently not.

"I love you, baby," she whispers to her daughter as she collapses against the wall. She crouches low to avoid the thick smoke pouring into the room. "I'm sorry I failed you."

She's given up. Something she never thought herself capable of. But when push comes to shove, she's just too tired to fight for her own life.

Lily will be okay without her. Her mum is looking after her. Maybe she can sue the hell out of the production company and pay for Lily's treatment. It's better this way.

A blinding light washes over her and takes her away.

Chapter 18

<u>Marty</u>

This is the Landlord. Congratulations, housemates, you have successfully completed this task. Luxuries will be returned in due course.

Marty springs from the sofa, shoving Jack to the floor, who remains with a grin plastered across his face. "We did it!" Jack says stupidly, looking around at the rest of the housemates. "We did it!" He rushes toward the kitchen as if the cupboards might magically replenish themselves.

"But at what cost?" Gaz asks Marty, pale and wide-eyed. He runs to join Marty at the Confessions Room door, where Marty is hammering.

"It's locked," Marty tells him. "Victoria, are you okay in there?"

The housemates crowd behind them, whispering words of anguish among themselves.

No reply. Marty turns to Gaz. "What do we do?"

Gaz grits his teeth and pulls Marty aside, bracing himself to charge at the door. He looks to Marty for approval—who nods.

"One... Two..."

The snap of the lock inside the door halts him mid lunge and he stumbles forward clumsily.

Marty follows Gaz as he rushes down the corridor into the Confessions Room itself, smoke billowing out behind them. "Victoria? Holy shit, Victoria!" Gaz cries out, pushing the chair out of the way.

Marty strains to see deeper into the room. He cannot see Victoria behind Gaz's enormous frame. "What's going on? Where is she? And why does it stink of smoke in here?"

Gaz squats down, and Marty can see for the first time. Victoria is slumped in the corner, her limbs tucked close to her body. She's sobbing into her hands. When Gaz tenderly brushes the hair from her face, Marty sees that her skin is clammy and grey, her pupils dilated with shock. She flinches at his touch as if human contact burns.

Marty joins Gaz in crouching down. "Hey, you're okay now." He breathes, but his words feel like lies. He has no idea what happened in here, but he *does* know that he's looking at a truly broken woman. Victoria is far from okay.

Victoria doesn't make a sound, just continues to cry silently into her sleeve. Marty throws Gaz a glance before resting a hand on her shoulders. "It's over now. We've got you."

But she doesn't move, and Marty looks to Gaz for help. Gaz shrugs before taking a deep breath. He nudges Marty away. "I'm getting you out of here, honey." He pulls her closer to him and hooks one arm under her legs and the other around her back. "Come on."

He hoists her up, and Marty presses himself against the wall to let them pass.

"What happened to her?" Susan asks as the three move through the living area, heading for the bedroom. "Where's the fire?"

Marty spins around. "What the hell do you think happened to her? They tortured her in there. Fucking *tortured* her. And we let it happen so we could get some damn food." He turns to Jack. "Was it worth it, eh? Pleased with yourself?"

"Mate, I didn't think..."

"No, you didn't think. You never do."

"Don't blame *me*! I didn't hurt her."

"But you didn't stop it either. And you wouldn't let me stop it."

"Oh, come on, there must have been a part of you that thought it was bullshit too, or you would've fought harder. If you really thought she was being tortured, you could've beaten me to get to her."

Marty holds his breath. Jack's right. Jack's grip was strong, yes, but Marty has been in real fights—street brawls where broken bottles and boots became weapons, where you fought or you died. But something inside him had hesitated just now. Some part of his broken brain that whispered: *What if you're wrong? What if it's fake and you blow the task? What if you fail again, like you always do?*

The coward in him had chosen the most selfish option. Had let Jack hold him down while Victoria suffered. Had prioritised food and comfort over a friend's pain.

Did he think it was all fake? Did he hold back? Maybe his fear crippled him, leading him to believe everything would be fine. Because he's a coward.

His heart sinks into his stomach as self-loathing floods through him. This is who he really is—not the reformed musician trying to make amends, not the loyal friend, not the boy his parents once loved. He's the same selfish coward who chose drugs over loyalty, who let his band implode, who destroyed everything he touched.

The bag of coke in his sock drawer calls to him now with renewed urgency. Because this is exactly the pain he used to medicate away—the crushing weight of his own inadequacy, the knowledge that when it mattered most, he chose himself, his fears, over everyone else. Again and again.

His hands shake as he follows Gaz into the bedroom, leaving everyone else to talk amongst themselves.

Just one line. Just one.

Gaz places Victoria on her bed where she immediately turns on her side and folds herself into a tight ball. Gaz strokes her hair with great care. When Marty approaches her, her eyes snap to his, crystallising his shame.

"You're okay!" she gasps. She sits up then and grabs Gaz's arm. With her other hand, she reaches for Marty's and grips it tight. "You're okay?"

"We're fine," Marty sits on the end of her bed, next to Gaz, bewildered. "Victoria, we are fine. What happened to you in there?" He examines her carefully. Despite smelling of smoke, there are no burns, no signs of physical damage whatsoever. "What did they do to you?"

"What did they do to *you*?!"

"Us? Nothing! Nothing happened. We just had to sit and wait." Whilst listening to Victoria's screams. How will Marty ever be able to tell her he stood back and let her go through that? What kind of man is he?

He isn't a man. He's a nobody. His eyes flit to his side of the room, to his chest of drawers that harbours his secrets.

"But I heard you screaming. Gaz, you were calling out 'fire'." She closes her eyes. "I could smell it. There was smoke."

Marty looks at Gaz, even more confused.

"Sorry, honey, but that didn't happen. None of that was real." Gaz speaks so softly, so gently, Marty cannot keep his eyes off him.

"There was no fire?" Victoria breathes. "It wasn't real?"

Gaz begins to say something but changes his mind and looks away. Gaz is no doubt riddled with guilt, like he is.

"Victoria," Marty says using his gentlest voice to mimic Gaz's. He cups her small hand with both of his, swallowing it whole. She looks him in the eye with such desperation his heart cracks in two. He let her down so badly. He needs to learn from this. "Everyone is safe. We're safe. You're safe."

Victoria cries. "I gave up Marty," she gasps. "I gave up on her."

"On who?"

"Lily! I thought I was going to die in there, and instead of fighting to get out, I crawled away and waited for it to happen." Her cries become thick, wet sobs. "I'm a terrible mother."

Marty grabs her shoulders. "Look at me," he tells her, forcing her to meet his eyes. "You are not a terrible mother. You have been fighting for her for years. Just look at what you're going through for her." He gestures around him. "You're in *this* hellhole for a start. And you didn't give up. You tried to get out. You were locked in, and there was nothing you could do. That doesn't mean you gave up. You just ran out of options."

Victoria stares at him through wet lashes as if staring directly into his soul. Her eyes widen and her mouth drops open. "How do you know I was trying to get out?"

Marty lets go of her shoulders, and she backs away from him. "You heard. You heard everything." With each word spoken, her voice increases in volume. She looks to Gaz. "Did you know too?"

Gaz swallows and looks like he's about to cry. "We didn't think it was real. We thought the Landlord was messing with us."

"So you... you didn't help me? You left me in there."

Marty jumps up to escape her flailing arms. "I tried! I tried to get to you, but Jack wouldn't let me. He wanted to pass the task..." He knows it's a feeble excuse, but he's got nothing else.

He knows what will help him right now. Though it might just destroy him too. It's a precarious balance of emotions, and right now, taking a step towards the drawers is far more alluring than staying clean.

Victoria

The betrayal cuts deep. Victoria knows these people owe her nothing—they've only known each other for a few days. They barely know each other at all. But do they not have even a touch of humanity? Enough to reach out to help someone in such huge distress, such apparent danger? Are people so cruel, or just these people?

"Leave me alone," she says, falling back into her pillow.

"Victoria, please. We thought it wasn't real. And it wasn't! The fire wasn't real."

"Well, I thought it was real! Which is why I was begging to get out. Because I thought you all were burning to death, and I wanted to get to you. I wanted to help!"

"Victoria ..."

"Leave me alone!"

Gaz moves to Marty, who has shrunk back into the middle of the room. Gaz grasps him by the wrist. "Come on. We should go."

"We'll be back to check on you later, though." Marty calls out as they exit the bedroom.

Pulling the covers over her head, Victoria bites down onto the fabric and cries. She can't be here anymore. Her time in this house must end.

Chapter 19

<u>Henry</u>

Henry takes a sip of his tea and holds the hot liquid in his mouth, savouring the burn on his tongue. He leans back in his chair, pulling the cup close to his face as he watches everyone digest the news of Victoria's despair. Her trauma dissected by their casual conversation.

"How were we to know it was real? This house is so messed up," Evangeline says defiantly, though her words are coated with guilt. She didn't say a word during the ordeal, frozen by the horror. After Victoria was saved, Henry heard her sobbing in the toilet. Pressing his ear to the door was risky; he doesn't want to look like an old pervert, but he's fairly sure no one saw him.

No one is listening to her musings, so Henry motions her over. "Evangeline, come and join me."

Did she just recoil? How strange. Henry was always under the impression that they got along. Though she has grown particularly close to Charlie, or is it Amber? Has Charlie said something to her?

He shakes those thoughts away. Fear breeds irrationality, and he needs his head screwed on tight.

"Please, keep an old man company. All of this hasn't been good for one's mental state."

Evangeline hesitates a moment longer before joining him at the dining table. "Happy you've got your tea back?" she asks him, a pathetic attempt at conversation. Henry notes her lack of depth.

Henry never acts on impulse. His deeds are calculated and executed with precision. His pleasures stem from true desire, never whim. Every word is weighed and examined before leaving his lips.

So when he listens to Evangeline, he drinks in every part of her. How she chose the seat across from him rather than beside him, the colossal dining table a barricade between them. How her eyes dart everywhere but to his face. How she angles slightly to the left, poised for flight.

She knows something. Amber has been whispering in her ear.

"How are you holding up, Evangeline?"

"Oh, good, you know, considering ..."

Henry nods and takes another sip of his tea. "Considering we're trapped somewhere between delirium and hell?"

That draws a smile, her discomfort waning just a little. "Something like that."

"You and Amber seem to be getting along?"

Her head jerks towards him. "So? That's not a problem, is it?"

"Oh, I've just seen you two spending time together, that's all. It's nice, friendships in such dire circumstances."

Her cheekbones redden slightly; she's more beautiful than ever. "I guess so. Though I prefer to call her Charlie."

"Is that so? I don't think I have seen Charlie properly for days. Amber seems to have taken over somewhat."

"I wouldn't know. I just talk to her like she's one person, you know?"

Henry nods knowingly. From what he's seen of Evangeline, she has so little depth. She wouldn't be able to look past the surface of someone to get to their deeper complexities. She's too one-dimensional. "And what is it you and *Amber* talk about?"

Her pink cheeks darken to crimson. "Just *stuff*."

Henry chuckles. "You young ones. So very few words. I guess you reserve them for when you're on screen."

Evangeline laughs, though she sounds unsure. "I suppose."

"And pray tell, have you and Amber ever discussed me?"

"No. Why would we?" Her words tumble out far too quickly. Henry doesn't like the stabbing sensation in his stomach.

"Surely you've talked about all your fellow housemates. It's only natural. So what has she said about me?"

"Nothing." Again, too quickly.

"Come now. You can't offend me. You don't get to this age without developing a thick skin."

Evangeline sighs and looks outside, where the rest of the housemates have gathered to discuss the events of the day. Victoria remains sequestered in the bedroom. "Look, she's just wary of you, that's all. She just said I should keep my wits about me when it comes to you."

"And what's your take on that assessment?"

Her shoulders relax. "I think she's batshit crazy. It's hard to take anything she says seriously."

"I see." Henry nods, studying the elegant line of her jaw, the smooth column of her throat that disappears into a generous bosom. He wipes the corner of his mouth with his thumb.

"Well, I shouldn't keep you. Thank you for humouring this old man."

She hurries away.

Henry has heard everything he needs to know.

Marty

Everyone is celebrating in the garden, and it's pissing Marty off. He came out here for a quiet smoke, and everyone followed him out, babbling about how great it is they can eat tonight, how Charlie has her meds again, how Jack can shave his face with his fucking four-hundred-pound razor.

Like any of it matters!

Like Victoria means absolutely nothing.

Wankers, the lot of them.

Gaz approaches, looking sheepish. "You alright, mate?"

"Ah yeah, fucking boss. I'm glad everyone is having such a nice time. As if Victoria didn't have to pay a massive price so Susan can have her face cream back!"

The other housemates turn to look at him. Gaz notices and waves them off. "Look, mate, what happened was horrible. Just *shit*. But Victoria is going to be fine, and dwelling on it isn't going to make living here any easier. We're hanging on by a thread as it is, Mart. We need to grab what joy we can."

"At Victoria's expense?"

"No! You know it's not like that. But we didn't do that to her, Mart. The Landlord did. He's to blame, not us!"

"Oh, fuck you, Gaz. You're telling me that wasn't our fault? All we had to do was go to that door and reassure her. Tell her it was safe."

"You heard what she told Susan. They were blasting sounds in there. Fire, us screaming. You think she would've heard us through the door? You think the Landlord hadn't thought about that?"

"But we didn't even *try*. We should've tried."

"Yeah well, as cruel as it sounds, it's done now. And Victoria's okay, Charlie said she's eating a bowl of Coco Pops in bed."

Marty laughs sardonically. "You think she's fine because she's acting normal? You haven't got a clue, have you? You're as thick as the rest of 'em."

"Come on. I don't want us to fall out."

"Nah, I can't do this anymore. You're just as bad as the rest of them."

"Really? Because from where I was standing, you didn't help her either. And sulking about it now isn't going to change anything."

Gaz has hit a nerve. Marty knows he's speaking the truth, but his back straightens all the same. "I tried ..."

"Did you? Did you really?"

Marty steps back, stubs out his cigarette and flicks it to the ground. He knows the truth. They all do. "I didn't try hard enough," he whimpers, covering his face with his hands.

Gaz reaches for him, an attempt to smooth things over, but Marty shoves him away. "Don't touch me."

Gaz raises his hands in surrender. "We need to put this behind us. We can't let this drive us apart. Because we're friends, right? Me, you, and Victoria. We'll get through this together. We *have to* if we're to survive here."

Marty stares at him, his breathing laboured, tears stinging his eyes. His guilt over Victoria isn't Gaz's fault; he knows that. He also knows that when he's upset, he acts like a prick.

"We're not friends. We're just two strangers dumped in this shithole and forced to get along. I wouldn't look twice at you on the outside."

"Marty, I know you're upset, but..."

"You're nothing but filth. You film yourself having sex; don't come to me with the moral high ground."

"Excuse me?"

"C'mon, you can't tell me the porn industry is all sunshine and rainbows. It's fucking disgusting, that's what it is. Those poor women."

"Hang on a minute. You think you know everything about me? Well, F.Y.I, I never fucked a girl on screen. Marty, I performed in gay porn. And the only person abused on those sets was me." His voice cracks. "I didn't *want* that job. I was pushed into that world when I was fifteen."

His shoulders heave with the effort of holding himself together. "My dad produced those videos and, according to his messed-up view of the world, gay porn was where the money was at. I was a commodity to him."

Marty cannot breathe. "Fifteen."

"Yeah. So you can get off your pedestal and accept that you're not the only one who's had it hard. But sometimes, mate, we're just too tired to save anyone else when the lifejacket we're wearing is weighed down by rocks."

He turns on his heel and walks away, leaving Marty standing alone in the wreckage.

Chapter 20

> @TortureRequest: Can you do something with the pretty blonde? She's been too comfortable lately.
>
> @VIPMember_Gold: The musician looks weak. Easy target. Break him down more.
>
> @EliteAccess: Why is the old man so calm? Either he's hiding something or he needs more pressure.
>
> @PremiumUser_X: The nurse is too strong. Find her weakness and exploit it. Make her beg.

Henry

This is the Landlord. It's time for another task. Please make your way to the pantry and collect the required items.

Henry, being the only person with a modicum of motivation to play the game, reaches the pantry first. He surveys the racks before him and claps his hands with glee. This should be fun. Susan steps in tentatively behind him and fingers the clothing.

Each item of clothing is labelled, and Henry hands them out with a flourish. The nature of the task soon becomes glaringly obvious. They change into their costumes and wait impatiently on the sofas.

"I'm not looking forward to this," Susan mutters, who has swapped her usual polka dots for orange overalls.

Thank you, housemates.

Victoria raises a middle finger and slouches deeper into her seat. Henry thinks she looks magnificent in her crisp white shirt, black slacks, and mirrored glasses.

Today you're going to take part in a game I like to call 'Cops and Robbers'. Half of you are police. Half of you are criminals. Your uniforms should make your role abundantly clear.

Henry wipes a smudge off his sunglasses and glances around the room. The group has already divided naturally. The orange jumpsuits (Susan, Gaz, Evangeline and Charlie) on the left, and the uniformed officers on the right.

Henry's only disgruntlement is having Jack on his side. It would have been rather fun to order Jack around for the day.

Yesterday drained him. The drama of Victoria's fright sapped Henry of his energy so much so that when he woke up this morning, he almost didn't get out of bed. This task has certainly lifted his spirits.

Prisoners, make your way to the garden where you will find your cells.

Jack dangles his handcuffs from his little finger, grinning. "Sorry guys. Bye bye!"

"Fuck you, Jack," Gaz spits.

"Now, now, Landlord's rules, not mine. No need to get so bitchy with the guards."

The prisoners shuffle out reluctantly while the guards await further instructions.

The game begins now.

"That's it?" Marty asks. "How do we know if we've completed the task?"

"I suppose we simply have to maintain order for a predetermined amount of time," Henry offers, sending the guards into a contemplative silence.

"Look, Jack, let me handle Gaz. You'll only wind him up, and we need him to cooperate," Marty tells him. He glances at Victoria. "We need this to go smoothly."

"Right, shall we see what situation our fellow housemates have found themselves in?" Henry stands, offering a hand to Victoria. She takes it and hauls herself up, making Henry stumble.

Convincing Victoria to take part was no easy feat. Susan literally dropped to her knees begging. They're in a constant state of stress, terrified of the consequences if they don't comply.

Jack smirks. "Hey, the police have gotta do what they've gotta do to keep the bad guys in line!"

"Don't be a twat. Let's get through this without any drama."

"Tell your mate that, not me. He's the one having a go every ten minutes."

"Because you wind him up."

"Not intentionally." But Jack's grin suggests otherwise.

Marty

They find the prisoners locked in individual cells in the garden, with drizzle falling through the bars. They're already soaked. Evangeline shivers, on the brink of tears. "This is stupid," she grumbles.

"It won't be for long," Henry reassures her.

Victoria goes to Evangeline's cell, reaching her fingers through the bars. "You don't have to do this. We don't have to do any of this."

"Don't encourage her to quit. We're not quitters!" Jack's voice rings with false cheer.

"Shut up, Jack. You of all people should know how dangerous these bollocks tasks are."

Jack glances at his bandaged hand—the smell growing more rancid by the day. His pain threshold is impressive, though getting his pills back has certainly put more of a spring in his step.

"It's okay," Evangeline tells Victoria, clasping Victoria's fingers in her own. "I'm more scared of what might happen if we *don't* take part."

And that's the awful reality. Damned either way. Though Marty suspects Evangeline's right, they're more at risk if they piss off the Landlord. He throws a meaningful glance at Gaz, pleading with him to behave. But Gaz looks away, turning back to Jack with hatred etched in his scowl.

Brilliant. This should be fun.

"I need a wee," Susan announces.

"Go then," Gaz tells her.

"You think I can? Prisoners can't just wander out of their cells."

"She's right; someone should escort her," Charlie says. "We need a wee too."

"We?"

Charlie blushes. "Sorry, I mean me. Just me."

Marty watches Charlie with growing concern. Despite getting her pills back, her personalities have been switching constantly. It's happening so frequently no one can keep track anymore, and Marty can't help but wonder if she's taking the right dose. Has Amber got too much control? "Right, Vic, you okay to take them?"

Victoria shrugs and unlatches both gates. "Take your time and get warm," she says. "That's an order."

Charlie giggles. Amber, definitely Amber.

Standing around in the drizzle loses its appeal quickly. Henry and Jack, utilising their freedom as guards, drift indoors, leaving Marty to watch over the prisoners.

Susan and Charlie return from their toilet break and engage in quiet conversation between their cells.

"So, what's your plan when you get out of here?" Marty asks Gaz.

Gaz scoffs. "You mean prison or the house?"

"What's the difference?"

Evangeline laughs and shifts closer in her cell to hear better.

Gaz looks away. "The plan was to use this to get exposure, get noticed for auditions. I had this stupid dream of being a movie star. The next Jason Statham."

"And now?"

"Fuck no. I hope I never see a camera ever again. I thought I could handle it after... well, you know. But actually, maybe I should stay away from all of that. Being on TV has hardly been a good move for me."

"Look," Marty says, addressing the elephant in the room. "I'm so sorry about yesterday. I didn't mean to... I was just so angry."

Gaz waves him away. "Forget it. We should just move on. We've got enough to deal with in here."

Marty nods, still unsure. "What about you, Evangeline? Going to sign the biggest advertising deal in history after this?"

"Ha! Who'd want me to represent their brand? The morning-after pill?"

"Don't be like that. That's probably all forgotten by now."

"Doubt it. Anyway, I think I want to do something different. Something more meaningful. You know? Maybe I'll follow in Victoria's footsteps."

"Nursing?"

Evangeline blushes. "It's just an idea. Okay, probably not nursing. Something easier."

"You'd make a great nurse," Gaz tells her with a beaming smile. He looks good wet, very sexy. Very Marty's type.

"What about you, Mart? Any big plans?"

Marty sighs, looking up to the sky. "Honestly? I just want to hang out with my parents for a bit. Maybe go fishing with Dad. Help Mum cook a Sunday roast."

Evangeline crinkles her nose. "Is that it?"

"Is that it?" Marty mocks. "Is there anything better than being with the people you love?"

Awkward silence follows. "You must really love your parents."

"There's nothing miraculous about that, is there? To be honest, it's not even about love. I just want to see them again. It's killing me, missing them like this. I feel like I've got no genuine connections, you know?"

Gaz and Evangeline nod, but Marty suspects they don't have a clue. They're both privileged in their own ways. They both have their looks, ambitions, a leg up in life. And good for them. You *should* take the love of your family for granted; roll around in it until it seeps into your soul so deep, it'll never leave you.

Something Marty forgot years ago when he traded their love for the thrill of drugs.

Chewing his cheek, he silently vows to flush the cocaine the moment he goes inside. Enough's enough.

"Grubs up!" Jack calls out, carrying two trays outside. Victoria is close behind, clutching two more. Henry brings up the rear with metal flasks coated in smudged fingerprints.

"You cooked lunch?" Marty cannot recall having seen him in the kitchen.

"No, deliveries today. Ours is inside. Take the lid off this for me."

Marty obliges.

Gaz peers inside. "What the fuck is that?!" He sounds ready to vomit.

"Some sort of stew?"

"It's grey."

Marty raises his eyebrows. "Henry's grey; doesn't mean he isn't delicious."

Henry bursts into laughter, giving the joke more enthusiasm than it deserves. Still, Marty smiles at his own wit.

"It smells like root vegetables," Jack says, his nose hovering over the dish. "And it's cold. Here, take one." He passes the dish through a hole in the bars. Gaz takes it begrudgingly.

One by one, the prisoners sample their meals. Hours have passed since they last ate, and they must be starving, but they each reject the food.

"Right, better go. Ours is getting cold." Jack motions for the rest of the guards to join him inside.

"Don't worry, guys, I'll share mine," Marty tells them with a wave.

"No you won't. We're not failing this task because they can't stomach some stew. Don't be so soft."

"Jack, don't be a dick. We don't even know what the rules are."

"Me, a dick? Play the hero and failing this task would be a bigger dick move."

"We all know what happens when we forget compassion," Marty gestures at Victoria. "And what happens when you stick to the so-called rules." Now he gestures at Jack's hand.

"So we're fucked either way."

Henry interjects. "I'd rather risk following rules that might not exist than deliberately breaking them. Giving the prisoners our food might seem gracious, but what if they're punished worse because of it? What if none of us can eat afterwards?"

"They have names, Henry. They're not 'prisoners'."

Henry shrugs. "Seems easier to use a collective noun."

Marty grunts and heads inside, letting the door slam shut in Jack's face.

Henry

It turns out Marty doesn't need to play the hero. The prisoners won't accept his food anyway. They've reached the same conclusion as Henry—it's better to see what happens if they behave themselves than discover what their punishment is for going rogue.

Henry chuckles. This is clearly an elaborate experiment, and the rats are performing exactly as expected. With manic confusion and turning on one another.

"Do you think we're doing enough?" Marty asks Henry now. "You know, to win the task?"

"What do you mean?"

"Do you think we're playing the parts convincingly enough?"

Henry shrugs. "There's no way of knowing. Though I suspect that's the whole point. What are your thoughts, Jack?"

Jack presses his lips together. Thinking appears painful for him. Obviously, he's unaccustomed to engaging his brain.

Instead of responding, he walks to the cells and drags his baton across the bars, the harsh rattle making everyone groan. "Right, you can't sit in there all day. You know what prisoners need?"

"To be left alone?" Gaz quips.

"Wrong. Exercise. Surely you of all people know that, Gaz?"

"You can fuck off. I'm not doing anything you tell me."

Jack positions himself inches from Gaz's cell. "You'll do exactly as I say."

Gaz sits down on the floor, knees bent, arms resting on his knees. "Make me."

To Henry's surprise, Jack walks away and opens Evangeline's cell door. "Come on, prisoner. Three laps of the garden."

"Oh, come on, Jack..."

"Do it!" Jack's scream erupts so loud that birds scatter from a nearby tree.

"Jack!" Marty warns.

"Shush! If we're passing this task, we need to play the game. Evangeline, run, now!"

Evangeline runs, her long legs Bambi-like. She does a lap of the garden in seconds.

"Again. Until I say stop." Jack watches her with a leering smile as he backs up to Henry. "There we go. She's a good girl. We'll pass this task because of her." His eyes never leave Evangeline. "I tell you what, Henry, she's a fine piece of ass. You know what I mean?" He chuckles. "Of course you do."

Henry opts to stay quiet. He has no intention of discussing his sexual preferences with Jack.

"Charlie, join her." Jack holds out his hand to silence Marty and Gaz. "They're fine. We just need to play the game. They're okay, and we'll pass. I've got this. Do some star jumps!"

Marty and Gaz watch awkwardly, unable to argue. Jack has a point. The girls are giggling now, part embarrassed, part joyful.

Jack groans over his shoulder. "Look at Charlie's little titties bouncing up and down."

Henry can't help smiling. He's been watching Charlie for a very long time. Always at a distance, always covert. To be able to just stare at her like this is liberating. Exciting.

"How far do you think we can push this?" Jack nudges Henry. "Reckon I can order them to make out?"

"Only one way to find out."

Jack bursts with laughter. "Henry, you dirty dog, you. I knew I liked you."

Marty glares at them both. Henry's eyes wide, the picture of confusion as if he hadn't said anything at all.

"Do a downward dog or something," Jack calls out. "Facing away from me."

"Fuck you, Jack," Charlie tells him.

"You can fuck me anytime, honey."

"Right, that's enough," Marty says. "Game over."

"Good idea. Back in your cells, ladies. I'll visit you later when everyone's asleep. Prisoners like a good gang bang, right?" He grabs his crotch and licks his lips.

"What the fuck is wrong with you?" Marty asks.

"What's wrong with *me*? Says the faggot."

Henry steps aside just as Marty launches at Jack. Jack sees him coming and dodges the punch with ease. He jeers. "Now, now. Guards turning on each other isn't a good idea."

"You're a pig, Jack."

"Oink."

Chapter 21

> @MadMen21: Just paid 3k to get them a pet. The Landlord better do it.
>
> @Member469: What like a cat or something?
>
> @MadMen21: I was thinking a dog, but yeah, whatever. Just pulling the money together to get them to kill it.
>
> @Member469: You're sick, man. Love it.

Marty

Marty's heart stops. He could swear the bag was in here. He was *certain* of it. Since arriving here, he's spent days avoiding this drawer one minute, then opening it the next. Lovingly running his fingers over the bag before shoving it to the back, out of sight.

No, the bag of blow was definitely here.

And now it's gone.

He yanks the drawer from its runners and tips the contents onto the floor, dropping to his knees to rummage through his boxer shorts and socks.

"Everything okay in here?"

Henry.

"No, it isn't!"

"Anything I can help with?"

"You can start by leaving me alone." Marty's tone cuts sharper than intended. Shocked at himself, he pauses and closes his eyes. "Look, sorry man, just having a rough day."

Henry approaches cautiously. "Yes, well, it can't be as bad as Victoria's."

It's a simple observation that cuts deep. Marty knows he has plenty to be grateful for; he hasn't had a hard time in here. But that's exactly what's crushing him. The guilt makes everything unbearable. He's painfully aware of how selfish that is, but when you're walking on a tightrope, you have to tread carefully.

He sighs, a deep, desperate sound. "I was looking for something. I'm sure it'll turn up." He's anything but sure. If the bag isn't here, it means someone has taken it. Unless he goes around asking and giving himself away, he can only hope that person stays quiet about his little secret.

He's kicking himself. If only he'd had the balls to flush the drugs earlier. The second he found them. None of this would be happening.

But then, he's always been weak. Weak and pathetic.

"Well, I'll leave you to it. You know where I am if you need anything."

Marty grunts and begins gathering his scattered belongings.

"Guys, we've got a situation," Victoria calls through the door.

Victoria

"I don't see what the big deal is. You can get another one?" Jack stands in front of the cells, waving something. "You want to win this, don't you? And you want the house to be clean? Two birds, one stone."

Victoria enters the garden with Marty trailing behind. She hears him gasp. "Jack and Gaz had a little disagreement."

"What the hell? I've only been gone a few minutes."

"Jack's perversion stepped up a notch too far, and Gaz kicked off. Jack handcuffed him to the bars."

"And the toothbrushes?"

"Jack thinks prisoners should clean the house. Why they need to use their toothbrush, I don't know."

Jack spins to face them. "For authenticity! We won't pass this if everyone just sits around having a nice time. I caught Susan having a cup of tea inside!"

"I got chilly!"

"You're a prisoner! Act like one!"

Susan tuts and crosses her arms. "You're not my boss."

"My uniform says otherwise, dear."

Marty's heard enough. "Give me the toothbrushes. They're not cleaning with them."

"Fine, they can lick the floors clean. I know Evangeline likes a good lick." Jack wiggles his tongue between his fingers at her.

She rolls her eyes and turns away.

"I'm going to fucking kill you," Gaz growls.

"Is that a threat, mate?"

"Are you deaf? Of course it's a fucking threat."

"Hear that, Landlord? The prisoners are acting out. Maybe a punishment is in order." Jack approaches Gaz's cell, sneering. "Or are you winding me up hoping you'll get a seeing to in the shower? Is that it? You jealous of me and Evangeline? Well, drop your soap all you like, mate, I won't touch your kind with a barge pole. Disgusting."

Gaz spits in his face, the thick foamy glob splattering his cheek.

Jack yanks the cell door open, bending the latch back. "I'll fucking kill you!"

Marty rushes forward, grabbing Jack's shoulder and yanking him away from a braced Gaz.

Victoria cannot make sense of everything. Limbs are flying. Charlie and Evangeline are screaming, having abandoned their cells. Gaz is kicking out randomly, trying to connect with Jack, his arm straining against the handcuffs pulled so tight the cell is tilting. Henry is trying to convince Susan to stay in her cell.

Victoria doesn't know what to do. What's the protocol here?

She clutches the locket at her throat.

This is the Landlord. The...

But Victoria misses the announcement. It's cut off by the brawling men's roars.

"Shut up!" she yells to no avail. "Stop fighting!"

Nothing.

Acting on instinct, she pulls her baton from her belt and smacks it against the bars of Evangeline's cell. The ringing echoes around the garden. "Will you boys stop acting like little pricks!" Her voice is shrill, cutting through the chaos. Finally, she catches their attention, and everyone freezes mid-action.

The scene would be funny if there weren't so much to be fearful of. Jack and Gaz's relationship has become so volatile, it's frightening to be around. They're no longer walking on eggshells; they're walking on IEDs.

"The Landlord was saying something. We missed it because you're acting like big babies."

Marty pulls back and scratches his head. "Sorry," he mumbles.

Gaz inspects his arm where the handcuffs have carved a deep ring around his wrist. Blood drips on the grass. "Sorry, Vic," he says with sincerity. "He deserved it though."

"Just stop, Gaz." Victoria sounds so tired. "I think the Landlord said the task was over. I can't be sure though."

"Did we pass?" Jack asks hopefully. His bandage has come loose, and Victoria is shocked by the oozing welts on his hand. If the Landlord doesn't respond to her requests for more antibiotics soon, Jack might lose his hand.

Victoria shrugs. "No idea."

Your reward is in the pantry.

Jack cheers, but everyone else moves sluggishly into action. Marty releases Gaz from his cuffs while Henry opens Susan's cell with a coy smile. They all trudge inside.

"What do you think it is?" Jack asks, the fight forgotten. How can someone switch emotions so quickly? From pure rage to excitement in the blink of an eye is no easy feat. It's disconcerting.

Before they reach the pantry, snuffling sounds come from the gap beneath the door. "What was that?" Charlie asks, clutching Evangeline's hand.

Henry chuckles and pushes to the front. "I think we might have a little visitor!" He pushes the door open.

Joy bursts in Victoria's chest as the golden labrador puppy comes rushing out, little paws prancing in excitement to explore. She's beautiful.

Evangeline reaches the puppy first, scooping her up, her face radiant with happiness.

Despite everyone gushing over the dog, Victoria's eyes automatically find Henry. He's staring at Evangeline with an alertness that's frightening. There's something behind his stare, something she's seen him give Charlie too. Something malicious. Something dangerous.

She files that nugget of information away for later. The puppy has bounced to her feet, and she cannot resist a cuddle.

Though her happiness carries a melancholic guilt. Lily would love this. Her daughter has an amazing love of animals. Her compassion for every pet, every bug, every multi-legged creature—be it real, stuffed on her bed, or drawn into a Disney film—they're all the same to her little girl.

She'd make a great vet one day.

If she gets that chance.

Victoria breathes in the puppy's fur, memories of her little girl flitting through her mind at super speed.

"What shall we name her?" Susan cuts through the images in Victoria's head like a knife.

"Cuddles!" Evangeline shouts, sounding just like a little girl.

"That's a shit name," Jack tells her. "Just because she's a girl dog, you think she should have a pathetic name? Call yourself a feminist?"

"Shut up, Jack. It was just an idea."

"How about Jessie?"

Susan's suggestion floats through the group like a warm breeze. Everyone smiles and nods.

"Jessie is lovely," Gaz agrees. "She looks like a Jessie."

"She looks like a dog to me," Henry says. "But yes, Jessie suits her somehow."

"How long do you think the Landlord will let us keep her?" Charlie asks.

The question hangs uncomfortably in the air. The Landlord isn't one for kind acts. What's the catch?

"Let's just wait and see, shall we?" Susan says cheerfully.

<u>Henry</u>

The day has been an amusing one. Henry sure does love games, especially when he's winning. Being a guard gave him an intoxicating sense of power—a sensation he usually enjoys privately, so restraining himself for the sake of his audience required considerable effort.

His housemates have no business seeing Henry's true colours.

The puppy is sweet enough; any fool can see that, but is all this cooing and fawning really necessary? It's only a matter of time before she pees on the carpet, and Henry is adamant he won't be cleaning it up.

Though he is curious about the Landlord's plans for this little creature. The Landlord isn't particularly nice to his tenants, and Henry just knows this won't end well.

Then there's the matter of Susan. She's scheming; he can practically smell the deceit on her. Her refusal to meet anyone's eyes. Her stuttering. She's nervous. She knows something is about to happen.

As predicted, the Landlord calls her into the Confessions Room, apparently to collect toys for Jessie to play with. She emerges with a sour expression, red-eyed from tears, trembling lips, and darting eyes betraying her terror.

What is she up to now?

He waits until she's alone. "So, care to divulge what you know?"

She turns to him, startled. "What do you mean?"

"What's the Landlord planning with the mutt?"

"How am I supposed to know?" she snaps.

"Oh, don't play the fool, Susan. It makes you look even more ugly."

Her top lip curls. "Leave me alone, Henry. I can't be bothered with your nonsense."

"No? That's a shame. Want to hear my favourite game?"

Susan turns with raised eyebrows, her lips slightly parted.

"Hey, everyone!" He calls out, easily commanding attention. "Susan has something she'd like to share."

"Don't Henry. They'll punish me," Susan hisses under her breath.

Everyone waits expectantly.

"Well? What is it?" Marty asks. "Everything alright?"

"Yes, yes, Henry's just being silly."

"You sure about that?" Henry asks sweetly.

"Yes."

Henry spins her away. "I assume you'd prefer to tell just me what you know?"

Susan sighs heavily. "They might kick me out, Henry. I can't risk it. You don't understand—I need this. I've been working my ass off, and I'm on the cusp of something huge."

"If you tell me, they *might* kick you out. If everyone discovers your secret, you most certainly will be. Make your choice."

Susan thinks this through, her face contorts into something comical. She eventually grunts and leads Henry outside, away from eager ears. "If I tell you, you have to play along, understood?" She looks up, a plea for forgiveness from the powers at be.

Chapter 22

<u>Henry</u>

As Susan promised, the Landlord announces Jessie's dinner time. Henry pulls up a chair for a front-row seat.

After much protest, Evangeline wins the right to feed Jessie, despite Charlie (Amber) claiming she deserves the honour because Evangeline has been 'hogging' Jessie all evening.

Evangeline pulls the lid off the plastic container. Henry catches Susan's eye.

"How much do I give her?" Evangeline asks, the fork hovering over the brown sludge.

"Give her all of it; she's a growing girl," Susan tells her, eyes closed.

Evangeline obliges, making cooing noises at the food slops into the bowl. "Who's a hungry girl then?" she asks the impatient dog, who is drooling over the kitchen floor.

The dish clatters down as Jessie dives for the bowl, devouring the brown, smelly meat in seconds. She eats so quickly, Henry is surprised she doesn't vomit it back up.

Now, that would spoil the fun.

Everyone goes about their business. Now they wait.

It doesn't take long. Charlie comes inside from the dark garden; cheeks flushed with cold and the dog in her arms. "She seems exhausted, poor thing."

Jessie certainly looks tired. Her head lolls back, tongue hanging from her mouth.

"You sure she's just tired? She looks sick to me," Gaz says, stroking Jessie behind the ears. "Lay her down."

When Charlie releases her, Jessie tries to stand, but her legs slide out from beneath her. She collapses into a golden puddle.

"What's wrong with her?" Evangeline demands. "Charlie, what did you do?"

"What did *I* do? I didn't do anything!"

"You must have done something. She was fine before you took her out for a wee."

Henry steps forward. "Now, girls. I'm sure there's a logical explanation."

Susan coughs behind him—a plea for Henry to keep quiet. But that's not going to happen. Henry is bored. Henry wants to play.

"What was in her food?" he asks innocently.

"Don't know. It came in a box. I just scooped it out."

"Susan? Do you know what was in the box?"

"Why would I know?"

"You collected it."

"Yes, but I didn't fill it, did I?"

"I suppose not. But given your track record, you might have *adjusted* it somehow."

"Shut up, Henry," Susan snaps.

"Oi, let's not fall out." Jack turns to Henry. "What are you talking about?"

"Oh, nothing. Just the silly thoughts of an old man." But the glint in Henry's eye suggests otherwise.

"No, you're hinting at something, and I think you need to grow some balls and spit it out." Jack looks down at Jessie, who is panting heavily, eyes closed, foam forming on her lips. "It might help us with Jessie." He crouches to run a hand over her head. The softness of his action, jarring against his harsh personality. It seems Jack does have a heart after all.

"Come now, you're telling me a clever man like yourself hasn't pieced it together?"

"Henry." Jack's growl carries a warning. Henry needs to be careful here before ending up with a bruised face to match Marty's.

"Susan spiked the punch the night of the party. That's how Victoria got so drunk."

The accusation hits hard. Everyone exchanges glances in silence before settling on Susan.

Victoria slams her palm down on the table, making everyone jump. "I knew I wasn't drunk! I don't get wasted that easily. But Susan? Was it really you?" She looks away, racking her brain for memories of that night. "You made the punch."

Susan backs away, wringing her hands together.

Henry grins at her.

"Why would you do that?"

"Victoria, I ..."

"I drank the punch," Evangeline squeaks. She looks as though she might throw up. "*You're* the reason I did those things that night?"

"Oh please, you did those things because you *chose* to. I didn't force you on Jack. Besides, you had loads of things to drink, not just the punch."

Evangeline's mouth drops open. "I thought I was drinking juice! I never would have... Susan, I never would have slept with him if I weren't so messed up."

Jack scoffs. "I am standing right here, you know."

"Shut up, Jack. This isn't about you."

"Really? Kinda sounds like it is."

"Leave it, mate." Gaz presses a hand to Jack's shoulder.

To Henry's surprise, Jack follows Gaz's order and sits down on a stool at the breakfast bar.

"Look, I am sorry, okay? I didn't *want* to do these things." Susan looks at the Confessions Room door, horrified.

Charlie strokes Jessie's plush fur, murmuring reassurances. "I think she's dying."

"So why did you?" Evangeline barks at Susan, not hearing Charlie.

"And what other things have you done?" Henry interjects.

"Nothing."

"No, you said 'these things', plural. Do tell, what else have you done?"

Susan's posture crumbles. "The night I was sleepwalking." She turns to Evangeline. "I was taking a lock of your hair."

Evangeline's fingers rake through her hair. "Why?!"

But Susan merely shrugs. "Landlord's orders."

"Anything else?" Henry asks, not caring if his housemates can see how much he's enjoying this.

"I had to keep Jack in the box game for as long as possible. I didn't know he was going through *that*." She motions to Jack's hand. "If I knew it was that bad, I would've stepped away. I swear to you, I didn't know what was going on. Just that I had orders and had to stick to them."

"Wait, did you kill the dog?" Marty suddenly shouts, visibly upset. Something is bothering him tonight; he's jittery and unpredictable.

"No!"

"Look at her; she's hardly the picture of health."

Victoria goes to lean over Jessie, who is no longer panting. She presses a hand to the tiny dog's chest. "She's still alive," she tells them. "But only just."

"What did you do to her?" Marty asks again.

"It wasn't me."

"What did you do?!" Marty's roar makes Henry's hair stand on end.

A tear falls down Susan's cheek. "Please don't. You're scaring me."

"Then fucking tell us!"

Susan bustles and moves away from the group. "I can't do this anymore. I want to go home, but they won't let me. I've asked over and over. I wanted to stay; they promised me so much. But now I don't care about any of that. I just want out." Susan's entire body sags. "But they won't let me out. I've tried the door; it's locked. We're trapped here."

"I knew you were dodgy." Marty slaps his thigh.

"We all did," Gaz laughs. "She's hardly a talented actress. Though the whole spiking thing is seriously messed up." He reaches for Victoria's hand, but she ignores it.

This is news to Henry. He raises an eyebrow. He thought *he* was the only one with even a modicum of intelligence to piece together Susan's story.

"It didn't take a genius to work out," Gaz tells him.

"I didn't know," Evangeline says quietly.

No surprise there. Evangeline isn't particularly sharp when the subject matter isn't herself. Good thing she has her looks.

Susan wipes a tear with the back of her hand. "I'm an actress. I signed up to stir the pot, not to watch people get *hurt.* I'm as confused as you are." She struggles to catch her breath.

"What is wrong with the dog, Susan?" Charlie growls. Charlie's innocent glow has vanished, replaced by Amber's darkness. Her eyes have sunken into her skull, her top lip raised on one side. She looks demonic squatting on the floor.

Susan stutters. "I'm sure she'll be fine."

"Bullshit. What's wrong with her?"

Victoria stands and places her hands on Susan's shoulders. "Tell us, Susan. I might be able to help her. Did you poison her? Does she need to be sick?"

"I'm telling you, she's fine! It's just a sedative. I think. It was meant to scare you, to make you all act crazy. Why, I don't know. We're all acting crazy enough as it is."

This is the Landlord. Could Evangeline please bring Jessie to the Confessions Room immediately for urgent veterinary care?

"Wait," Susan says. "It's just a sedative. I swear that's what they told me. She's fine."

But no one is listening. Evangeline has Jessie in her arms, rushing her away, followed by Gaz and Marty.

Charlie leans into Susan's ear. Henry has to strain to hear her. "If anything happens to that dog, *I'll kill you.*"

Henry cannot contain his glee, his laughter catching the women's attention. "I wouldn't laugh if I were you, old man," Charlie tells him. "You're first on my hit list."

Chapter 23

<u>Henry</u>

Everyone has been insufferably glum since the dog left yesterday. They're all moping around being miserable, as if she actually mattered. Don't they realise it was put in here purely to torment them? If they possessed any intelligence, they'd brighten up instead of letting the Landlord think he's winning.

It's been a tedious day for Henry. Susan's apologies dominate every conversation, sucking the life from the house and making everything boring. And Henry is fed up with the incessant chatter; he longs for something more stimulating. Another task would be lovely. He rather enjoyed yesterday's cops and robbers game, yet he can't help but think it ended prematurely.

Jack has made a simple casserole for dinner, and it smells divine. Henry practically salivates as he takes his seat, waiting for Susan to serve him before tucking in without so much as a 'thank you'.

No one has really spoken to Susan since her big revelation, despite her efforts to be cordial and friendly, frantically trying to win back their affection.

It isn't working. Relationships here are tenuous at best, but they were all they had. Now that she's lost their trust, she'll never get it back.

Susan remains oblivious to the extent of the damage she's caused, however, and Henry has enjoyed allowing her to wait on him hand and foot—fetching drinks, bringing blankets when it's chilly, even taking over his bathroom cleaning duties this morning.

He picks up his cutlery, and just as he spears his food, the speakers crackle.

This is the Landlord. An ominous pause follows; the speakers continue to crackle. Enjoy your dinner!

The housemates sit frozen, scanning each other. No one moves. The Landlord has never been randomly *nice* to them before, and the cheerfulness of his last comment is menacing at best, downright dangerous at worst.

"What's in the food?" Marty asks Jack.

Jack sneers at him in disgust. "You think I did something to the food? Why would I sabotage my own efforts? I'm a chef, not a fucking idiot. You should be asking that woman there." He jabs his knife at Susan, who hangs her head.

"I haven't been anywhere near the kitchen," she blushes. "I swear! Promise you I haven't."

"Alright. Just asking," Marty says, poking at his food.

Jack scrapes his chair noisily. "Yeah, well, you can keep your mouth shut and eat your food."

Gaz laughs. "How can he eat with his mouth shut?"

Jack shoots him a venomous look. Gaz laughs but does as he's told.

Always grumpy, this Jack guy. He cannot claim it's because he's tired though. It's not as if he lacks sleep. The Landlord had to sound the alarm four times this morning before Jack gave up on his lie-in. Henry just hopes the Landlord punishes Jack alone for his insubordination rather than the entire house. That would be grossly unfair.

Henry takes the first bite. He's hungry, and the mounting paranoia in the house is becoming ridiculous. Jack cooked the food and hasn't tampered with it. Henry knows this with certainty—Jack is a terrible liar.

"Well, this is simply divine," he announces as everyone watches him chew with various degrees of horror on their faces. "The tarragon is perfect!"

As if breaking a spell, the clink of cutlery tapping against crockery fills the room as everyone follows suit. Henry doesn't swallow—he waits. He isn't foolish.

Someone else can take that chance.

This is the Landlord. Could Charlie please come to the Confessions Room for today's nominations?

A chorus of groans and dismayed talk sounds around the table.

"At least try to pretend you're happy for me," Jack tells them.

"Happy for what?" Henry asks.

"For avoiding eviction. We're all voting for Susan, right?" He smiles, pleased to be off the hook. Or so he thinks.

"I doubt you'll be allowed to vote for me," Susan says glumly. "Punishment for me spilling the beans. He's obviously keeping me here to make me suffer."

Charlie pushes away from the table, her chair making a terrible screech that sends Henry's hairs on end.

He watches as she disappears into the Confessions Room.

<u>Victoria</u>

Victoria sits on the sofa, waiting to be called in to nominate. She has no idea where to cast her vote, and she can feel her pulse hammering in her throat. There's no way she can vote for Gaz or Marty. They may have betrayed her, but they're still her friends. Without them in here, she doesn't know how she'd cope.

Jack and Susan are obvious choices, but which one? Jack may be vile, but he's transparent. Susan is the dangerous player in this game. But now that she's exposed, the threat of having her in here has lessened.

But if they vote for Jack, the Landlord might kick Susan out anyway for breaking her contract. Or will Jack once more get immunity? He's obviously resonating with the audience outside to have won it once. God knows how, maybe he's a sympathy vote? Or is his disgraceful behaviour so entertaining the viewers cannot bear to see him leave?

It doesn't matter. She doesn't know what to do.

There's another problem she's battling with, though.

There's no way she can enter the Confessions Room. Not after what happened last time with the fake fire.

She remains on the sofa, waiting for Marty to exit the Confessions Room. Evangeline and Charlie whisper in the kitchen behind her whilst cleaning the dishes.

Victoria is hungry. She has barely eaten since her trauma. Her appetite has completely vanished.

Gaz sidles over. "Want me to prop the door open whilst you're in there?"

The longer Victoria stays in this house, the more attractive Gaz becomes. But she's unsure if it's enlightenment or a desperate need for affection that has made her come to this realisation.

"I don't think the Landlord will allow it."

"Then he doesn't get your nomination."

"And what do you think he'll do to me if I refuse?"

Gaz looks away.

If Victoria knew the punishment was immediate eviction, she'd refuse to take part in any of this nonsense. She'd have her bags packed right now.

But punishments mean pain and anguish in this house, and defying the Landlord isn't worth it. There's nothing to gain from pissing him off.

"What do you want to do?" Gaz mumbles. "Because I've got your back. Whatever you decide."

"Help me scale the walls?"

He grins. "Yeah? I'll throw you over."

"You may have underestimated how much I weigh."

"And you, young lady, are underestimating how strong I am." He flashes her a bicep and poses with a pout. "See?"

Victoria laughs, her terror of the Confessions Room dissipating just a little.

"There you are. I wish I could make you smile more. It looks good on you."

His words touch her in places that have been left abandoned for so long. She reaches for his hand.

This is the Landlord. Could Victoria please enter the Confessions Room?

The walk seems to take forever, like she's entering the gallows. She slides into the tiny space, glancing around for clues of potential torture. "Landlord, can I prop the door open, please?" She knows the answer before she's even asked, but it's worth a shot.

You cannot.

Victoria presses her lips together and nods, watching the door slide shut. She closes her eyes, waiting for the click of the lock snapping into place. It doesn't come.

Although, as a show of support, the Landlord will not lock the door on this occasion.

Her relief is palpable. She blows out a deep breath and sits on her hands.

She'll just make this quick. Get it over with. "Okay. I want to nominate Susan. She spiked my drink the night of the party, and that's unforgivable. I just can't trust her."

She can hardly breathe. It's as if invisible smoke is entering her lungs again. Her ears strain for the cry of despair from outside.

"Can I go now?"

You may return to the house. Thank you, Victoria.

When the door is open just a centimetre, Victoria pushes out of the room, rushing straight into Gaz's arms.

"Hey, you okay? Did they do anything to you?" he asks, pulling her into his chest and wrapping his arms around her.

"No, I'm fine. Just freaked out," she tells him, absorbing every bit of comfort his embrace offers. In a bid to banish her panic, she focuses on this moment and this moment alone.

"You're okay," Gaz breathes into her hair. "You're okay."

"What happened?" Marty appears, looking petrified. "Did they hurt you?"

Victoria pulls away and straightens herself. "No, no. I'm just being silly. I need to calm myself down."

This is the Landlord. Could all housemates gather on the sofas?

Chapter 24

<u>Marty</u>

Nomination results—it has to be.

Marty prays he's going home. Eviction seems to be the only way to escape here. Most housemates have begged to leave, and the Landlord has refused every request. There's no door to break through except the one they entered, and from what he remembers, at least three more doors stand between them and the outside world.

They could try climbing the walls, but they're impossibly high and edged with razor wire. The wounds inflicted might be worth it if he could guarantee freedom greets them on the other side. But knowing the Landlord, there'd be another layer of horror to break through.

On day one, that old woman, Gloria, was evicted. She left in mysterious circumstances that they haven't talked about since. Probably because they're too afraid to speak it out loud.

Did the Landlord hurt Gloria?

What kind of show is this anyway? At the audition, he was led to believe it would be aired on mainstream television, though now he knows that can't be true. There's no way the BBC or ITV would broadcast this horror show. No, he suspects this is purely for dark web entertainment. He keeps this idea to himself; he doesn't want to cause a panic.

"Who do you think it'll be?" Evangeline asks, looking petrified. Probably thinking the same thoughts—what happened to Gloria the night she was nominated?

"It has to be Jack or Susan. No idea which one," Marty tells her, not bothering to keep his voice down.

"Who did *you* vote for?"

"I'm not going to tell you that."

Evangeline scrunches her nose. "Fair enough. I just hope it's not me. I don't want to go out there." She gestures toward the open garden door.

"You'd really want to stay in here?"

"After what I did? You're kidding, right? They'll slaughter me."

Marty takes a deep breath. "You've got to stop being so hard on yourself. What you did was a mistake. A mistake made a million times before by millions of people. Sleeping with Jack might not have been your finest moment, but you've learnt from it. Besides, you think we don't all have our demons?"

"Yeah, but you haven't shown yours on T.V, have you?"

Marty thinks of the drugs he had stashed away. Everyone must have seen. But they'd also seen him resist. He didn't take a taste. Even if he came so damn close.

He can understand Evangeline's fears. If he'd have taken the coke, being outside would have removed the hazy memories and rose-tinted glasses—it'd be out there forever, for him to see, for people to show him.

He can't think of anything worse.

This is the Landlord. Today's nominations are now over, and I'll return with the results in due course. First, as a reward for her role in the Confessions Room task, Victoria is to receive a gift. Victoria, do you accept?

<u>Victoria</u>

A gift from the Landlord? Is that wise?

She looks at everyone in turn, waiting for someone to decide for her. Gaz clasps her arm. "Take the gift. We won't let them hurt you."

Victoria grimaces. It's noble of him to say, but it's a promise Gaz cannot keep. How can you say you'll protect someone when you have no idea what the dangers are or when they're coming?

"I don't know," she whispers.

"It might be information on Lily?" Henry offers. Victoria sees Marty wince in her peripheral vision. He thinks this is a bad idea. But he doesn't offer any advice; he knows this decision has to be hers.

She closes her eyes and thinks of her daughter.

If this gift concerns her, and she turns it down, can she ever forgive herself? Hasn't she sacrificed so much already? Isn't a little pain worth it? As the days slip by, her desperation reaches new heights. She would lock herself in the Confessions Room with the house burning around her just to know Lily's okay.

"I accept your gift, Landlord. Thank you."

The faint static blaring through the speakers dies, leaving the room feeling suddenly cold and vast.

They wait. Everything in here is a waiting game. A power play by the Landlord. A way to keep them on edge. Stressed and impatient.

"Well? Is that it?" Jack barks. His bandage looks sodden with a yellowish-brown liquid. Victoria feels sorry for him. No one deserves to be left in such a painful mess.

Five minutes pass; the Landlord doesn't return. Jack leaves to have a cigarette.

"He's probably arranging the call," Susan says, squeezing Victoria's shoulder gently. "He'll be back."

Victoria hopes so. But a huge part of her is filled with dread. She doesn't like that the Landlord is taking his sweet time. It gives him more opportunity to conjure something horrible.

<u>Henry</u>

By the time bedtime rolls around, Henry is exhausted. He's unsure of the time, but it must be approaching midnight. Way past his usual bedtime. But he'd simply grown too comfortable on the sofa and couldn't bring himself to move.

When he enters the bedroom, he stops dead.

"Oh no!" he gasps. The room looks barren. He counts four.

Four beds.

Eight housemates.

It doesn't take a genius to work out what the Landlord is orchestrating.

Marty bustles in behind him. "Ah shit. What happened in here?"

"Well, I'm no rocket scientist, Marty, but I think this might just be our punishment for Jack's selfish need for extra sleep this morning."

Marty groans. "For fuck's sake."

"Indeed."

"Right, tell you what, I'll share with you. Only you can have the bed; I'll sleep on the floor."

"That's very generous of you."

Marty shrugs. "I've slept in worse places."

"You've lived quite an interesting life, haven't you?"

"That's one way of putting it."

Henry slips into the bed nearest the bathroom, whilst everyone else piles into the room.

No one knows how to handle the altered sleeping arrangements, and Henry watches from his bed, overjoyed by the confusion.

<u>Victoria</u>

Victoria watches Evangeline cling to Charlie's arm, claiming her bed-mate. She's not sure if Evangeline has made the right choice, Charlie is so unpredictable. Victoria would rather pair with Susan. At least she's a little more stable now. Or at least she thinks so, who knows what's going on in any of these housemates' heads.

Susan, however, is heavily hinting at sharing a bed with Gaz. She can't blame her; sharing with Jack isn't even an option, and Gaz is probably the tastiest housemate to bed share with.

Victoria shakes off these thoughts. Now's not the time for pathetic fantasies.

"Vic," Jack says, sidling over. "Looks like it's me and you."

Victoria scowls at him. "Don't you dare come anywhere near me. You think I'm sharing a bed with you? This is all your fault, you big idiot. You should have gotten up when the Landlord told you to. You can sleep in the bath for all I care."

"What, with this?" He gestures at his mangled hand. "You're a nurse, you wouldn't do that to me."

"No, I would, and I am. Want to fix your image on the outside? Don't you think it's time you started?"

Jack laughs. "My image is torn to shreds. There's no coming back from that. Might as well have a little fun with it." He has the audacity to wink at her, turning her stomach.

"Get away from me," Victoria growls. She sees Gaz watching from the other side of the room.

Jack steps closer. "Can't handle the sexual tension, eh?"

"I swear to God I will ram that hand up your arse if you don't get away from me."

Gaz steps forward at the same time as Jack, but his heroism isn't required. Victoria reaches out and grabs Jack's injured hand, making him squeal a noise so high-pitched it could belong to a little girl. She gives it a deliberate squeeze. "Get away from me, Jack."

"The Landlord won't let you get away with this."

Victoria laughs. "You think the Landlord gives a shit? Jack, he was the one who did this to you in the first place! This was no *glitch*. You're on your own." She grips his hand tighter. "We all are. Now, I suggest you make yourself a little bed on the sofa, because that's where you're going to be for the foreseeable."

Jack whimpers.

"Yes?"

"Yes!" he yells. "Yes, okay!"

She releases him, and Jack scuttles off, clutching his burned hand protectively. He mumbles something under his breath that Victoria doesn't catch. She doesn't care—she's more concerned with her laboured breath. She *hates* confrontation, and what she did was beyond reckless.

Though she's proud of her bravery, despite fearing Jack's retaliation. She can't imagine he'll react well to having his masculinity tarnished.

"Nice work," Gaz tells her, beaming. "He deserved that."

"Yeah," Victoria says, watching Jack pull a spare blanket out of a cupboard before carefully selecting the plumpest pillow from the remaining bed. "I guess we just wait and see if he gets revenge."

"Nah, I won't let him."

Victoria welcomes his reassurance, but it does nothing to soothe her nerves. She shakes it off. Glad to be sleeping alone tonight, she gets ready for bed.

Chapter 25

Victoria

Victoria has been listening to the sounds of sleep for what has felt like an eternity, though it's most probably just an hour. Without clocks, time has become this slippery, unknowable thing, and it sets her teeth on edge. She's someone who lives by schedules—patient rounds, administering Lily's medication, making sure she is pulled in the right direction on the right day. Her irritability is so high she worries the weight of it all is slowly suffocating her.

She turns to face Evangeline, lying in the bed a few feet away. Victoria can just make out her curves in the emergency lighting. Her mouth hangs open, her head tilted back. It's a very unflattering pose.

Victoria smiles. Sleep humbles even the most appearance-conscious person. Evangeline was brought down a peg the night she slept with Jack. The other housemates still whisper words of disbelief about her actions, but Victoria knows better. When you're broken inside, you'll do absolutely anything to keep yourself together. Evangeline must have been in pieces to have hoped Jack would hold the answers she needed.

That and under the influence of something. Fuck Susan.

Victoria makes a mental note to get to know Evangeline better. When she first entered the house, she clung to her, hoping she'd absorb some of her popularity. That plan was soon abandoned when Victoria could not stand being near Evangeline for longer than necessary. But here in the dark, she sees the child in her. And every child deserves to be held tight through their pain.

She rolls over to find a figure standing by her bed. She sits up with a gasp, her heart hammering against her ribs.

"Shhh. It's just me. Budge up," Gaz whispers in her ear. She catches a whiff of the faint scent of mouthwash on his breath.

Victoria hesitates.

"Come on. It's freezing out here."

She scoots over onto the cold side of the bed, and Gaz slips in beside her, leaving a polite gap between them.

"What are you doing?!" Victoria admonishes. "You can't be in here."

"No? I beg to differ."

"Gaz..."

"Sorry. Susan keeps *touching* me. It's freaking me out."

"Touching you?"

"Yeah, she's a fidget, and she keeps throwing her arm over me like I'm a big teddy bear."

Victoria giggles. "Well, you *are* soft and squishy."

"Oi. I work hard to maintain this physique. I'm toned. Hard. Soft and squishy... pfft."

"Yeah, yeah. How come you're still awake?"

"You didn't hear my Susan story? What's your excuse?"

"I don't know. Since the Landlord promised me a gift, I keep assuming I'll get to speak to Lily. I've been imagining hearing her voice." She swallows. "I'll probably just get a bag of jellybeans or something."

"Maybe."

"Well, either way, I'm too scared that if I fall asleep, I'll miss it."

"The Landlord won't do that."

"You really trust the Landlord?"

"No. Not one bit."

"Exactly."

"Okay. How about this—I promise to be an extra pair of ears. You sleep, and I'll wake you if the Landlord calls you into the Confessions Room."

"And what about your sleep?"

"I'll be okay. I don't need beauty sleep like you ugly bunch."

Victoria whacks him in the chest, giggling. Henry grunts in his sleep, and they hold their breath, but he just rolls onto his back and resumes his soft snoring.

"Whew," Gaz breathes. "Close one."

"Don't want to be caught in bed with me?"

"Now, now. Someone's getting cheeky. You'll get me all excited."

Victoria realises her hands are pressed against Gaz's chest. She contemplates pulling away, but his skin is so warm, so smooth, so comforting.

It's exciting.

It's dangerous.

She feels giddy with desire, and it feels good.

"So, what do you think? You sleep, I'll keep watch."

"You promise you'll look after me?" She doesn't know why she says it. She never felt incapable of protecting herself. Since Lily's piece-of-shit father abandoned them, she had faced life with her head held high and her heart warm with love for Lily. She never needed anything else.

But right now, she longs to let go of all that. Of the hurt, the stress, just everything. Just for tonight. Just for now.

"I'll look after you," Gaz whispers, kissing her lightly on the forehead, pressing comfort into her skin.

Victoria lifts her chin and places her lips on his. He freezes for a second before pulling her into his thick arms. She wraps her leg around his waist, making him groan quietly into the darkness.

His tongue finds hers as she parts her lips, her fingers wrapping around the back of his head, pulling him closer to her. A moan threatens to pour out of her very soul as he pushes against her, demonstrating everything he has to offer.

And she takes his offering with everything she has.

***

Gaz is gone by the time Victoria wakes. Interestingly, the Landlord didn't wake them with his obnoxious alarm this morning. Another way to confuse and disorient the housemates.

Victoria pulls her blanket up to her chin and closes her eyes. Try as she might, she cannot get what happened last night out of her head.

It was a mistake; she knows that. She cannot let a man steal her focus from her little girl right now. But to allow herself one night of passion in this hellhole? She can't feel bad about that.

Can she?

As fun as it was, as necessary as the release was, guilt for Lily still gnaws away at her stomach.

"I brought you tea," Susan says, standing uncomfortably close as she places the mug on the bedside table. "Sleep well?"

"Very well, thank you."

"Lucky you! I had Gaz fidgeting all night, I didn't sleep a wink."

"No?"

"Until he left the bed, that is."

Victoria cringes inwardly and grabs her cup to have something to occupy her hands. She avoids making eye contact, too afraid of what she will see in Susan's expression. Mockery? Jealousy? Disgust? None of them are welcome.

"You okay, love? You look mortified."

"No, no. I'm fine. Just missing Lily, I guess. Hopefully, he'll put me out of my misery today."

"Yes, well, hopefully he'll put all of us out of our misery today. Hopefully, he'll just evict me." Susan walks away to deliver Henry his drink.

Victoria had forgotten about the eviction. What's the hold up? It would be nice to know where she stands. Maybe she'll be seeing Lily soon enough after all.

Marty

Marty has been locked in the toilet cubicle for forty minutes, his forehead resting in his hand, sweat clinging to his skin.

He pulls back and stares at his trembling hands. Knowing the bag of cocaine was in the drawer had been a comfort blanket—a high-pressure, painful comfort blanket. Now that it's gone, he feels lost. Like a close friend has died.

Before, he had a choice, a way out. Now he's on his own, and he's panic-stricken.

He thinks of Carl's promise before he came in here. The hatred blazing in his eyes as he shoved Marty back over the car park railing, six stories up. A gust of air breezing past his exposed neck.

"You killed my boy, and now you're going to pay for it." The restraint it took Carl not to push him off, to face his death. He wishes Carl had done it; things would be easier for everyone if he were dead.

"Two more weeks," he whispers to himself now. "Just survive two more weeks and win. Then all this will be over." And if he doesn't win? He sighs.

He leans back, his spine pushing into the wall.

Someone hammers on the door, making him jump. "You going to be much longer? Jack made a right mess of the other toilet. There's no way I'm peeing in that smell." It's Charlie.

"One second!" Relieved to escape his tumultuous thoughts, Marty stands, flushes the toilet for believability, and exits. "Don't worry. No smell in there."

"Why are you gays so much more considerate than straight guys?"

Marty can't help smiling at her brazen question. "I'm not sure if sexuality affects the smell of shit."

"No? Maybe." She disappears into the toilet, the click of the lock shutting her off from the rest of the house.

Everyone is in deep conversation when he enters the living room. "What's going on?" he asks Henry, who is watching from the sidelines as usual. Always analysing. Marty would love to know what's going on in that balding head of his. Is he as innocent as he seems? Surely not. Everyone has skeletons in their closet.

"No idea," Henry says. "I just walked in, and you could cut the tension with a knife in here."

Marty goes to stand by Gaz. "Do you know?"

"Amber just dropped a bombshell and then fucked off to the toilet."

Marty raises an eyebrow.

"She thinks Gloria is hidden behind the wall in the main bathroom."

Marty laughs, but it's cut short by Gaz shaking his head. "Don't, mate. It's really shaken Evangeline. Apparently, Amber can smell Gloria rotting in there."

"Shit. That's messed up."

"Exactly. And you know what's worse?" Gaz looks at Victoria, who has her arm wrapped around Evangeline's shoulder. There's longing in his eyes. "She said Susan was the one who put her there." He bites his lip. "I think the house is making her crack up."

"More so than she already is?"

Gaz shoots him a withering look of agreement.

Susan is sitting alone, shaking her head. She looks as if she has run out of protests.

Poor Susan. Marty knows she isn't capable of killing someone and stashing them inside the walls of the house. It's a ridiculous idea. But when everyone is already doubting her, this must be crushing.

"Susan, you okay?" he asks her quietly, taking the seat beside her.

"I did no such thing. That girl is crazy."

"We all know that." He offers a warm smile. "Look. Amber likes shocking people. But you know what? She takes it too far to be believable. This will be forgotten in ten minutes."

And, as if on cue... *Could all housemates gather in the living area for Victoria's very special message?*

Chapter 26

<u>Victoria</u>

Her heart stops. She cannot catch her breath.

Someone takes her hand and guides her onto the sofa. They sit beside her, resting a huge hand on her thigh. "You've got this," Gaz whispers in her ear.

Victoria looks him in the eye. He gazes down at her so earnestly she has to fight the urge to rest her head on his chest.

"I'm scared, Gaz."

The speakers hiss, making Victoria sit up straight. She strains her ears, desperate for Lily's delicate voice to fill the house. She closes her eyes and breathes out.

This is the Landlord. Victoria, Lily's doctor would like to speak with you.

Lily's doctor. What?! This cannot be good. Why would she need to speak to Lily's doctor? Has her SMA worsened drastically whilst she's been away?

She suddenly feels cold, her body shaking uncontrollably. Gaz reaches for her hand again, but she pushes him away. She doesn't want him right now; she just needs to know Lily is okay.

Dr Chattergee, one of Lily's consultants, clears his throat over the speakers. Victoria knows that nasally cough anywhere. "Miss Steeple?"

Victoria leaps up from her chair, her hands pressed into a prayer position. "Dr Chattergee! How is she?"

"As you know, before you left, Lily was in a strong position. Well, we've had to admit her to hospital."

Victoria gasps, but Dr Chattergee quickly interrupts her panic. "Just to be clear—she's doing fine. No need to panic. Lily contracted pneumonia, but it's under control now."

No need to panic? Is this doctor insane?! Her baby is sick! This wasn't supposed to happen. When Victoria left, Lily was stable, she was happy. Victoria would never have left if she had thought for one second Lily would deteriorate so drastically.

The full weight of her decision to enter this house hits her so hard she falls back onto the sofa. Regret is the hardest feeling to live with, and it's truly agonising. She wants to rip it out of her chest and throw it at the Landlord.

"I need to leave," she announces, glancing around as if a taxi might appear.

Marty pulls her back down to reality. "Hear the man out. Get all the info before deciding what to do next."

That makes sense. She'll get all the information before leaving, so she knows what she's facing outside. She'll know how hard she has to fight for her release.

Dr Chattergee explains: "Victoria, I know how frightening this must sound, but I want you to know that we caught this very early. Lily came in with what seemed like a simple cold, but because of her SMA, we're always vigilant about respiratory symptoms, as you know. Her oxygen saturation dropped slightly, so we admitted her straight away.

"We started her on IV antibiotics, and she's responding beautifully. Her fever broke yesterday, and her oxygen levels have been stable with minimal supplemental oxygen.

"More importantly, her respiratory muscle function hasn't declined. She's been able to clear her secretions well with the chest physiotherapy, and she's even been chatting away to the nurses. In fact, Lily has a message for you. I recorded it on my phone."

Victoria squeals with apprehensive joy. Marty, sitting on her other side of Gaz, breathes out a joyful laugh. She leans forward to block him out. As much as she's glad to have him here, this moment is hers alone.

"Hey Mummy," the sweetest, most angelic voice fills the room and floods Victoria's heart. She gasps and clutches her chest, absorbing every note, every sound, every precious timbre of Lily's sweet voice. "I just wanted to tell you I'm okay and I love you. Nana let me eat ice cream for breakfast!" She ends with a little squeal that makes Victoria laugh. "I miss you, though."

"I miss you too, sweetie," Victoria whispers.

"Oh, and Mummy? Daddy says hi."

The crackle cuts out. Lily is gone.

And Victoria's world implodes.

Victoria's Confession

"Let me out!" She doesn't bother sitting down. She gives the Confessions Room chair a shove. It wobbles but fails to fall over, much to her dissatisfaction.

"Is something bothering you, Victoria?"

"It's time to go. I'm done. Let me out."

"And why is that?"

"You heard her! I need to see Lily. I need to know what's going on out there."

The crackle dies away, fading into nothing.

"Landlord!"

The hesitation intensifies her fury into unimaginable potency. She curses and kicks the wall.

"The Landlord is contemplating, Victoria. Please refrain from damaging my property."

"Fuck your property."

"Then consider your request denied."

"No! Look, I'm sorry, okay?" Victoria sits down, the image of a good girl. *"I'm behaving, please let me out. You said we could get out if we put in a formal request. Well, this is my formal request."*

"Victoria, the rules did indeed state that you can request to leave. That rule has since changed."

"Changed..."

"Housemates can only leave if the Landlord deems it acceptable. Right now, your exit isn't acceptable."

"But Lily!"

"Goodbye, Victoria."

"No! Don't go!" But the speakers go silent, and the door slides open.

<u>Henry</u>

Victoria went barrelling into the Confessions Room so fast her fist left a small mark in the plasterboard where she hammered on the door release button.

"Oh my," Henry squeaks, capturing Susan's attention.

"What do you think that was about?" she asks him. "Her little girl sounded happy?"

He sneers at her. "How am I supposed to know? I'm not privy to every aspect of Victoria's life."

"Alright, calm down. You just seem to be in the loop with a lot of things. No need to be so arsey. It must have something to do with the girl's dad." She frowns and nods to herself. "Yeah, must be that."

Evangeline flops down next to Susan, cupping a bowl of Coco Pops in one hand and a spoon in the other. "You think she's upset the dad's back on the scene?"

Henry smiles. "Ah, we were just speculating on that," he says, assuming for kinder tone. Susan scowls at him, but he continues with a smile. "I should imagine it's rather concerning to have someone walk back into your child's life when they initially wanted nothing to do with her."

Evangeline pouts, but only with concern now. She isn't posing for once. It has been interesting watching her mask slip. Evangeline has gone from prom queen to tragic innocence in such a short time. But is she a victim of the house, or has she just been released from the pressures of social expectation?

"Maybe it's a good thing having him back? Every child should have a father," says Susan.

"Not true," Evangeline cuts in. "I was better off without mine. I know that for sure. He disappeared when I was little, ran off with his secretary. Classy right?"

Ah, daddy issues, Henry thinks. He was right. It makes perfect sense. Her incessant need for approval. Sleeping with Jack was probably a disturbed attempt at winning the approval of a man her father's age.

A broken bird. So delicate. So vulnerable. Such a pity.

"Do you have children, Henry?" she asks, startling him. "I imagine you'd be a good dad."

Henry shakes his head. "Sadly not. My wife wasn't blessed in that department. It wasn't meant to be."

"So you tried?"

Henry bristles at Susan's question. He has no desire to discuss the intimate details of his life with her.

"We did," he admits. "For many years."

"I'm sorry, Henry," Evangeline murmurs.

"It's okay, my dear. I'm fulfilled with other... pastimes."

Evangeline tips her now-chocolate milk into her mouth. A little drips down her chin, and Henry takes it upon himself to dab it with his handkerchief.

"Told you you'd be a good dad," Evangeline tells him, her cheeks pink. "You're one of the very few nice ones."

Susan scoffs. Henry and Evangeline turn to her. "Are you okay, Susan?" Evangeline asks. Of everyone, she seems to be the most forgiving of Susan's role in the show.

Henry leans forward, concerned. "Yes, Susan, is everything okay? Any more secrets you wish to divulge?"

Susan just scowls at Henry and makes her excuses before disappearing outside.

"What's her problem?" Evangeline asks.

"Between you and me, I don't think Susan likes me very much."

"Oh, you're being paranoid. How can anyone not like you?"

"Amber doesn't?"

"Yeah well, Amber isn't real."

Henry smiles, satisfied Amber has released her clutches of Evangeline. "I don't know. I just think Susan has more secrets stashed away. She's a cunning woman."

"Rubbish. She's admitted to being a pawn in the game, not the puppeteer. And I believe her."

"Oh, come on. You're a clever girl; you must have noticed. Her disappearances in to the Confessions Room, her obsession with staring at the cameras. She's more in control than she's letting on. She knows things."

Evangeline looks pained as she considers this. Eventually she nods, her mouth agape. "Now that you mention it..."

Henry wonders how much longer he has before the Landlord kicks him out for meddling. Or is it good for views? Is that what's keeping him here? He hopes so, because he isn't ready to give this up. Unlike all the other housemates, he's enjoying himself. He hasn't made a fool of himself begging to go home.

This is the Landlord. Susan, as a result of the nominations, you have been evicted. You have one hour to pack your belongings and say your goodbyes.

<u>Victoria</u>

The news of Susan's eviction makes Victoria's blood boil. Nothing in this damn house makes sense. It is *imperative* that

Victoria leave right now, but her demands have been denied. Whereas Susan wants to stay and she's being kicked out?

Victoria is livid.

"You can't keep me here against my will!" she screams, tipping the contents of her underwear drawer into her suitcase. Gaz paces the room. Having promised to help escape, he's been wracking his brain and checking for secret passages for the last five minutes while Victoria rants at the Landlord.

Marty comes barrelling in. "Right, I reckon, between me and Gaz, we can charge the doors. Gaz is a big boy. I'm, well, I'm a stupid lad and as my mum used to say, 'no sense, no feeling'."

"You think?" Victoria asks. "There are like four doors to get out of here. We'll be stopped before we make it through the first one."

"It's our only option," Gaz says, nodding. "The perimeter fence is too high. We could stack some chairs, but the razor wire looks lethal. It's worth a shot though, right?"

Victoria sighs. "This isn't a house—it's a fucking prison."

Susan steps into the room, zipping her wash bag. "You okay, duck?"

"No, I'm not fucking okay," Victoria snaps.

Susan raises her free hand. "What's the urgency? I don't get it."

Victoria punches her pillow. "That man is the biggest arsehole on the planet. That's the urgency."

"Lily's dad." Gaz clarifies.

"Don't call him that. He was a bad decision and a sperm donor. That's all."

Susan tentatively touches Victoria's arm. "Is he a bad person, love?"

Victoria swallows, her eyes desperate, pleading for Susan to understand without having to say the words out loud. "He was the worst. I didn't know him that well when we hooked up. I'd seen him in the local pub a few times; we made eyes over the bar, you know? But I never intended for anything to happen."

"Mistakes happen. We've all been there. Just look at Evangeline," Susan reassures.

"That's just it. I don't think I made a mistake. I can't remember. One minute I was leaving the pub. The next I was waking up at his house."

There's a pregnant pause as everyone contemplates Victoria's admission.

"Oh, darling," Susan groans. "You poor girl."

Gaz presses his hands to the top of his head and blows out hard. He looks like he's in physical pain.

"I just thought I'd had a few too many drinks and made some stupid, drunken choices. At least, that's what he led me to believe."

Silence rings in Victoria's ears. She's sealed off, utterly alone. The world beyond her, the house, no longer exists. She's back in that apartment, waking to find herself lying beside the man she thought was attractive just the night before. But now, the morning after, he makes her sick.

She just can't remember why.

"Morning, sleepyhead," he'd said with a grin. "Last night was just magical."

Victoria didn't know what to say. She just stared at him, mute.

"I've got to go to work soon, but I made you a coffee." He motioned at the mug on the bedside table as if it was the most thoughtful act in the world. The sentiment is clear: drink and get out.

He disappeared into the bathroom then. The second Victoria heard the shower burst into life, she ran.

She didn't even know his name.

She didn't see the man for a long time after that. Nine months exactly.

She spotted him before he saw her. She tried to sneak away, but, trembling from shock, she stumbled off the kerb, drawing his attention.

They made eye contact. Victoria's cheeks burned. Fury at having been 'caught' with her baby? No. Horror at seeing the man who slept with her without her consent? Also no.

No, she was frightened. Frightened that he would connect the dots and lay a claim on her little girl. Her one chance at happiness through the foggy darkness.

From then on, she kept seeing him everywhere. She learnt his name was Daniel, an estate agent, married.

He sniffed around her for a while. Pretended he wanted to be a father. Claimed to be 'figuring things out'.

Until Lily was diagnosed with Spinal Muscular Atrophy at three months old, and then he ran away so fast Usain Bolt would have been impressed.

She's been battling this alone ever since. She won't pretend she wishes he was around; she's *glad* never to see him again. Though if she's going to wish for something, she'd shoot for the moon and wish to have more support. Support from a man decent enough to deserve Lily.

It's amazing how someone as beautiful as her little girl could be fifty per cent DNA of a monster. A nature vs nurture debate at its finest.

"You need to get that man away from Lily. You need to leave," Susan whispers, dragging Victoria from her memories. "Come on, I don't know how long I have until he kicks me out of here." She moves to leave the room.

"Where are we going?"

"I'm getting you out of here, duck. Call it an apology for lying to you all."

Chapter 27

<u>Henry</u>

Susan runs into the kitchen, past a bemused Jack, who steps out of the way with a scowl. "I hope you're not looking for biscuits; Henry just ate the last one," he calls out as Susan, Victoria, Gaz, and Marty rush into the pantry, all four of them squeezing inside.

"I had just three biscuits. Just because I had the last one, it doesn't mean I'm the greedy guts," Henry calls back, following the crowd. "What's happening in here then?" he asks the group, standing just outside, propping the door open with his foot.

"Nothing you should concern yourself with, mate," Marty tells him. "You could get yourself in a lot of trouble if you stick around."

Henry chuckles. "I've done worse things, I'm sure."

Marty gives him an odd look, part confused, part impressed by Henry's lack of concern about angering the Landlord.

"Shut the door, Henry," Susan says sharply. "We don't need to invite the whole house in here."

Henry obliges, bristling at Susan's tone. Now isn't the time to complain, though—he wants to be involved in this. Whatever *this* is. He pushes his way in, pressing against Marty.

"Right, see this here?" Susan opens a large cupboard and reaches inside, pushing food staples out of the way. "It has a false back." She reaches in further with a grimace, and Henry hears the unmistakable click of a catch unlocking.

"Holy shit. Susan, what are you doing?" Gaz says, ever the most eloquent of the group.

Could Susan please come to the Confessions Room?

"He knows," Marty says.

"Of course he knows—he has over a hundred cameras in this place." Henry mocks. Marty pulls a face as if refusing the truth will make all the cameras vanish.

"Right, Vic, time to go," Gaz tells her.

Victoria peers into the opening. "Where does this go?" she asks Susan.

Susan shrugs. "No idea. It's how they've passed stuff *in*. I have never used it to get out."

Everyone hesitates, looking at each other uncertainly. "Come on, you'd better go before the Landlord puts a stop to all this," Susan urges.

"Who's to say there isn't someone waiting for me on the other side?"

"There probably will be. But at least you'll be out. It's easier for them to keep you locked in than to force you back in once you're out."

Gaz shrugs. "Makes sense."

Henry bristles. "Why has no one addressed the fact that Susan has kept this from us? A secret way out sounds like the perfect thing to share with a group desperate to escape." He cocks his head to the side.

"Not now, Henry. We haven't got time for this."

"Yeah, and sorry, Henry, but we don't need to go over the whole mole thing again," Marty says, peering into the cupboard. He pulls a bag of pasta out of the way.

"Thank you, Mart." Susan turns to face Henry. "I know I've done wrong. I'm trying to make up for it now, okay? Now be quiet."

This is the Landlord. Susan must come to the Confessions Room immediately. The remaining housemates must gather in the living room.

"Go now," Susan urges. She pushes her way towards the door. "I'll go to the Confessions Room and try to buy you time."

Just then, the pantry door swings inward, hitting Susan in the face. She stumbles back clutching her cheek, a muffled moan sounding through her fingers.

Charlie stands outside, the sunlight making her silhouette glow. "What the fuck is going on in here? The Landlord sounds pissed."

"Nothing, we're just leaving. Come on, living room," Susan says, grabbing Charlie's arm to guide her aside with one hand, the other still clutching her face.

A curious look passes over Charlie's face. It's as if a shadow passes through her eyes. Henry recognises this look now: Amber taking over. Her eyes lock onto his, hatred pouring through them, burning him.

She's been more intense lately, more *enraged*. A ticking bomb.

She bares her teeth at him.

Quick as lightning, she raises her arm in the air, and a glint of metal flashes above her head.

A paring knife.

Victoria screams. Gaz pushes forward, shoving Henry to the side, bumping his head against the cupboard overhead. He groans and rubs his injury as the screams erupt all around him.

He forces his eyes to refocus on the chaos and finds Susan lying on the floor, blood spreading from her abdomen, merging with the multi-coloured polka-dots on her dress.

@Connoisseur: FINALLY! Someone's dead. The first of many! The knife work was artistic. Chef's kiss.

@DeathCollector: Downloaded in 4K. That blood spray was magnificent. When's the next elimination?

@VIP_Diamond: Worth every penny. The screaming was authentic. More like this please.

@Anonymous_Mega: Transferring £10k. This is exactly what I wanted. Kill the influencer next. I bet she squeals like a pig.

@LiveLeak_Veteran: Better than anything on the internet. You've got a new permanent subscriber.

@RichSadist_001: My wife and I watched this together. We haven't been this entertained in years. A real turn-on.

Chapter 28

<u>Marty</u>

All hell breaks loose.

Marty doesn't know where to look, what to do, or who to help. His eyes fix on Susan, bleeding out on the tiled floor. Charlie stands open-mouthed, pure horror etched on her face. Tears create rivulets through the blood painted across her cheeks. She's still standing over the Susan, watching her die.

"Get help!" Marty hears himself calling. "Get paramedics in here NOW!" The knife is lying on the floor, and he kicks it away, out of Charlie's reach.

But no one in green overalls comes rushing through the doors. There's no response whatsoever, not even the crackle of the speakers.

It's as if they're stranded here, alone and surrounded by hell.

Marty's heart hammers in his chest, fighting for his attention. His breath comes in thick, wet rasps.

Gaz leans over Susan, pressing down on her wound on her stomach. Jack rushes in with clean towels. When the door opens, he can see Evangeline standing in the living room, crying into her sleeve, while Henry hasn't moved a muscle inside the pantry—he remains transfixed on the red blood pooling around his feet.

Victoria! She'll know what to do.

But Victoria is nowhere to be seen.

Marty is relieved to leave the scene as he rushes into the bedroom. It's like entering a sanctuary. It's quiet in here, and he has to fight the urge to climb into bed and pretend like none of this is happening.

But there's a woman dying out there. He can't just leave her.

"Victoria!?" he calls out. She isn't in the bedroom, and he rushes to peer around the bathroom door. It's empty. "Victoria!"

Running now, he goes to the garden. There's no one here except Evangeline, who has moved outside and is lighting a cigarette with shaking hands. "I can't be in there," she cries. "I'm sorry."

Now is not the time to comfort Evangeline. Marty heads back inside. "Has anyone seen Victoria?"

Henry strolls out of the pantry, looking pale. He points through the propped-open pantry door, over Susan's body, at the cupboard with the false back.

Marty's jaw drops open. "She left?"

Henry nods. There's a strange urgency about him that doesn't inspire sympathy. If anything, Marty feels a little frightened looking at Henry right now. It's almost as if he's *hungry*. For what, Marty doesn't know.

Marty heads back into the pantry, carefully stepping over Susan and Gaz, who is swearing and coated in red. He looks into the cupboard and glimpses a long corridor ahead. He leans in as the door slams shut, missing him by millimetres. Someone's out there.

"Shit," he gasps.

"What?" Jack asks, scratching his sweaty head, still standing just outside, too afraid to step into the crime scene, his eyes not leaving Susan.

"Victoria's gone."

Henry

Henry is wringing his hands together on the sofa. He doesn't know what to do with himself, and he cannot take his eyes off Susan. He breathes a sigh of relief when Gaz gives up the fight and leans away from Susan. That was all very stressful.

"She's gone." Gaz sounds stunned. Distraught. The poor lad obviously has never dealt with a dead body before. Though few people have, Henry supposes.

Jack claps Gaz on the back. "You did good," he stutters. "But what do we do now?"

Jack has surprised Henry. When push came to shove, he was helpful, quick-thinking, and entirely unselfish. Maybe he isn't the complete arse Henry assumed. Just ninety-nine percent arse.

"I need to speak to that bastard!" Gaz rises from the floor and stomps over to the locked Confessions Room door, raging. "You happy now?! She's *dead*. And it's your fault."

Not strictly true, Henry thinks. The blame should surely rest with Charlie, or is it Amber? Where is she anyway?

He finds her sitting underneath the dressing table in the bedroom, sobbing uncontrollably. Henry pulls out the stool for a better look at her. "Charlie?"

"I didn't do it!" she cries. "I didn't do that."

"I know, darling. I'm assuming Amber was to blame?"

Charlie looks up at him, bewildered. The poor girl looks utterly confused. She looks him up and down with wide eyes. "Your hands aren't red. Henry, mine are red! They're dirty!"

"I think most of us are messy." He doesn't want to use the word 'blood' in case it sends her into a panic. "Why don't you come out of there, and we can wash our hands together? I'll help you." He holds out his hand, and she takes it tentatively.

All housemates must gather in the bedroom immediately.

Henry and Charlie freeze as the remaining housemates hurry into the bedroom. Gaz is soaked with blood—Henry cannot take his eyes off him. The red is so gloriously vibrant.

"They've got help," Marty is saying hopefully as the doors lock with a heavy thunk. "They'll be in there now, saving her."

"A bit late for that, though, isn't it?!" Gaz yells. "She's already dead."

"Maybe you got it wrong? Maybe she's okay."

Gaz gives Marty a look of derision, but exhaustion immediately takes him. He's too tired to fight back and slumps to the floor. "I tried to save her."

Marty sits carefully beside him and hooks an arm around his shoulders. Jack moves away as if he might catch homosexuality. There's the Jack Henry has come to know and love. Jack's far more interesting when he's angry and inappropriate.

Jack catches Charlie's eye and realisation forces him back. "You..."

Charlie whimpers and cowers behind Henry's small stature.

"You did this..."

"Now, now, Jack. You don't want to do something you'll regret."

"Regret?! Henry, she's a *murderer*."

"Yes, and the police will deal with the matter, not you."

"You really feel safe around her?"

"I feel safer having Charlie behind me than having you in front of me."

"How dare you compare me to that psycho?"

"Does Charlie look dangerous to you?" Henry spins to reveal Charlie now crouched on the floor, her hands over her ears and eyes squeezed shut. "Look, I understand you're angry. Scared, even. What happened in there..." Henry scratches his head. "It was overwhelming, to say the least. Yes, we should keep an eye on Charlie, ensure we're safe, but it isn't our place to punish her."

Silence follows. There's a lot to take in. So much to process.

Evangeline garbles something by the bedroom door.

"Sorry, darling, what did you say?" Henry asks her.

"She wouldn't do this," Evangeline says, louder this time. "Charlie wouldn't do this." She's visibly shaking, her eyes wild. She reminds Henry of someone else. One of his girls from long ago.

Marty stands and pulls Evangeline into a tight embrace. "Come on, bird, this'll all get sorted. It's all on camera. We just have to pull together and figure this out. You'll get out and back to your boyfriend in no time."

Evangeline melts into Marty, then scoffs. "*Boyfriend*? Oh please, I couldn't give a shit about him, and he cares even less about me."

"Oh? Okay then." Marty looks around the room, bewildered that his words of comfort missed the mark so completely.

"I tell you what, when all this is over, I'm burying myself in my bed and never coming out," she says.

"Sounds like a plan," Marty grins. "Might do the same." He glances at his drawer. Again. Henry squints at him.

"Where's Vic?" Evangeline asks, pulling away from Marty to look around the room.

Marty sighs and looks to Gaz. "She's gone."

Henry expects Gaz to look saddened at losing his friend, but only relief brightens his face. "She got out?"

Marty nods. "I can only assume she did. She's not here, anyway."

"Oh, thank God for that."

The locks draw back in the doors, making everyone jump.

"Time to face the music," Jack announces.

Chapter 29

<u>Marty</u>

One by one, the housemates enter the bathroom to get cleaned up. No one is in a rush to face the aftermath of Susan's death. Of her murder.

Marty isn't sure how he feels about Charlie right now. She doesn't look like the type to kill someone. Even Amber, though more volatile, isn't a killer, surely?

She's such a slight girl, weak in stature, weak in mind. Then again, as Marty knows all too well, the weakest minds are often the most dangerous. To others, maybe, but more likely to themselves.

Henry is right, though; there's nothing they can do in here. They need to leave it to the police. They'll arrest her. If they ever get out.

Jack sidles over as Henry gently leads Charlie into the bathroom, the last to get clean. "Marty, we need to do something about this. I can't just stay here with that woman knowing what she's capable of."

"You think she's capable of overpowering you? I thought you were all man?"

The jibe doesn't hit. "Oh please, I can't sleep with one eye open, Marty; none of us can."

"So what are you suggesting?"

"I think we need to keep watch, you know? Me, you, and Gaz, take it in turn to be on guard, just in case she flips again."

It might not happen often, but Marty cannot deny that Jack is speaking sense. Charlie might be delicate in stature, but she's troubled and incredibly dangerous. He nods. "Alright, you're on. I'll speak to Gaz, and we'll work out some sort of rotation."

"Great. Good. Right, shall we go and see what's out there? They took her away, right? I mean, I was never a fan of Susan, but living with her body is, you know, fucking disgusting."

This man sure has a way with words.

Jack needn't have worried. Susan is gone, as are the floor tiles she bled out on. Nothing remains except dark-tinged concrete patched with dried floor glue.

Marty heads to the cupboard and gives the back panel a mighty shove, but it doesn't move. He groans in exasperation.

"You think she lived?" Evangeline says, creeping up behind Marty and making him jump. "You think they got to her in time?"

"Erm, maybe." There's no chance Susan was resuscitated. Marty saw her before they were locked in the bedroom—there's no way she was still alive. He's seen skin that shade of pale grey before. No, definitely dead.

They leave the pantry, Marty ensuring the door is firmly closed behind them, and finds everyone slumped on the sofas clutching tea made by Henry. Jack has abandoned his tea for an empty glass, the bottle of whiskey in front of him on the coffee table. He nudges the bottle with his foot. "Want some?"

"Nah mate. Don't drink."

"Even now?"

Marty shrugs. "Even now."

They sit in contemplative silence. Charlie sits on her own by the garden door, tucked into a ball on the floor.

"So what now?" Evangeline asks.

"We get the fuck out of here," Gaz tells her, his eyes hard.

"How?"

Gaz leans back and places his hands behind his head. "Marty will help me over the wall."

"I will?"

"Course you will. You want out of here, don't you?"

"You'll get ripped to pieces. It's razor wire."

"I couldn't give a shit. Better than staying here one second longer." He laughs bitterly. "Man, I was such an idiot. Thinking this would be my lucky break. Get noticed. Get a movie deal."

"We all had our reasons." Marty tells him. "I doubt any of them seemed reasonable in hindsight."

"I came in to grow my brand," Evangeline says glumly. "I was such a shallow idiot." Her cheeks are tear-stained, and she shudders with every in-breath.

Marty shakes his head. "Not true, Evangeline. Your brand is your business, and a bloody successful one. You're good at what you do. That doesn't make you an idiot."

"*Was* my business. Not anymore."

"Well, the world is your oyster."

"Yeah, if I get out of this alive."

Evangeline's words hang in the air between them.

Gaz downs his tea and tops the cup back up with whiskey. "I hope Victoria's okay."

"I'm sure she'll be on her way back to Lily by now."

But no one looks hopeful. The producers clearly have no morals—they're hardly going to whisk Victoria off to her happy ever after.

What must the viewers be thinking about all this? Was this all planned from the beginning? Is this what is classed as *entertainment*?

What the fuck has he signed himself up for?

He sits up straighter. If Victoria can get out, they all can. They have to.

Gaz is staring thoughtfully at the pantry door, most probably thinking the same as Marty. The panel at the back of the cupboard was made of thin wood, it won't take much to punch through it.

"Gaz, fancy a biscuit?" he asks, jerking his head toward the pantry. No need to invite everyone. If they're going to do this, they have to act quickly—before the Landlord stops them.

"Starving." Gaz says, taking the hint. "I could kill for a custard cream." He winces. "Sorry, bad choice of words."

All eyes turn to Charlie, but she remains slouched by the door, deaf and blind to her surroundings.

Marty and Gaz stand.

As they reach the kitchen, a hammering sounds out from behind them.

"What was that?" Gaz asks, jerking around to face the Confessions Room.

Jack stands but doesn't move. His fists clench in preparation of whatever drama the Landlord is about to unleash, the whiskey making him look dazed.

The knocking comes again, now with more urgency.

The door slides open, and someone comes barrelling through, stumbling into the living room and falling to the floor.

"Victoria!" Evangeline calls out, rushing to the figure on the floor.

Victoria looks up at Evangeline. Her face is covered in blood, bruises forming around her swollen eye. She groans and rolls onto all fours. "I didn't get out," she whimpers.

"Holy shit, Victoria." Gaz helps Victoria upright and takes her to the sofa. "What happened to you?"

Her eyes are wild. "I don't really know. One minute I was climbing through that hole in the cupboard. The next thing I know, I'm back here."

"Come on, what happened?" he urges Victoria, sounding furious.

"I saw a corridor. It was dark, but I could tell it was empty. I thought if I ran, I would find a fire exit and I'd be free!"

"But you didn't," Jack states the obvious.

Victoria shakes her head. "The next thing I knew, someone stepped in front of me, and everything went black." She motions to the purple bruise across her head where she was apparently knocked unconscious.

"I'm going to kill them." Gaz punches the back of the sofa, making Victoria wince. She looks terrible. Her left eye is almost swollen shut, her nose is slightly crooked, and her words are slurred between bruised lips. Whoever roughed her up did a good job.

Gaz marches around the room, yelling at no one in particular as Victoria lies down on the sofa, closing her eyes. She looks so tired, so resigned to her fate.

Marty kneels before her and strokes her hair.

"I want to go home," she whispers.

"I'll get you home," Marty promises.

She doesn't look like she believes him. Then she gasps as if realising something for the first time. She sits up, frantically searching the room. "Is Charlie okay?"

"She's fine, considering," Marty says. Victoria never fails to amaze him, always so considerate, so sweet. Marty turns to look for Charlie, but she's gone. Alarmed, he scans the room. Jack is standing sentinel at the toilet door. Catching his eye, Marty raises his eyebrows—a question. Jack nods. Charlie is in the toilet. Doing God knows what.

Marty releases the breath he's been holding.

"What happened to Susan? Is she okay?"

Marty looks at her bruised eye and split lip. He desperately wants to spare her the truth, but what would be the point? Someone is bound to tell her in the next few minutes, and at least he can tell her with a little sensitivity. Besides, everyone in this house needs to be prepared for what might come next if they are to survive.

"She's dead, Vic. I'm so sorry."

Victoria nods, reaches forward for Jack's glass on the coffee table, and pours the contents into her mouth.

"Poor Charlie," Victoria finally breathes. "She must be so freaked out."

"*She's* freaked out?! Come on, Victoria, with everything that's happened to you, don't you think you should save some of that sympathy for yourself? She killed Susan!"

Victoria looks him in the eye. "No Marty. Charlie didn't kill Susan."

Chapter 30

<u>Marty</u>

"Is that so?" Henry appears behind them, his sudden appearance startling Victoria.

"Yeah, she definitely looked like she *wanted* to do some harm, but I swear she dropped the knife while it was still in the air. I saw her. She didn't stab Susan."

Marty shakes his head. It was chaos in such a confined space; he didn't see what was happening. He looks at Victoria, who is watching him with conviction. "So who did then?" he asks her.

Victoria shrugs. "I don't know; I was out of there. But I do know one thing for sure—they're still in this house with us."

Marty and Victoria both turn to Henry, who shifts uncomfortably. "I hope you're not suggesting it was me."

Marty shakes his head. "Course not. It was madness in there, bodies everywhere." Blood is on everyone's hands. "It could have been anyone."

"Not Evangeline," Victoria says. "She didn't enter the room. It wasn't me either; I was by the cupboard."

Marty blows air noisily through his lips. "You're saying we're living with a killer. One who isn't insane and living with two people in her head? I don't know whether that's a good thing or a bad thing."

Charlie steps out of the toilet then, and all eyes turn to her. She looks truly broken. Jack follows her into the bedroom. Did Jack stab Susan? Is he doubling down by 'guarding' Charlie to hide his guilt? It's possible.

Marty wants to suspect Jack; he's the easy scapegoat. But Jack might be a bit of a prick, but is he a killer? Marty doesn't think so. He doesn't think Jack is capable of taking a life.

But then who else could have done it?

Gaz? He was right there in the thick of it.

Surely not. He's so kind and big-hearted. And what motive did he have? He was upset with Susan for lying about her position on the show, but he wasn't so angry he'd kill for it. Was he?

Then the same could be said for everyone in here. No one liked Susan, not really. Then her mole revelation added to their dislike, morphing it into mistrust. A dangerous concoction.

But Susan didn't deserve to die.

Henry moves away to the kitchen and fills the kettle. Marty watches him carefully. Henry is acting oddly. Jumpy. Yet there's something else there too. Pleasure? Amusement?

Did Henry kill Susan?

Henry

Henry wonders if Marty knows.

He's so sure he'd been subtle. In fact, he promised himself he'd leave well alone, but when the opportunity presented itself, it turned out he simply couldn't resist.

He can feel Marty's eyes boring into the back of his head, making his cheeks feel hot.

Still, it was worth the scrutiny. It has been a long time since Henry had experienced the ecstasy of tasting blood, and he was hungry.

Henry remembers exactly when the hankering for blood began. He'd always been drawn to anything gruesome—horror films, traffic accidents, roadkill.

He was just seven years old when he came to realise his fascination with the macabre could be satisfied.

He can remember it as clearly as it was just yesterday. His mother was slicing potatoes for dinner when the knife slipped, easily cutting through her hand and exposing bone. She ran off in search of something that would stem the blood flow, leaving blood spattered across the kitchen counter.

Henry was drawn to the red droplets like a bee to nectar. Without thinking, he dipped his finger into the blood and sucked it clean.

A rush went through him like nothing he's ever known. He'd cleaned the kitchen before his mother returned. Oh, how pleased she was with him.

But did Marty see him take a taste of Susan's nectar? Did Marty see him scoop some onto a spoon and savour the mouthful, his pleasure spilling into a groan?

Surely not; he would have said something.

Because Henry isn't delusional. He knows what he does is wrong. He knows some might view it as strange, even. Which is why he goes to great lengths to satisfy his cravings whilst maintaining absolute discretion.

It's why he draped a cloth over the camera in the pantry. Not really to 'save the viewer' from the body as he'd explained to the Landlord out loud, but to save himself. He doesn't want to be seen, his hobbies exposed. He has no explanation for his actions, and he isn't prepared to provide one. He shouldn't have done it, but the temptation was too great.

He now feels sick with worry. How could he have acted so recklessly?

Then there's the mystery of Susan's killer. If Victoria is correct, if Charlie did not take Susan's life, then who did?

It's no great loss. Susan was hardly a sterling housemate. But the conundrum bothers Henry. He doesn't enjoy being kept in the dark.

Not when he's hungrier than ever.

Victoria

"I need to talk to Charlie. Woman to woman," Victoria tells Jack, who is standing guard outside the bedroom door where Charlie has gone for a lie down, alone. Victoria can see her through the gap in the door, curled up in bed, seemingly asleep.

"You're not going in there on your own."

"Why are you playing the gentleman now? You've been a pig this entire time."

"Look, I might be a little controversial when it comes to sexual tastes. I get that. But that girl *killed* someone. I take safety very seriously."

"But not a girl's consent?"

"Evangeline was up for it, Victoria. Don't twist what happened."

"And those young girls you played with in your restaurant?"

"They were paid well. They took the money like greedy little pigs." Jack looks around.

This is not the time for this argument. "I'm going in there." She pushes past him, but he grabs her wrist, stopping her.

"I'm going in there with you then."

"No, stay here. I need her to talk to me, and you hardly inspire vulnerability and honesty."

Jack leans against the door frame, his arm blocking entry.

"What's going on?" It's Gaz, riding in on his white horse. As much as Victoria appreciates Gaz having her back, she doesn't need him here to provoke Jack and start a fight.

"Leave it," Victoria snaps. He looks at her with wide eyes, but to his credit, he takes a step back and watches through narrowed eyes.

Victoria turns to Jack. "Look, let me in, and keep watch at the door. I'll be fine." Without another word, she pushes past Jack's arm, leaving him standing there with his mouth agape.

Charlie is facing away from the door, but it's clear from her shaking form that she's crying.

"Charlie," Victoria murmurs. She gets no response. "Charlie?"

Charlie lifts her head but doesn't turn to face her completely. An invitation? Victoria hopes so.

Despite knowing Charlie wasn't holding the knife when it was thrust into Susan's abdomen, she can't help feeling a little scared. Charlie and her other persona are volatile at the best of times. Who knows how she'll respond under such intense pressure?

"Can I sit down?" Victoria says with utmost caution.

Charlie makes a noise that resembles approval, and Victoria takes a seat on Susan's bed. Or what used to be Susan's bed. The thought makes her balk.

"Charlie, are you okay?"

"No," Charlie whimpers. "I'm so confused, Victoria. I'm so sorry. So sorry."

She looks so young, her distress drawing out the little girl inside her. Victoria feels the urge to stroke her hair but thinks better of it.

"Charlie, why were you holding the knife like that? What were you thinking?"

"I wasn't," Charlie cries. "Amber was."

"So what was Amber thinking?"

Charlie looks into Victoria's eyes, the picture of innocence. There isn't a bad bone in this poor girl's body. Her mind, however, now that's corrupted by all kinds of unknowns.

"She said it's time to punish." Charlie sits up.

The sudden movement makes Jack flinch by the door, but Victoria raises a hand and he remains where he is. "But you've got to believe me. I never expected her to do what she did, and I couldn't control it. I thought she was just trying to scare everyone. She's like that sometimes. Stupid."

"I love her, but she can be really horrible. Never dangerous, though. At least I didn't think so."

Victoria leans back, deep in thought. Charlie thinks she killed Susan. She was wielding the knife after all. The poor girl must be so lost.

But Victoria knows what she saw. Everyone was running riot, scattering everywhere.

She felt the cool breeze wafting through the exposed hatch, and a sense of calm came over her, bringing a pure sense of clarity. It was as if everything slowed down.

She saw Henry dodge out of the way as Charlie rushed toward him. Then the knife came down only to be released before it made contact.

Charlie dropped the knife *before* Susan was stabbed. And that's when Victoria had made her escape.

"Charlie, you didn't kill Susan."

Charlie looks up at her through wet eyes. "No, Amber did."

"And you know that for sure?"

Charlie blushes and looks away. How much does she miss when Amber takes over? How much of her life, of her memories, has slipped through the cracks?

"You can't be sure, can you?"

"I remember grabbing a knife from the knife-block. I remember everyone screaming..."

"But you don't remember stabbing Susan?"

"Well no. Sometimes I block things out. I think it's a sort of coping mechanism. I want to forget the things she's doing to me."

Victoria sighs. "That doesn't mean you should make assumptions. Charlie, you didn't kill Susan. I saw you drop the knife and back away—there's no way you could have killed Susan."

"You saw what happened?"

Now it's Victoria's turn to blush. "Well, no, not exactly. Not all of it. But, Charlie, you have to believe me. *You dropped the knife* and got the hell out of there. The look on your face was not that of a killer—you were shocked, disgusted. You had no intention of killing Susan."

Victoria is so damn sure it wasn't Charlie. She knows what she saw. She can feel it in her heart: Charlie is not a killer—she didn't do this.

Someone else did.

Charlie continues to just stare at her. "I didn't kill her?"

"That's right!"

"I dropped the knife."

"Exactly!"

"So who did?"

"That's what we need to figure out."

Chapter 31

<u>Marty</u>

"Looking for something?" Henry asks over Marty's shoulder, his mouth mere centimetres from Marty's ear, making him pull away in fright.

They're in the main bathroom. Marty is rummaging through everyone's drawers. It *must* be here somewhere. Cocaine doesn't just vanish into thin air. Someone has taken it, and Marty needs to know who.

He NEEDS that bag.

He resumes his search.

"Marty, you look... frantic. Is there anything I can help you with?"

"Leave me alone, Henry. This isn't the time."

"Look, I know Susan's death has been hard on everyone, but we need to remain calm, or we'll implode. They're devising a plan to escape out there. We'll get out."

Marty laughs manically. "You think we're getting out? How can we escape when they're watching *everything*?! Wherever we turn, they'll be there waiting to push us back."

"Yes, well, we're being murdered now. The game has changed. We simply must get out."

"Oh please, we've been dying since day one; it was just easier to ignore it, to pretend it didn't happen. Sweet Jesus, that poor woman. Gloria. We should have put up a fight then, *before* it got to this level of crazy."

"We weren't to know. People don't *die* on television, Marty."

"This isn't a T.V show! This is some sort of sick experiment."

"I think we've all reached that conclusion now. Well, maybe not Charlie; she's a tad too loopy to connect the dots," Henry chuckles.

"What do you have against Charlie?"

The question jolts Henry. Every time Charlie is in the room, Marty has noticed Henry watch her with an odd look. It's hard for Marty to describe. 'Lustful' doesn't quite cut it, but there's definitely a worrying undertone.

"I have nothing against Charlie. She's such a *sweet* girl."

And there it is again—that look. It's almost like he's hungry.

Marty shakes his head. He doesn't have time for this. He spins around to resume his search.

Henry clears his throat. "Is *this* what you're searching for, Marty?"

Marty looks up at the mirror to find Henry standing behind him, brandishing the little plastic bag like he's won a prize.

Marty spins to face Henry, his breath caught in his throat. "Where did you get that?"

"Silly Marty. You're hardly subtle. I think the more pressing matter is, what are we going to do about this little predicament?"

"There is no predicament. I'm flushing it. Give it to me."

"If you were going to flush it, you would have done so already." He makes a clicking sound with his teeth. "So why haven't you?"

Marty runs his hand through his hair. "You wouldn't understand."

"I disagree! You're not the only one with addictions."

Marty raises an eyebrow. "Yeah?"

"Oh yeah, I struggle at times too."

What could this strait-laced, easy-going man be addicted to? Alcohol? Gambling? Porn? Yeah, porn. That would explain his fascination with Charlie.

"How do you stop it? The obsession?" Marty asks him, desperate for answers.

"There's only one thing I've found that helps keep the monster within quiet." Henry licks his lips and glances away.

"I feed it. Not much, not often, but just enough so that it doesn't take over my life."

Marty stares at Henry, his thoughts racing. *Feed the monster.* Feed it. Just enough to keep it happy, keep it at bay. Marty has always been an all-or-nothing kind of guy. He knew he was addicted, and he assumed that the only way to make it go away was to stop completely.

Is Henry right? Has he got it wrong all this time?

Henry smiles at him, knowing, confident. He's a well put-together man. He has a wife, a good pension from a successful career, he's clean, he's healthy, he's loved. Maybe he holds the answers Marty has been looking for.

The bag is still dangling from Henry's weathered hand. Henry looks at him compassionately. Henry understands. He gets it. He knows what to do.

Marty takes the bag.

Henry

Henry always knew Marty was an addict. Anyone with eyes in their head can see he's a troubled lad. He wears the face of a man who has weathered storms. His skin shows signs of battle. The way he touches his arms, scratches at them when he needs a fix. His hands that tremble when his past is mentioned. No, this young man has been through a lot.

Does Henry want to send him back there? Certainly not. He likes Marty! So why is he doing this?

Entertainment? Yes, sure. To test Marty? Probably. No, when he truly thinks about it, Henry's reasons are even more selfish. Self-preservation.

Marty is a clever lad. He watches people. And he's been onto Henry for a while now. Henry has noticed the way Marty observes him, the way Marty has noticed Henry's fascination for Charlie grow.

Because Henry doesn't have an *addiction*—that's for people wishing to play the victim card. The weak. No, his obsession is power. Pure and simple power. In any form too—from the everyday battle of decision-making on small matters, to the larger sense of power that comes from physically overpowering somebody. From taking everything from that person, every last drop of what makes them who they are.

That's when Henry is truly satisfied. That's when the monster in him can rest. Hibernate.

For a little while.

And yet the house has stripped him bare. It's made everything so incredibly hard. He has assumed that coming here would be the perfect way to maintain his obsessions, his passions.

Having watched Charlie from afar for so long has been fun, but the lack of proximity has been excruciating. This was the final push. The pièce de résistance before he could finally finish his task.

He could finally taste the sweet ecstasy of complete ascendancy.

But for now, until he can get out of here and take what he wants, he'll settle for playing with Marty.

No hard feelings.

He places the bag into Marty's eager hand and exits.

Chapter 32

<u>Victoria</u>

If Charlie didn't kill Susan, that leaves three people who could have committed the evil deed—Henry, Marty, or Gaz. None are likely suspect, but they're suspects, nonetheless.

Victoria runs her brush through her dripping wet hair, glad to be alone with her thoughts.

The pantry is a small room, leaving very little room for so many people. It was cramped, and all three men were pressed close to Susan. When Charlie came rushing in, they squeezed even closer, all eyes on Charlie. So, logistically, any of them could have done it. Victoria needs to examine the motive.

She loads her toothbrush with fluorescent blue toothpaste.

Susan didn't have any friends in here. She was tolerated, not loved. But that isn't a motive for taking her life. Or if it is, then it's a terrible one.

Gaz never really interacted much with Susan. They were always polite, having surface conversations about their mundane lives. In fact, Susan had clearly taken a shine to Gaz. Is that it? Susan was the only one who knew she and Gaz shared a bed that night. Was she jealous? Was there animosity between the two of them? It's far-fetched, but it's all she has. Maybe Gaz took matters into his own hands.

Then there's Marty. Polite, lovely Marty who wants nothing more than for everyone to live peacefully and with respect. There's no way he could have hurt Susan. Could he? She'd been caught lying repeatedly. Spiking drinks was serious, but was it bad enough to push Marty's buttons? Did she push him too far over the edge? Victoria doubts it. But then who knows what secrets Marty hides behind those shadowed eyes?

And Henry? That's almost laughable. Henry, with his slight frame and delicate hands, surely cannot have it in him to take a life. He might seem a little *odd* sometimes, but eccentricity doesn't equal killer. Henry and Susan had a strange relationship. They clearly didn't like one another, but there was nothing specific that could justify Henry killing her.

Victoria pulls on her pyjamas, wincing as she catches her pyjama top on her bruised eye, and climbs into bed.

She didn't think this place could get any worse. Missing her daughter was supposed to be the hardest thing she'd have to endure here, and the pain that brings is constantly excruciating. But to add the torture of the house on top of her suffering creates unimaginable stress. And now she's going to bed, knowingly sharing a bedroom with a murderer.

What the fuck has she gotten herself into?

Marty

Marty is high.

He couldn't bring himself to join everyone in the bedroom—it's too quiet in there, the tension too much to handle in this state.

He paces the garden, tilting his chin to look up at the moon. The rush floods him, so intense it's as if he could leap into the sky and dance across the stars.

It is as if an old friend has returned to him with excitable, immense energy.

He runs laps of the garden, feeling like he's winning a marathon, over and over. Lap after lap. He runs the pain away. He gulps in sweet, blissful air, laughing at the sense of freedom each breath gives him. It's beautiful. Why hasn't he noticed how beautiful breathing is before?

But the effects soon wear off. His limbs go heavy. His eyelids feel like weights attached to his head, and he flops down, relishing the damp grass pressing into his shirt. The chill making him shiver uncontrollably.

He feels dirty. The euphoria has curdled, and in its place sits shame that burrows deep and won't let go.

Nothing good can come from this. His disappointment in himself has taken up space in every cell of his body. He wants to cry, but it's as if he's forgotten how.

He has never felt more alone. For the first time in a long time, he has friends. Friends who like the true him, not the crazy, party-loving version that would sing too loud at parties and dance from dusk till dawn in the clubs. Just him—the true, raw him he thought had died a long time ago.

But he knows their friendship isn't real. It was all pretend. They were forced to act like they liked him because they're trapped here. They're not friends; they're cellmates, and as soon as they're out of here, they'll all go their separate ways. Marty will go back to the gutter.

Where he belongs.

He's shivering. Is he cold? Does he even care?

No.

He tries to hum a tune, but his voice sounds weird, too loud inside his head, so he stops, blowing air through his lips, making a raspberry sound.

He's bored. Should he wake everyone up? See if they want to dance? He giggles, imagining their reaction to the suggestion of having some fun. Miserable, the lot of them. He leans over to the side where the remaining coke sits lined up on a biscuit tin lid. He snorts another line through his left nostril.

He jumps up, eager to get everyone involved. Make them join the party. A song is playing in his head, and he moves with the bass notes, his arms flying over his head.

This is better.

The door to the house slides open, and Marty tucks himself next to the wall, giggling, praying to remain hidden in the shadows. He doesn't want to be seen. They'll know. They'll know what he's done. The bass still thuds between his ears, and he nods his head, his neck snapping back with each movement.

Whoever it is enters the garden, grass crunches unbearably loud beneath their feet. They head towards Marty. He holds his breath. But whoever they are, they don't approach. Instead, they walk away from him. Marty can see them now, looking up at the moon. Like a werewolf. Marty stifles a laugh and bops up and down in a squat position.

It's Gaz.

The seconds stretch forever as Gaz paces. His mouth is moving. Is he talking to someone?

Marty watches Gaz, mesmerised. He's always thought Gaz is hot; no one can deny that, not even Jack, the homophobic arsehole. But right now, lit by the moon, Gaz looks ethereal, a god sent from the heavens. Marty feels a little twitch in his pants.

He laughs, forgetting to be quiet.

Gaz spins around to peer into the shadows. "Who's there? Marty, is that you?"

Game over. Marty stumbles to his feet. He feels so *tall*. "Only me," he says with a flourish, jazz hands waving manically.

"Marty? Where the fuck did you come from? No one told me you were here." Gaz marches over.

"I just came outside for a bit. You couldn't sleep either?"

"No chance. There's too much going on, you know? How anyone can sleep through this is beyond me."

"Yeah."

"You okay, man? You sound weird."

"Yeah, yeah, all good. So you're not all cuddled up with Vic tonight?"

Gaz laughs softly. "You know about that?"

"Susan told me. She was pissed. You shag her?"

"Jesus, Marty, don't hold back, will you? But no, we didn't. We just kissed, had a cuddle, did *stuff*, you know?"

Marty doesn't know. He can't remember the last time he had that kind of romantic connection. His most recent experience of seduction usually just involved hazy memories and painful regret.

Marty changes the subject. "So, who do you think did it? Who do you think killed her?" He's speaking too fast. "Who do you think killed her?" he repeats, more slowly this time. Too slowly?

Gaz bites his lip hard. "Please can we not talk about Susan?"

"Sorry, man. It's all so shitty, isn't it? I mean, I knew coming in would be hard, but I figured hard wasn't necessarily *bad*. In fact, I thought bad might actually do me good. I never thought it'd be like this. So messed up."

Silence drifts between them. Marty's teeth chatter.

"Yeah, really hard." Gaz sits up straighter. "And for the record, I think it was Henry."

"Yeah, me too," Marty nods. "So what do you think we should do about it?"

"*Do* about it? That's not up to us. The police will sort it out."

"You think? Gaz, if the police had any idea what was going on here, we would've been removed from this hellhole a long time ago."

"True." Gaz sighs. "I'd love to know what's going on out there." He stares wistfully into the distance, his legs bouncing up and down.

"I think we should just kill him" Marty doesn't know where the words came from—some inner part of him he likes to keep locked away. A part of him that has woken up.

A buzz works its way from his toes to the centre of his brain. "Yeah? Eye for an Eye and all that."

"Don't be so stupid; you couldn't hurt a fly."

"I've decked Jack a few times."

"That's different. He deserved it."

"And a killer doesn't deserve to be punished?"

"You don't know it's him."

"Well, I know you didn't do it. And it wasn't me. So..."

"Marty, you're losing your mind."

"Am I? I actually think I might just be finding it at long last."

Gaz returns his gaze to the moon, contemplating Marty's suggestion. Marty feels excited. He's in the mood to shake things up.

"Nah, we can't do that. We can't stoop to his level."

Marty cannot hide his disappointment.

"You need to get some sleep, Mart. You're losing your head." And with that, Gaz wanders off back to the house, leaving Marty more determined than ever.

Chapter 33

<u>Victoria</u>

The room has swallowed all light. Not even the emergency lights are on tonight. There's a heavy atmosphere, weighted with anticipation. It's as if the house itself is holding its breath, waiting for something to happen.

Victoria senses everyone is lying awake, thinking over the events of the last few days. Occasionally Henry snores, only for the grunts to stop abruptly as if he's suddenly jolted awake.

Gaz walked out about half an hour ago, probably to find Marty. Victoria is tempted to join them, but it's cold outside and her bed is comfortable. She feels safer in her little cocoon somehow, as if the quilt can fight off the murderer lurking among them.

The bedroom door bursts open, and Marty fills the frame, his tall figure carved black against the silver moonlight streaming in behind him. A chilly breeze sweeps through the room, making Victoria pull the quilt up to her chin, shrinking deeper into the warmth of her bed.

He rushes toward the bathroom, but he stops, looms over Henry. Victoria feels nauseated. Something is about to happen. She just doesn't know what.

And where's Gaz?

Victoria blinks, refocusing her eyes to make sense of what's happening. It looks like Marty is leaning over Henry's bed, his arms out in front of him, rigid and pushing down. Pressing down on Henry.

A ragged gasp sounds out.

"Henry!" Victoria darts out of bed, rushing to Marty, who has his hands wrapped around Henry's throat.

"Marty, stop!" Victoria screams, pulling him away.

"I can't!" Marty laughs. "Henry is a bad man. Bad men need to be punished. I'm helping."

"No, Marty. Not like this, please!" Victoria can hear shouts and screams behind her. An immense weight comes barrelling over, knocking her out of the way.

Jack.

He smashes into Marty with such force that they both hit the wall with an incredible bang.

Henry writhes on his bed, fighting for breath. Victoria goes to him, urging him to remain calm and focus on taking deep, controlled breaths. A request made in vain, but at least he knows she's here for him. That he's safe now.

"You can't do this!" Jack is shouting. "This isn't you!"

"He deserves it. He killed Susan!"

"That doesn't make *you* a killer!"

"So you think he did it too?"

"Well, if it wasn't him, who was it? Always thought he was a creep."

"Well, I happen to think *you're* creepy! That doesn't mean you're a murderer." Evangeline screams hysterically from across the room. Charlie is sobbing behind her, her face a shade of crimson, her eyes dark.

With Marty's outburst, Charlie's breakdown, and Evangeline's distress, Victoria wonders what permanent damage the Landlord is inflicting on their mental state. PTSD is pretty much guaranteed at this point.

The door swings open once again. "What's going on in here? Mart?" It's Gaz. Victoria can see the bewilderment on his face in her mind's eye. "Fuck, I only left you two minutes ago—how are you fighting with Jack already?"

"He tried to kill Henry," says Charlie, her voice monotone through her distress.

"What? Marty, mate, I thought you were joking."

Marty is bouncing up and down on one foot.

Victoria is outraged. "You planned this?!"

Gaz looks incredulous, his eyes wide and his palms out in a gesture of innocence. "No! We were just chatting, you know? Imagining what we would do if we could help. He wasn't actually supposed to go ahead with it. Henry, you okay?"

"Yes," Henry grunts, though his voice is weak and raspy. He sounds far from okay.

Victoria wishes she had her medical bag with her. She needs to check Henry over—a difficult task when it's still too dark to see properly. "Evangeline, sit with Henry. Come and get me if anything changes, if he blacks out, if his breathing becomes laboured, anything."

"Okay," Evangeline stutters, unsure of the responsibility.

"Marty, come with me," Victoria says to the shadows by the wall.

"I'll come too," Jack says through gritted teeth. Victoria can just make out him gripping his bandaged hand. He must have hurt it during the brawl.

"No, you stay here and watch Charlie. Gaz can come with me."

"Okay, fine," he agrees. Victoria was expecting him to put up a fight. His hand must be really hurting for him to give up so easily.

She pulls on her dressing gown to fight off the cold and leads her two friends into the garden, knotting the belt tight around her.

The second they're outside, she rounds on Marty and whacks him on the chest. "What the hell is wrong with you?"

But Marty doesn't say anything. He stands staring at her, his eyes distant and glazed. His eyes dart around as if he can't decide where to look. There's a stupid smile on his lips like he's about to tell an unbelievably funny joke. Victoria has seen that look before at work.

"Marty, are you *high*?"

Marty tries to look shocked and fails spectacularly. He laughs and starts jabbering on about Henry and how *shifty* he looks.

"Sit down before you fall down," Victoria instructs, shunting him backward onto a bench. "Talk to me. What happened tonight?" She looks to Gaz, but he shrugs, his eyes ringed with red. Has he been crying? That's a matter to deal with later.

"I can't do this," Marty states matter-of-factly. "I need to go now."

"Yeah, we all do. But, Marty, what happened? Why did you do that to Henry?"

A minute ticks by. Two. Three. Who knows how many more? Victoria and Gaz watch Marty as he works through every emotion on his face. His eyes light up as he sings to himself. Looking surprised as a thought enters his head he hasn't had before. His mouth working constantly as if having a private conversation with himself.

Eventually he slumps forward. Gaz reaches out and catches him before he falls off the bench and hits his head on the slabs. "Because I'm a bad person, Vic. I do bad things." Though his words lack conviction. He looks very pleased with himself.

"That's not true."

Marty laughs sadly. "You have no idea, do you? What I've done." He whispers. "You don't know what I'm capable of. I killed someone. A kid. Sixteen years old."

Victoria stares at him. "What?"

"Jamie Morrison. He was my dealer's son? Loved the band. Loved me. Followed us everywhere. Like to help out sometimes." Marty's voice cracks. "And I gave him the drugs that killed him. Just shared my stash like it was nothing. Like he didn't matter."

He slumps a little, the effects of the cocaine morphing into a sadness so deep he might just cave in on himself. His eyes close.

"Oh, Marty." Victoria swallows the ball in her throat. She isn't sure what the right words are. The truth is, she's disgusted with Marty. How can someone play with a child's life like that? But then she's seen what drugs do to people, how they can strip the morals from the nicest of people. "That was an accident," she finally says.

"*I killed him*, Vic. There's no such thing as accidents when you kill a child. There's nothing but evil—pure, stupid evil." He groans. "Poor Henry! I shouldn't have done that." He sounds heartbrokenly sad. "I don't know why I do anything. I'm just a loser. A massive, pathetic loser."

"You're not a loser, Marty. But you need to tell me—what have you taken?"

"Coke."

"And where did you get it?"

Marty shrugs, laughing. "No idea. I found it when I came in here."

Victoria takes a second to gather her thoughts. She glances at Gaz, who shrugs. "You're saying it was planted in here?"

"It certainly looks that way. I'm such an idiot." Marty cries like a tired child, soft and sorrowful.

"Marty, for what it's worth, I don't think you're an idiot," Victoria says softly, resting a hand on his shoulder.

"Look what I did, Vic! Look at what I *am*!"

"We can talk about what you did another time. But what you are? Marty, I think you're an addict who has gone weeks fighting an urge to take a drug that he has kept hidden. I see absolute strength in that, not a loser."

Marty looks into her eyes. "Really?"

"Really."

"Thank you, Victoria," he says with no conviction. He looks up at Gaz, who's hovering awkwardly in the background. "You two make such a nice couple." His voice is leveling out.

"We need to get out of here. This house is going to be the death of us all, one way or another."

"We can't, though, can we?"

Victoria closes her eyes. "I think we can. We just have to grow some balls."

"What? You know how to get out?" Gaz asks behind her, relieved.

But Victoria cannot say—the Landlord is watching and will stop them. She needs to take matters into her own hands.

Chapter 34

Henry

The sun is just appearing over the horizon when Henry awakens. He lifts his head and winces, the horrors of last night hitting him like a sledgehammer. His fingers drift to his throat, pressing on the bruising. It makes his eyes water.

He glances around the room, relieved to find no sign of Marty. Tempting him with the drugs was a ridiculous mistake born from a menacing heart. He never imagined it would lead to that. Lesson learned.

Thankfully, someone has left him a cup of water on his bedside table, a straw poking out of the top. He takes a sip. Swallowing is agony, like someone has scraped the inside of his throat with shards of glass.

His quilt shifts, startling him. He spins around to find the cause. Evangeline lies beside him. Sweet Evangeline must have fallen asleep on his bed last night.

She was such a gem. Checking on him constantly, listening to his breathing, worrying. At one point she even pressed her hand to his heart. "It's racing!" she had said. Of course it was racing—having her so close, *touching* him, it was almost too much to bear.

Charlie may be the object of his intentions, but that doesn't mean being around Evangeline comes easy to Henry. He's still a predator living amongst such easy prey.

He breathes her in now. She smells like candyfloss mixed with something rich and heady, as if the child within her is fighting against the adult version. He focuses on the sweet scent, breathes it in deeply. His mouth waters.

She looks like a doll. Porcelain skin, rosy cheeks, full red lips. Her hair could do with a wash, but it is still golden and thick, lying over her rising chest.

A small whimper escapes her lips, and her eyebrows crease. Probably dreaming of the house, of the pain it is putting them all through.

He thinks of Charlie. Of the pain he will put her through. He looks at Charlie and imagines his knife slicing through her white skin. How easily it slits beneath the tip. How her flesh gives way to muscle underneath. The blood oozing through, dripping to the floor around his feet.

But will he get the opportunity to satisfy his cravings? Or will the house kill him first?

His thoughts now turn to his wife, Brenda. What would she have said if she had known what he was thinking? Maybe she *does* know. Who knows what happens beyond the grave?

Evangeline turns over to face away from him, and Henry has to fight off the disappointment.

He brings his fingers so that they hover inches over her skin, tracing the curve of her neck, the heat emanating off her making him tremble. He's salivating.

Two seemingly dead already. Gloria and Susan. Henry cannot grieve them, for he does not care.

Though he is jealous. *Someone* got to take their lives. Whoever it was got to feel the intense power of life slipping through their hands. They got to experience the joy of the knife breaking skin and working through soft flesh, nicking bone en route to deeper organs.

Did Charlie kill Susan? He doesn't think so. He knows Charlie. She's too timid, too coy. She isn't strong enough in body or mind to make such a huge decision.

No, he thinks Marty did it. After last night's antics, he's the obvious choice. He's clearly unstable.

His hand hovers over Evangeline's shoulder and wanders down to her waist. Her pyjama top has risen just a few inches, exposing the tantalising two dimples in her lower back.

He swallows and resumes his path. Over her hips. To her thighs.

He permits himself to wonder what it would be like to make love to a woman like Evangeline. He imagines it would be theatrical, a game of pretend. Not that she'd ever sleep with someone like Henry. She'd only ever go for the prettiest trinkets or the most popular on the internet. A kind heart and stability probably haven't even crossed her mind for a potential suitor.

Brenda was always good in bed—he'll give her that. That was probably the only thing he liked about her. The rest of her was abhorrent. Always moaning, putting him down, making him look a fool in front of friends. Well, he had the last laugh.

The stroke killed her slowly while Henry watched. Smiling, enjoying the alarm on her face as she slipped away in the most frightful panic he'd ever seen. She shouldn't have been so nosy. Maybe the shock of learning Henry's secret wouldn't have made her spiral like that. It was all her fault really.

Such a glorious day.

He needs to get up. Every second he stays beside Evangeline, the grip he's kept on himself slips, unravelling the control he's fought so hard to maintain. The Landlord has all the power in here; he's made that abundantly clear. And Henry is suffering.

The game being played is brutal. The Landlord has abandoned the rules, and the consequences are inconsistent and harsh. So what's stopping Henry from just doing what he longs to do? It's not like the producers are revealing what is happening to the public, or the police would have been in here long ago.

And if he stays here, he'll probably die. Because now he sincerely believes that's the Landlord's true plan. How else will he get away with all this? He will have to kill them off to destroy the evidence.

What would they tell their families? Not that Henry has any family to tell.

If he's going to die, he might as well die happy. Right?

He's shaking violently. His hand has moved back up to Evangeline's face, the tremor bringing him mere millimetres from touching her cheek. He doesn't have the strength to pull away. He can already taste her.

Sweet. And moreish.

He brings his face to hers and breathes her in, desperately trying to quench his thirst. Though her scent does nothing to fight the urge—if anything, it *feeds* it.

"Henry? What are you doing?"

He jolts back, alarmed at her whisper. How long has Evangeline been awake?

"Henry?" she repeats when he cannot form an explanation. "Were you *smelling* me?"

"I must have been asleep!" Henry blurts, feigning confusion. He blinks furiously.

"No, no, you weren't, Henry. You were smelling me."

"You were what?!"

Oh great, Jack, Mr Volatile, has got involved.

"I was doing no such thing. You must have got it confused, Evangeline. Maybe you were dreaming. Hardly surprising given the stress we're under."

She looks at Henry through piercing eyes. "You look weird."

"Well, that's just rude." Henry gets out of bed. "Now, if you don't mind, I need to visit the bathroom."

"Stay right there," Jack orders. Where is everyone? Gaz, Victoria, and Marty are not in the room; only Charlie is here, sitting up in her bed, the covers pulled up to her chin and her eyes wide with horror.

"I'm going to the toilet," Henry says defiantly. "I'm an old man, and I can't hold my bladder like I used to. You'll know what that's like soon enough."

"Evangeline, get away from him," Jack orders. She obliges. "Now, you're going to tell me what you were doing, or I swear to God I'll force it out of you."

"You'll do no such thing."

"Wanna bet?"

Jack approaches Henry with clenched fists. Henry winces, his throat on fire.

A loud siren blares through the speakers, shrill and unrelenting. It ricochets off the walls, drowning out Jack's demands.

Oh, thank God, the Landlord has come to his rescue.

"FIRE!!" someone screams from just outside the bedroom. "FIRE!!"

Chapter 35

<u>Victoria</u>

Victoria was out of options.

She stands back and watches the flames climb the walls, licking the ceiling. The heat is already intense. Smoke curls in ferocious tendrils along the ceiling, and Victoria watches with fascination, as if she has all the time in the world. She's disconnected, like she's watching this on a screen, not living it.

The irony is lost on her.

Orange light dances in the mirrors that no doubt hide multiple cameras and equipment. It's spectacular. A dance of twists and coils, its rhythm erratic and seductive.

Memories of Lily drift through Victoria's mind. She cocks her head to the side, allowing her thoughts to wander wherever they please.

I'm doing this for you, baby girl. She's getting out. She's done here. Whatever happens now, it's all for her.

The sirens blare from every direction, startling Gaz and Marty from the sofa where they fell asleep in the early hours of the morning with their heads on each other's shoulder.

Gaz jumps up and drags Victoria away from the raging heat. "FIRE!!" he screams, waking the rest of the house.

"Victoria, what did you do?!" Marty asks, his eyes wide with horror.

"What choice did I have? If we can't climb the walls, we have to tear them down."

"You'll kill us!"

"No. They won't let that happen."

"Yeah? You sure about that?"

Victoria isn't sure. Not even a little. She digs her heels in firmer. "This is our way out, Marty. I know it."

"I hope you're right, Vic, for Lily's sake. She needs her mum."

"Screw you! *She's* the reason I'm doing this. It's ALL been for her. Don't you dare make out she isn't the reason I breathe, the reason I get up every day and fight."

"Come on, you two." Gaz grabs Victoria's hand, squeezing too tightly. "This isn't the time to be arguing. Vic, no one is questioning your loyalty to your daughter. But we need to get out of here."

The heat bites at Victoria's skin, leaving it raw. She lets Gaz pull her into the garden where the others wait, terror carved into their faces.

"Right, guys. It's all going to be okay," she tells them.

"What happened?" Jack asks. They don't know she started it. That's good.

"No idea." Victoria looks away to avoid eye contact. She needs them to be on her side, to listen to her. "But this is our chance to get out."

"Is it?" Evangeline's voice wavers between hope and doubt. "What if the house just burns down around us? Takes us with it?"

"It won't." Victoria is relieved to find that she sounds more certain than she feels. "It'll burn. Then we'll walk right out."

Henry laughs, his voice dry. "A big, burning hole in the wall. You want us to walk through a mouth straight to hell."

"We are already in hell!" Victoria screams. "Don't you see that?!"

Henry nods slowly; he can just make out the flames creeping toward the kitchen's gas hob from their vantage point at the back of the garden.

"What other option did we have? We can't just sit here waiting for the Landlord to let us out. He clearly has no intention of ending this."

"You don't know that," Charlie says. She looks pale as death.

"I know that two people are dead, and they didn't give a shit. You think they'll let us tell the police what has happened in here? They've been playing with us! We're not here to entertain; we're a sick experiment. They're not going to let us go. Trust me."

"You don't know Gloria is dead," Charlie says, though the whimper reveals her uncertainty.

"The blood!" Victoria screams. "She was at the very least hurt. And you think they just let her out of here, free to tell people what's going on? She's a witness of something dark and dangerous. They didn't let her go, trust me."

The window behind Victoria cracks. The group duck in unison as glass shatters, showering them in glittering shards.

Victoria swallows her horror and stands back up. "I don't know about you, but I will not let them win. *I'm* in control of my life. Not them."

"Here here!" shouts Henry over the fire's roar.

"So now what?" Jack asks, stepping away from the heat.

"We need to go in there and find a way out. Before they react and stop us."

"We can't do this," Gaz announces. "We have to stay. They'll rescue us."

"You don't really think that," Victoria snaps. "You're not that thick."

"Please, Vic. We can't go back in there."

"We're getting out."

Victoria spins to face the house. The smoke is so thick, she can't see inside. She doesn't know where the fire has spread, whether there's a safe path through.

But she runs anyway.

Chapter 36

<u>Marty</u>

"Vic!" Marty's voice catches in his throat as he chases after her. The smoke, now billowing from the broken window. It fills his lungs, making him cough. He stops, unable to see how to enter the house, how to get through the fire. "Vic!"

She's gone—swallowed by the inferno. A hand grasps his wrist. "Don't even think about following her in there," shouts Gaz over the roar.

"We can't leave her!"

"You want to die for a stranger?"

Marty can't believe what he's hearing. Gaz is supposed to be her friend, not a *stranger*. He yanks away, disgusted.

"I mean it. She's got no chance. Don't make her fatal mistake yours too."

Gaz has never looked so ugly. "Fuck this," Marty mutters under his breath. He braces himself, holding the bottom of his t-shirt over his nose and mouth, and he runs into the house.

The heat slams into him like a wall, knocking him back. Every instinct screams at him to turn around, but his fear calls louder. He has to reach Victoria.

Crawling, he pushes on, forcing his eyes open to see through the thick black smoke. Each breath scalds his throat. He doesn't stop. Can't. The heat presses in from all sides, but fear drives him on.

The living room flickers in and out of view through the smoke, lit in orange bursts as flames leap toward him. Floorboards groan beneath his feet, protesting each step with a warning snap. With a hand outstretched, he fumbles blindly forward. "Victoria!"

Behind him, outside, voices call desperately, trying to pull him back. No chance. He's committed now. It's the right thing to do.

Sweat pours down his skin. Somewhere ahead—a cough. He surges toward it, lungs burning, driven by a primal need to fight.

"Vic?"

A movement catches his eye through the smoke. A figure hunched down and pressing forward. "Vic!"

She flails her arms wildly at him. "Go back, Marty. There's no way through."

The fire swallows her words, but he catches their meaning. He inches toward her. She isn't leaving. She's still searching, so desperate to escape she's willing to burn alive trying.

Marty won't let her fight alone.

He moves closer, but a deep groan stops him in his tracks. It's like the Earth itself is splitting open.

The wall on his left gives way. Not in slow motion, not with a warning, but all at once. Plasterboard explodes outward, knocking him down. He loses focus. All sense of direction.

He's done for.

Flames flicker overhead; it's almost beautiful, the way they tease each other with their terrible grace.

"Mart." Victoria's voice is right beside his ear. She's crawling to him, pulling him back to the present. Her skin is blackened, her voice choked. They're out of time. "Mart! Come on!" She tugs at his arm, and he forces himself up, meeting her determined eyes.

The fire seems to spiral inward, pulling them with it.

The wall. It's gone.

A corridor lies on the other side.

Chapter 37

<u>Henry</u>

The fire has spread around the remaining housemates. They're huddled together in the back of the garden as the inferno edges towards them, as the flames grow, looming over them. They're frozen, watching the house where Marty just disappeared.

"What are we going to do?" Evangeline asks. Henry is shocked to realise she isn't crying. Horror does strange things to people.

"We only have one option." Jack has been searching frantically since they got here, desperately looking for anything to help them get out. "We have to wait to be saved."

"They're not coming though, are they?" It's Charlie, her voice flat. "We're going to die here."

"It'll be over soon," Henry says darkly. "Besides, maybe dying isn't all that bad." He doesn't know why he says it. Has he given up? Or does he just want one last shot at winding them up? Probably both.

"Oh, fuck this," Gaz growls, stepping away and stomping over to the hot tub. Is he really taking a dip right now? He squats down and pushes at the side panel of the tub, his jaw set with grim determination.

To Henry's surprise, the panel pops off. Gaz flings it aside before slipping into the hole left behind.

Jack swears and rushes to the hot tub. Charlie and Evangeline press against Henry's side, sharing his reluctance.

An explosion sounds behind them. They crouch in terror. There's no time to dither. Shaking off his shock, Henry grabs Evangeline and Charlie by their hands and pulls them to their escape.

Chapter 38

<u>Marty</u>

The corridor is long and slopes steeply downward, underground, the cool air a blessing on his scorched skin. Marty's flesh feels tight against his muscles. It's blackened and raw.

They run until their breath runs out and they collapse, coughing violently. Victoria drops onto all fours, her body convulsing with such force Marty is worried she'll tear herself apart.

"Come on. We need to keep moving," Marty tells her, trying and failing to pull her up. He doesn't know where they're going; he just knows he needs to get out right now. No good can come from sticking around.

Victoria struggles to her feet. Her hair is matted, her skin charred, her clothes are singed and ragged. But she keeps going, a pillar of strength.

The narrow concrete tunnel leads them away from the house before joining a wider passage that branches left and right. With no time to decide which way to go, Marty drags Victoria to the left.

They keep pushing forward as smaller tunnels join from the direction of the house, forming a wheel shape.

"We're back at the beginning. Surely." Victoria wheezes. "We're running in circles."

"I think you're right." There are no markers to tell them where they are, but they must have circled the house by now. The heat coming from the corridor leading back to the house drifts towards them.

Marty's heart sinks. He sends a silent prayer for the rest of the housemates' escape. The thought of their screams makes his stomach turn.

"Marty, Victoria!" Charlie's voice echoes behind them. They spin to find the five remaining housemates rushing toward them, Gaz leading the way.

"You're okay!" Evangeline cries, falling into Marty's arms. He gives her a little squeeze before setting her back upright. They don't have time for this.

"Which way?" Jack asks.

"The path just goes round in circles or back towards the house," Marty tells him. "There must be another way out. We're missing something."

"Why don't we ask *him*?" Charlie asks, pointing at Gaz. Her eyes are sharp, the eyes of Amber.

What could Gaz possibly know? He's as lost as the rest of them. Isn't he? Jack's glare suggests otherwise.

"Gaz?" Marty asks.

Gaz looks away, scowling.

Victoria reaches for his hand, her fingers delicately brushing his. "Gaz? What's going on?"

He pulls away. "Nothing. We should find a way out." His eyes are dark and contain a fury. A fire within him burning strong.

But why? What's happened? Marty cannot take his eyes off him. He's different somehow, but he cannot place his finger on what's different. He's still Gaz, the Gaz they all know and trust, yet there's something pulsing through him. Something angry and sinister.

"Nah, don't give me that fake 'I don't know what's going on' crap," Jack barks. "You knew exactly how to get us out of there. This whole time, we could've got out."

Gaz scowls and turns away.

"What's going on?" Victoria asks, sounding horrified.

"There was an escape hatch on the side of the hot tub. That *prick* waltzed right up to it and opened it like it was nothing." Jack jabs Gaz in the chest, making Gaz shunt backwards. "You need to tell us what you know. Now."

Gaz sighs, studying the floor. They wait. He shakes his head, and when he looks back up, he's smiling sweetly. "Sorry guys, but I can't do that."

Victoria steps away as if he's made of the fire they've just escaped. "Gaz? What do you know?"

"I know you're not getting out of here."

Marty can't believe what he's seeing. His friend is morphing before his eyes—the kind, jovial nature is melting away, replaced by something cruel and wicked.

"Gaz, wait..." Marty splutters.

"Call me Gareth."

Quick as lightning, Jack has Gaz by the throat, pinning him to the wall. "I don't give a shit what your name is, you're going to tell us how we get out of here or I kill you."

"You won't do that. I'm your only hope."

Jack's grip tightens. "At least I'll die knowing I've made you suffer."

Marty presses a hand on Jack's shoulder. "Don't. He'll need to get out too. He'll have no choice but to lead us out."

"Yeah Jack. Don't be so selfish," Gaz jeers. "Marty has a point. He's wrong. But he has a point."

Jack has the decency to look around before letting Gaz go.

"Don't hurt him, Jack," Evangeline tells him. "He might be our only chance."

"I agree with Marty and Evangeline," Henry agrees. Amber throws Henry a venomous look and moves away from him.

"Gaz," Victoria says carefully. "I don't know what's going on, but if you know something, you have to tell us. I need to get to my little girl. You know that."

Gaz locks eyes with her. A hint of his former self flickers behind his eyes before vanishing. "I know, Vic. But believe it or not, I simply don't care."

Victoria's mouth drops open, but no words come out. Marty is stunned. Every fibre of his body screams exhaustion, and the pain of his singed skin is taking hold. He's afraid he's going to pass out.

He can't. Not when they're this close to getting out. He needs to get Victoria out. And poor Evangeline. He's got to get the help Charlie so desperately needs.

Part of him agrees with Jack. He wants to inflict pain on Gaz, to wipe that cocky smile off his face. But when he looks at this man, he sees only Gaz. Not the mystery of this *Gareth* he claims to be.

An explosion rings out from the direction of the house. The group screams. "We don't have time for this bollocks." Marty shouts. "There must be a way out! Look for a way up, a ladder, a door, anything we missed."

Victoria

Gaz walks ahead of the group with a swagger Victoria's never seen before. He's gained a dangerous arrogance in the last few minutes.

Who is this guy? This Gareth. Is this another Charlie/Amber situation? Surely not. Charlie is unique; there can't possibly be more than one.

That leaves one option, and she doesn't like it.

Gaz is a liar. A fraud. He knows more than he's letting on.

"Gaz?" she asks, catching up with him. "Gareth. Please tell me how we get out."

"No can do," he says, voice low enough for her only. "I can't do that."

"But why? I thought you were my... friend?" She lets her voice simper. A bid to win him over.

He tuts at her. "Typical woman. Oversensitive to the slightest bit of affection."

Victoria swallows, her fury growing in the pit of her stomach. He really thinks she cares about a damn kiss and cuddle in bed? She swallows her pride. "How dare you?" she forces a sob. "How dare you use me like that?"

He grins at her. "I enjoyed myself. So did you. That's all there is to it."

"I thought we were friends. Closer than friends."

"We've never been friends, Victoria."

Jack glances over, trying to hear what they're saying with creased eyebrows and concern flooding his rugged face.

"I thought you could be my boyfriend." Her crocodile tears sting her dry eyes. "Lily needs a dad. She would've loved you."

"You think?" Gaz laughs.

Well, no, but Victoria will not admit that. "Yes. You're funny, kind, and you have a big heart. We could have dated for a while, seen where things went. Then I could've introduced you to Lily."

"Lily. Don't you ever get sick of saying that name? It's all you ever fucking talk about."

Victoria stops, aghast. Who is this cruel man? And more importantly, how has she not seen him before?

"I'll never get sick of saying her name. She's my little girl."

"Look, if you're trying to win sympathy, you have another thing coming."

"You'd really do that to a sick little girl? Look, Gareth, you know something. Is it Susan? Is what happened to her putting you off telling us?"

Gareth stops dead and bursts out laughing. "Susan? She was an idiot. Don't you dare compare her stupidity to my brilliance. Wash your fucking mouth out."

"She died! How can you be so cruel?"

"She should have played the game better. I brought her here to help me orchestrate everything. She failed spectacularly."

Victoria cannot talk. She cannot breathe. Gaz *brought her here*; he orchestrated all of this. Everything that's happened comes rushing at her all at once. Gloria's disappearance. Jack's mangled hand. The spiked drink. The poor puppy. Susan's death.

Was this all him?

Every cell in her body rages. Her muscles tighten under painful skin. She leaps forward, pushing Gaz against the wall, her fingers around his throat. "How do we get out, you sick piece of shit?"

"There she is. The ballsy woman that turns me on so much." Gaz runs his tongue over his top teeth. "And I'm not telling you."

"So what's your plan, Gaz? Let us all die down here?"

He shrugs. "Not *all* of us. I have no intention of dying." He shoves her away with ease.

In her peripheral vision, Victoria sees Marty way ahead, oblivious to what's happening. He stops and waves the rest of the group over. She can see his mouth moving, but can't hear his words over the fire's roar coming from the house.

Jack and Evangeline run ahead to catch up with Marty.

But where's Henry and Charlie?

Victoria glances back to find them behind her—Henry is on the floor with Charlie straddling him, pinning him down, yelling into his face, her words drowned out.

Chapter 39

<u>Henry</u>

Twice in one day. Henry isn't having much luck.

First Marty's fingers incapacitated him; now Amber's fury renders him useless.

Henry is an old man. He isn't as weak as he likes to make out, but his body isn't as strong as it used to be.

The first time he met Amber, he was struck by her height—a good foot taller than him—and an athletic physique. She was strong. Taking her required careful orchestration. Though when the reward is as great as Amber, a three-month wait was worth it.

Watching her, learning her routine, her friends, her weaknesses. Until the day finally came.

She was crying into her phone. Apparently, her boyfriend had broken up with her for someone else. She was waiting for the bus miles outside town, begging for him to take her back.

When she'd finally hung up, Henry took his chance. He sent her a message from his fake Facebook account, letting her know there was a party nearby. He'd set the account up months before, using the image of some jock in the States with a pretty face and spectacular abdominal muscles. Amber had accepted the friend request in minutes.

She'd looked confused before shrugging and abandoning the hope of catching the bus back to the student halls. She turned, presumably to walk to the taxi rank nearby, but seconds later she was bundled into the back of Henry's Volvo, incapacitated by shock and a bloodstream diluted with alcohol.

He pushed the syringe into her neck with ease.

Now she brings her fist down on Henry's face. He feels his cheekbone crack.

"I know who you are, you sick bastard," Amber spits in his ear. "You've been following Charlie for months. I recognise you. What do you want with her?"

Well, that's interesting. Amber doesn't recognise him as her killer.

"I don't know what you're talking about."

She spits in his face. The thick globule lands on his lip and slides down his cheek. "Don't play dumb, you sick fuck!"

Henry can see Amber then, as if Charlie has disappeared completely. He can see the look of terror on Amber's face as she realises he'd strapped her down in his basement, the floor and walls lined with thick white plastic.

She had screamed. Pointlessly. There was no one around to hear her.

"Shh darling," he whispered into her ear, stroking her hair from her face. "No one can hear you."

She pushed up with every ounce of strength left in her, the leather straps around her wrists and ankles barely moving. "What are you going to do with me?"

"My sweetness, we're going to play a little game."

Now multiple hands appear, drawing his focus to the present. They pull Amber off him. He breathes deeply and shuffles away from her. "Oh, thank God. She's lost it. She's crazy!"

Gaz laughs in the background. "She sure is."

Amber screams, high-pitched and hysterical. "He's Charlie's stalker. She's been paranoid for months. And he's *here*. Living with her this whole time."

"Charlie please. This isn't the time. Whatever's playing on your mind today, we can deal with it on the outside," Marty tells her.

Henry longs to pat Marty on the back.

"No! Don't you get it? He can't leave. He should burn down here—it's the least he deserves."

"Come on, you silly bitch. I can't be bothered with this." Jack touches Marty's elbow, capturing his attention. "Did you find a way out?"

"Don't you *dare* ignore me!" Amber screams, stamping her feet. "He's not who he says he is. He's been walking among you like an innocent old man. But he isn't. Please! He isn't."

Her eyes lose focus as realisation hits her hard. "Oh my god. It was YOU! You killed me."

Henry forces himself not to smile. It's amusing to watch Charlie trying to work everything out from Amber's perspective. He'd love to know what's going on in that damaged mind of hers.

All eyes turn to Henry. He merely shrugs, looking tired and dejected.

Victoria speaks up. "Okay, we hear you. But we'll deal with this when we're out, okay? He'll get what's coming to him, I promise." But the look she shoots Henry suggests otherwise.

"You don't believe me," she whimpers. "Victoria, Amber is dead because of him."

"Look, if we delay, we'll *all* be dead."

Amber pants, her shoulders heaving. "Fine," she agrees, a snarl on her lips. "Fine. But keep me away from him."

"Deal."

But no one does. No one cares. Because no one believes her.

Henry creeps up behind her and presses his lips closer to her ear.

"You know what I did after I killed your sister?" Henry whispers into Amber's ear. "I cut her into tiny pieces. Then I *ate* her. You were next, Charlie."

Chapter 40

<u>Marty</u>

What the hell is going on with Charlie? She's more broken than Marty realised, and he's eager to get her help before she harms someone.

Maybe she killed Susan after all. Maybe Victoria got it wrong. He wishes he had eyes in the back of his head. There's too much going on in here he isn't privy to.

"It was along here somewhere." His hands roam the wall, frantically searching for the switch he discovered just before the commotion with Henry.

It was flush against the wall, nearly invisible through the smoke. It's so small, so subtle.

His fingers brush over the tiny dent. "Got it!" he shouts, hooking his finger under the pull-switch.

"I wouldn't do that if I were you," Gaz tells him, though his voice sounds slightly panicked. Marty doesn't know what's going on with him, but he does know they haven't got time to figure it out now. The smoke is thickening by the second.

He tugs the switch. A hatch opens overhead, and a ladder slides down the wall. His heart leaps with joy. "I'll go first! Check it out."

He is up the ladder in seconds and pauses at the top. "Everyone up. You need to see this."

Gaz is next through the hatch. "What the fuck do you think you're doing? You can't be in here."

But Marty sees him now. For the first time, truly sees him. Despite the muscles and bravado, he's weak. Terrified.

"What is this place?"

The rest of the housemates appear through the hatch behind Gaz, looking around the room in wonder.

Computers line the walls, screens everywhere. Files sit on desktops. A cup of coffee rests next to a keyboard, still steaming. Whoever was in here must have fled moments ago.

Evangeline gives a mouse a wiggle, and a screen illuminates. She frowns and pushes the chair out of the way as she expertly searches through the computer files.

She frowns and double-clicks a file titled *housemates*. She finds hers. "They know everything about me, guys. Everything!" She keeps flicking through the documents. "They even have my dad's information—*I* don't have his information. He fucked off when I was eight."

"They have a section on Lily too," says Victoria. She's leaning over another desk, clicking frantically. She blanches when an image of a young girl covered in tubes appears on the screen. She spins around, fury reddening her cheeks. "Gaz, you need to talk. Right now!"

Gaz presses his tongue to the inside of his cheek and cocks his head. He glances at Jack, who is moving across the room with purpose. "They're your housemate files. Of course, we have information on you. You agreed to this before coming in here."

"But how did you get *this* information? I have never told anyone Lily's dad's name. You have his full name, date of birth, a picture of his fucking passport."

Gaz shrugs, the picture of nonchalance.

Jack erupts. Roaring, he grabs at something on a desk. A knife. Quick as a flash, Jack is behind him, holding him back with his damaged arm, the knife pressed against Gaz's throat. "Tell us everything, you dirty cunt."

"Now, now. There's no need for that kind of language. I…"

But Jack cuts Gaz off mid-sentence by pressing the knife harder against his bare skin, drawing blood. "Who are you and what is this place? Where is everyone?"

Gaz presses his lips together in a poor attempt at dignity. "I don't know where my team is. They must have scarpered when the fire started. Needless to say, they won't be getting paid."

"And?"

"And what?"

Jack growls, and for the first time, fear flits over Gaz's face.

"Answer the rest of it. Who are you?!"

Gaz raises his hands and smiles. "I have always been honest about who I am. I'm Gaz." He clears his throat. "A.K.A Gareth Walters. Porn star and son to one of the biggest porn producers in the world," he says with a flourish, as if he's proud of himself. "You know this."

Jack scrunches his nose. "Walters? As in Bart Walters? I met him once."

"Ha! Of course *you* would know him, dirty fuck."

"Who you calling a dirty fuck!?"

Marty steps forward, holding a hand out to Jack. "Wait!" he begs. "We're not done here."

Jack throws Marty a look of frustrated venom.

"What is this place?" Marty asks, desperate for answers.

Gaz looks Marty resolutely in the eye. "Tell him to let me go or I'm not saying a word."

Jack looks around the group, bewildered at having to make such a big decision. Eventually he shoves Gaz away, still holding the knife out to him, a reminder of who has the power here.

Gaz brushes himself off, standing up straight. "This place is my inheritance," he says with pride. "When father died, he left me a tidy sum, and spending it on booze and jewellery quickly got boring. I needed something to occupy myself."

"So you locked us up? To mess with us? Because you were bored?"

"Something like that. I have always been fascinated by human behaviour. I'm a people watcher."

"Seems a little extreme."

"No, Marty," Gaz barks, spittle flying through the air. "What's extreme is what I had to endure because of my damn father. He made me do despicable things for the money. When he did, it was only right that I got to spend it how *I* wanted. I decided to play a game."

"We're not toys, Gaz!" Victoria cries. "You had me beaten up! My daughter could be seriously ill for all I know, and I've been in here for your entertainment?!"

Gaz looks at her with genuine sorrow. "Yeah, sorry about that. They weren't supposed to beat you up so badly. I felt fucking awful. For a second I thought I'd lost control of it all." He laughs maniacally, looking around him.

"Rest assured, they were fired. Believe it or not, I quite like you, Victoria. You're spunky." He looks deep into her eyes, almost sorrowful. "As for your daughter—you made that choice when you walked through the doors. That's on you."

Victoria screams. She picks up a mug and smashes it into the closest screen. "Get rid of him," she tells Jack, who just stares at her with wide eyes. "Do it, Jack!"

Jack hesitates.

"Kill him," Evangeline mutters from her position away from the group. "Come on, Jack."

Jack steps forward, urging Gaz backward.

Henry laughs. Nerves maybe? All eyes turn to him. "Sorry, I didn't mean to laugh. Isn't this all a little ludicrous? We signed up to be on this show and now we're shocked about it?"

Sweat drips from Jack's brow, torn between what he wants to do and what his conscience is telling him. "Did you kill Susan?" he asks.

Gaz nods. "It was funny," he says with disgusting indifference. "The viewers loved it."

"What viewers? Who would watch this shit?"

"Don't underestimate the sick bastards who frequent the dark web. I bet you're friends with most of them, Jack. And you, Henry. How do you think I found you? Now you're an interesting guy."

Henry's lips pucker. His cheeks turn pink.

"So this was never aired on mainstream T.V?" Evangeline asks.

Gaz laughs. "Of course not! You think any T.V channel has the balls to air this? No, this is my baby, and only I have the courage to show what human nature is really like. My subscribers pay a lot of money to watch you."

"How much money are our lives worth to you?" Marty asks him.

"Oh, a *lot*, trust me. But this isn't just about the money—I've got more than I can spend already. This was more about showing people what entertainment really is: exploitation. My father put me in front of cameras when I was *fifteen*. Made me perform sick acts for other people's pleasure.

"The industry didn't care—just as long as people were watching, paying, getting off on it. Sound familiar? Show business isn't about giving people a chance for success. It's just one thing; taking desperate people and making fools of them for the audience's amusement. You all signed up thinking you were different, special. But you're just the latest victims in a system that's been abusing people for decades."

The housemates don't utter a sound, stunned into silence.

"The only difference is I was honest about what this really was—torture for entertainment. When this footage goes public, and it will, people will finally see what they've been consuming all along. Every reality show in the world will be questioned. Every competition will be scrutinised. I'm going to burn down the entire industry that made me, using you as the match."

Marty wants to throw up. His heart pounds hard in his chest, smashing against his ribs. "Back away from him, Jack."

Jack's mouth falls open, but he only hesitates for a second before walking away from Gaz, his singed bandage pulled close to his chest. He looks weak. Broken. No longer the big man in the room, he's shrunk down and timid.

"What are you doing, Marty?!" asks Evangeline.

"We're not murderers," replies Marty. "We won't stoop to his level. I'm assuming it was you who killed Gloria and Susan?"

Gaz shrugs. "Had to. Viewers' request. Besides Susan, my little helping hand, was causing too much trouble. So, it just made sense to kill her off early. She was a complication."

He coughs, clearing his lungs of smoke. "Oh, and that dog, Jessie? You don't have to worry about her."

"She's dead too?" Evangeline groans.

"What kind of monster do you think I am? She was sedated and released. She's fine."

Marty breathes deeply, unsure of their next move. "Evangeline, pass me that cord. I'll tie him up."

Evangeline leans over the desk and pulls a wire towards her.

"Ah, Evangeline," murmurs Gaz, his face lit with utmost glee. He looks crazed in the flickering light. "My viewers *loved* watching you, young lady. That peachy arse waving around in the air, begging that pig to fuck you."

The scream that escapes Evangeline's lungs is primal as she leaps forward, her shoulder barging into Gaz with such force he goes flying backwards.

The last thing they see of Gaz is his look of terror as he plummets through the hole, his limbs flailing, grasping at air.

Victoria slams the hatch down and slides across the bolts, sealing Gaz's fate.

Chapter 41

DAILY MAIL ONLINE

EXCLUSIVE: 'The Landlord' Reality Show EXPOSED as Sick Dark Web Entertainment - Millionaire Orchestrator 'Dies' in Fire as Police Launch Murder Investigation

By Patrice Mitchell, Entertainment Reporter

A fake reality show that lured contestants with promises of winnings and legitimate television careers has been exposed as a multi-million pound dark web entertainment scheme that sold footage of psychological and physical torture to wealthy subscribers around the globe.

Millionaire heir to Bartholemew Walters' porn production fortune, Gareth Walters, who posed as contestant 'Gaz' inside the house, has been identified as the mastermind behind the elaborate operation that resulted in at least two confirmed deaths.

DARK WEB HORROR EXPOSED

Police sources reveal that Walters, 30, charged premium subscribers to watch live footage of contestants being subjected to escalating psychological torture, physical harm, and staged 'eliminations.'

"This wasn't reality TV - it was a snuff film in the making," said Detective Chief Inspector Michael Harrison. "Walters was selling human suffering to the highest bidders on the dark web. The more extreme the content, the higher the price."

The operation generated an estimated £15 million from over 300 international subscribers, including several high-profile figures whose identities are being protected pending investigation.

CONTESTANTS USED AS HUMAN ENTERTAINMENT

What participants believed was a legitimate reality competition with major television potential was actually an elaborate death game. Walters used sophisticated psychological manipulation, staged events, and genuine violence to create increasingly disturbing content for his paying audience.

Using a fake production company called "Apex Entertainment Productions," Walters created convincing casting processes, professional-looking contracts, and rented legitimate office spaces to maintain the illusion of a genuine television production.

"He specifically targeted people with financial desperation, addiction issues, or personal trauma," DI Harrison explained. "These people thought they were chasing legitimate opportunities that could change their lives. Instead, they became victims in Walters' sick game."

POLICE CORRUPTION UNCOVERED

The investigation has also uncovered evidence of police corruption, with Walters allegedly paying substantial bribes to senior officers to prevent early intervention. Sources within the Metropolitan Police confirm that when families first reported concerns about their missing relatives three weeks ago, investigations were mysteriously called off within 48 hours.

"Walters had contacts in high places," revealed a whistleblower officer who cannot be named. "Phone calls were made, files were buried, and concerned families were told their loved ones were simply 'unavailable for contact due to filming commitments.' We now know at least three senior officers received payments totalling over £500,000 to look the other way or falsify police reports."

The Independent Office for Police Conduct has launched a separate investigation into the corruption allegations, with several high-ranking officers suspended pending inquiry.

VICTIMS AND SURVIVORS

Nurse Victoria Steeple, who entered believing she could win money for her daughter's medical treatment, was among six survivors rescued from the compound in the heart of Essex countryside. "They fed her false information about her child's condition to maximise her emotional distress," revealed a source close to the investigation.

The confirmed murder victims are pensioner Gloria Whitworth, 72, and part-time actress Susan Chambers, 41, who was stabbed to death in front of cameras for subscribers' entertainment. Gloria's body is yet to be recovered, and police are still searching the surrounding woodland.

Susan is believed to have been unknowingly recruited by Walters in a bid to help keep his identity secret whilst he played the part of an innocent housemate. A job opportunity that resulted in the loss of her life.

THE LANDLORD'S TRUE IDENTITY

Walters had been operating dark web entertainment sites since 2019. Using his wealth and connections, he created an elaborate fake production infrastructure that fooled even experienced entertainment industry professionals.

"The level of deception was extraordinary," said fraud investigator DS Caroline Walsh. "Walters spent months creating a completely believable production company. Even industry insiders would have been fooled."

DEATH OR DISAPPEARANCE?

Walters allegedly perished when contestant Victoria Steeple set fire to the facility in a desperate escape attempt. However, police sources suggest his death may have been staged.

"We have not recovered a body," confirmed DI Harrison. "Given Walters' resources and planning, we cannot rule out that his 'death' was another manipulation designed to help him escape justice."

SURVIVORS SPEAK OUT

Musician Marty Fletcher, who was deliberately supplied with cocaine to trigger his drug addictions, told police: "He played us all. Every conversation, every friendship—it was all part of his sick show. He knew exactly how to push each of us to breaking point."

Social media influencer Evangeline Cox, 19, revealed she was drugged before being filmed in compromising situations with another contestant—footage that was sold as premium content to subscribers.

INTERNATIONAL INVESTIGATION

Interpol has issued a Red Notice for Walters, who holds multiple passports and has properties in Dubai, Switzerland, and the Cayman Islands. His dark web operation had subscribers across Europe, Asia, and North America.

"This is human trafficking for entertainment," said Interpol spokesperson Maria Santos. "We're working with authorities worldwide to identify and prosecute everyone involved in this network."

The investigation has uncovered similar operations in development, suggesting Walters was planning to expand his human entertainment empire globally.

WHAT HAPPENS NEXT

The survivors are receiving intensive psychological support as they come to terms with their ordeal. Legal experts suggest they could be entitled to substantial compensation from Walters' frozen assets, currently valued at over £400 million.

Several high-profile figures have been questioned about their alleged subscription to Walters' content, though no charges have yet been filed against viewers.

"Gareth Walters turned human suffering into a commodity," said victims' rights advocate Kathy Chen. "Whether he's dead or in hiding, justice demands that everyone who paid to watch this horror be held accountable."

The case has prompted calls for stricter regulation of cryptocurrency transactions and enhanced monitoring of dark web activities.

INDUSTRY RESPONSE

The scandal has sent shockwaves through the legitimate entertainment industry, with casting directors and production companies reviewing their security protocols.

"This case shows how sophisticated fraudsters can exploit our industry's trust-based relationships," said industry body spokesperson Amanda Clarke. "We're implementing new verification processes to prevent similar deceptions."

More coverage: How the dark web trade in human misery operates - Pages 4-6 Comment: The sickening reality behind reality TV - Page 15 Investigation continues...

Chapter 42

ONE YEAR LATER

Victoria

The coffin is tiny, yet Victoria's grief knows no bounds.

She watches as they lower her little girl into the ground, not a hint of emotion on her face. Her heart is heavy, but her relief is light.

Lily's condition worsened significantly over the year. Her illness took the ability to use her legs, but no one predicted it would spread up her spine and compromise her lungs.

She gave a good fight. She was strong to the very end, and Victoria is so proud of her. She sang Disney songs and hung onto Victoria's neck. And she breathed in her mother's love with her last breath.

Lily was in pain. But she was brave.

Now Victoria owes her the same. She swallows the cry building in her throat and clutches her mum's hand.

Her mum sobs into a handkerchief, not listening to a word the vicar is saying. Though it doesn't matter what he says—he'll never capture the beauty that shrouded her little girl. Her warmth. Her cheeky humour. The glint in her eye when she thought she'd conned you out of two gummy bears when you'd promised her one.

She could have two. She could have had as many as she liked. Lily deserved the world.

The service ends, and they all head back to Victoria's mum's house. She's decorated it with balloons and Peppa Pig bunting. A funeral fit for a sweet little girl. If only she could be here to see it.

She sees Dr Chattergee talking to a woman Victoria thinks might be a long-lost relative. Dr Chattergee has been incredible, fighting for Lily's life until her very last breath. His involvement in Victoria's stay in The House was, of course, non-existent. A fabrication made to mess with her head.

All of it lies, all of it pointless, a waste of time when time was so damn precious.

Her grief feels like a living thing inside Victoria's body. She wants to claw it out. Scream until the pain dampens.

She can't stay here. She runs upstairs and slips into her mum's bedroom—a brief reprieve from the looks of pity and words of condolence that do nothing to ease her agony.

She picks up a pillow and bites down on the soft fabric. The release lessens her stress, even if her pain is still immense. Its tentacles have released their grip, just a little. Just enough to breathe.

"Sorry, your mum said I could come up."

Victoria spins around to find Evangeline standing in the doorway, looking sheepish. "Vic, I'm so sorry for your loss."

Victoria can only nod, tears swimming in her eyes. Seeing Evangeline standing here, the picture of health, is such a relief. She reaches out a shaking hand and pulls her friend in for a hug.

Evangeline squeezes so tight Victoria is worried she'll pass out. But the embrace feeds her with warmth, and she pulls Evangeline in even tighter. Besides, passing out won't be so bad. It'll make the day pass more quickly. Lily used to call sleep a time-machine.

"I can't imagine what you're going through," Evangeline whispers in her ear.

Victoria pulls away. "We've all been through a lot."

"Yes, but all with different outcomes. Yours is truly the worst. I wish I could make all this go away."

A whimper sounds from outside the door. "Sorry," Evangeline mutters before disappearing into the hallway. She comes back with a baby seat hooked over her arm. "I was praying she'd stay asleep. They never sleep when you want them to, eh?"

Evangeline's little girl is gorgeous, just like her mummy. Victoria reaches out and touches her chubby cheek. Blue eyes sparkle back at her. "Oh, Evangeline, she's *beautiful*."

"She's a handful," Evangeline laughs. She sounds bone tired—the kind of tired only a solo-mother can understand. "Worth every second though."

"Of course. No matter what they put you through, they're worth every single bit of it."

Evangeline locks eyes with Victoria as she pulls her little girl out of her seat and cradles her in her arms. "You mind?" she asks.

"Go ahead."

Evangeline unclips her bra and feeds a now-bawling baby.

"What's her name?"

"Briana. It means 'strong.'"

Victoria smiles. "Like her mummy."

Evangeline smiles but looks sadly down at her little girl, who is now suckling enthusiastically. "Victoria, you can't tell him."

Briana's father.

Jack.

Since they broke out of The House, Jack has had a tough time. He soon declared bankruptcy, and the world watched as the bank took his remaining restaurants, his home, everything.

The doctors even took his hand.

Last she heard, Jack was living in Dorset, a broken man. Humbled.

Victoria can understand why Evangeline wants to keep Briana a secret. At least for now. A child's upbringing is a delicate thing, and Jack is a cruel man with a lot of troubles—hardly a good time to bring them together. Jack needs to heal first.

Plus, Evangeline's mental state hangs on by a mere thread. If she were to introduce Jack's pain into her own, she wouldn't be able to cope.

And now she has to. Coping isn't optional when you have a little one to care for.

"Your secret is safe with me." And to be honest, Victoria doesn't have the strength to get involved.

Briana pulls away from Evangeline's breast and looks at her mummy with pure devotion.

Victoria's heart might just burst.

"You heard from Charlie?" Evangeline asks.

"She emailed a couple of weeks ago. She's in L.A., Checked into some sort of mental healing facility."

"L.A! Fancy!"

"I know. I think she could only get help if she escaped the paparazzi here. She needed anonymity. Poor girl is so broken."

Evangeline laughs gently. "To put it mildly."

They look at each other, their shared pain palpable. They'll never forget The House and the horrors it scarred them with.

It has since been revealed that hundreds of thousands of pounds were sent to Gaz's production company, buried amongst umbrella companies and offshore accounts. Victoria doesn't understand the logistics of it all, but she does know that the only way it was supposed to end was when they'd all been killed. Marty was next on the hit list, according to exposed production plans.

The housemates' vote had sealed Gloria's fate. Footage has since leaked of Gloria being dragged out when the lights went out. Someone sneaked through the Confessions Room door and placed a handkerchief over her mouth. She slipped into a drug-infused unconsciousness, scraping her head on the corner of the coffee table as she went before being dragged out by the intruder. The altercation took seconds.

Her body was discovered buried in a shallow grave about a mile away from the house.

Then Susan. There was no record of Susan's death in the production plans. It wasn't premeditated, just a spur-of-the-moment decision made by Gaz when everything started spiralling out of control.

Victoria makes a mental note to lay a flower at both women's graves.

The press made them a spectacle for a short while. Until they got bored and the latest scandal involving a footballer and a hooker turned their heads.

Fickle. That's what they are. The public is happy to consume the surface level of the stories they read, feeding their desire for gossip. But the depth of the stories doesn't matter; attention spans are too short. Ironically, that was the point Gaz wanted to prove.

"Come on. Let's get a Peppa Pig cupcake." She takes Evangeline's arm and leads her friend downstairs.

<u>Marty</u>

The pill rolls across Marty's palm, small and white as bone. He studies it with curiosity. It never ceases to amaze him that something so small can have such a tremendous impact on the world.

He hands the pill to Kyle. "You need to come back same time tomorrow, okay? Miss this appointment, and you'll breach your bail conditions. We both know what'll happen then?"

The young lad nods like a scolded child.

Marty's expression softens. "Kyle, I've been where you are, alright? You're here to make a change that'll get you back on track. You've got your whole life ahead of you. Don't fuck it up."

The nineteen-year-old looks into his eyes, regret and gratitude all over his face. "Thanks, man."

Despite this boy's crimes, Marty cannot judge him. He cannot judge anyone who walks through that door. Kyle reminds Marty of Jamie, the boy whose life was taken by the drugs Marty gave him. It's Jamie he is here for. A hope that he can make up for his past mistakes. Even just a little bit.

The Green Light Foundation was set up thirteen years ago—an organisation that aims to help criminals get clean before being sentenced for crimes committed. Kyle was caught with his hand in the till and panicked when the cashier raised the alarm. Huge mistakes were made. And now he's paying the price.

Marty doesn't know if Kyle will face a prison sentence, but he *does* know that prison will be a lot easier if you're already sober. He also knows that if Kyle isn't helped now, he'll likely end up dead before his twentieth birthday.

"Right, I'll get my supervisor to sign this off and you can get out of here." Marty stands and presses his hand to Kyle's shoulder.

Kyle touches his own hand on top. "Thank you," he mumbles. "For helping me."

"No worries. It's what I'm here for."

Marty leaves the room with his heart in his mouth. Leaving The House was both the best and the hardest thing he's ever done.

He still has nightmares that feature Gaz's screams as he fell through the hatch. He can still hear the weight of the metal lid as it crashed down, sealing away any chance of Gaz's escape.

The guilt eats at him, his mind taking the brunt of his anguish. Though deep down in his heart, Marty knows their actions, though harsh, were right. A man like that shouldn't be allowed to wander the Earth. Body or no body, Gaz couldn't have survived that. There's no chance in hell he's still out there. Right?

Gaz had orchestrated the entire thing for entertainment. Their lives meant nothing more than pawns to be moved across the screen. Well, if lives mean so little, what does it matter if Gaz lost his own?

His supervisor signs off Kyle's forms, and Marty returns to say goodbye to Kyle. He wishes him luck for his court case and offers a prayer for his rehabilitation to be as bump-free as possible.

Because Marty knows all too well how painful setbacks can impact sobriety.

Marty had two options when he left the house: crash or soar.

He chose to soar.

The House was evil. Gareth vile. But all that taught him he has a strength in him to walk through fire to save people.

So why couldn't he save himself?

He took that thought and ran with it.

And every day now he helps people who need saving too. He won't let drugs cause more hurt, destroy more lives. He longs to give back, and he'll spend the rest of his life helping people who are in the same boat he was sinking in not that long ago.

Marty will never forgive himself for causing the death of his dealer's son. The guilt will forever remain etched on his heart. But knowing Carl had provided him the drugs in the first place left a bitter taste in his mouth.

He knew what he had to do, and helping the police with their investigations of drug dealing in Liverpool was just the start of the rehabilitation of his conscience.

Only when Carl was arrested and charged could Marty afford to walk just a little straighter.

He's waiting for his bus home when his pocket vibrates. "Hello?" he says into the phone, wrapping his free arm around his chest to fight off the cold.

"Marty, hi."

"Who is this?"

"Jack."

"Holy shit, Jack! How you doing, mate?"

"Ah, you know, as well as you can be with one arm and mental scars so deep there's little left to fight for."

"Yeah, well." Marty hates speaking to Jack—a reminder of the damage The House caused. Marty decided to fight through the negatives and emerge stronger than ever before, but Jack took a different route. One that has led him to believe life has nothing to give. "So, what's up, Jack?"

"Oh, you know, just thinking things over."

"You been drinking?"

"No, not at all. Just having one of those days."

"Want to talk it through?"

"Not really." His tone suggests otherwise.

Marty's bus pulls up at the kerb and he gets on. Takes a seat at the back. "What you up to these days?"

"Same as always—fishing, scaring the kids with my hook hand."

Marty laughs at the imagery. "You don't have a hook hand!?"

"Nah, maybe I should. Might be cooler than being stumpy."

Awkward silence descends over them. Marty watches as workers hurry, hoping to reach home before the heavens open.

"Look, sorry, I don't know why I called you," Jack admits. "I think I just needed to talk to someone who was there, you know?"

"I know. Look, Jack, I'm here whenever you need to talk, okay? Don't go through this alone. And if you ever want to hang out, you know where I am."

Jack swallows loudly. Is he crying? "Thanks, man, I needed to hear that." He pauses. "And Marty?"

"Yeah?"

"I'm sorry. I was such a prick to you in that house. I don't know why. I had no right to judge you."

"Everyone judges, Jack. Even the most virtuous have their prejudices. At least you were upfront about yours."

"I was a dickhead."

"Yeah, you were."

They laugh, and Jack makes his excuses before hanging up. Marty sighs and presses his forehead to the cold glass. Will all of this ever end? Can wounds so deep ever scab over? It feels like with every move they make, the more the cuts tear wider.

"How is Jack doing?" The man sitting in front of Marty asks.

Marty knows that cool, calculated voice. His blood runs cold. "Henry?"

Henry turns around, his face tucked into his hood. He grins at Marty.

"What are you doing here?"

Henry shrugs. "Curious, I suppose. I wanted to see how you're getting on since the whole debacle in that house."

Marty leans forward so his face is inches away from Henry's. "I know who you are, *what* you are. How dare you have the audacity to come near me?"

After their escape from the house, Henry vanished. He's never given an interview. Never provided his side of the story.

Marty took it upon himself to investigate Henry when he finally had some breathing space after The House. Seven girls have gone missing in the ten years running up to the show. All university students. All investigated and eventually forgotten about. All vanished within fifty miles of Henry's hometown in the Midlands.

Could Henry have taken these girls? Marty will never know for sure.

But his research taught him that Amber truly existed. And he does know she's missed dearly by her damaged sister.

"You admit it then—you took those girls?"

Henry smiles pleasantly. "I don't know what you're talking about."

"If you're innocent, you wouldn't be running."

Henry's smile grows wider, his teeth glinting in the diminishing sunlight. "Who says I'm running?"

"Where have you been then?"

"I moved." Henry shrugs. "I needed a break from the carnival after the news came out about the house."

"You didn't kill Amber?"

Henry reaches out and presses the button for the bell. "This is my stop." He stands.

"Did you?!"

Henry reaches into his pocket and pulls out a small plastic bag. He takes out a slice of ham and slides it into his mouth. "I guess you'll never know for sure."

Marty watches Henry exit the bus, too shocked to move. The bus inches to the right to rejoin the traffic. The cars keep filing past, refusing to let the bus out, much to the bus driver's chagrin.

Henry crosses the road, head down, and disappears down an alleyway tucked between two buildings. He vanished into the darkness of the tunnel.

Something else catches his eye then. A smaller figure, flitting between the crowds, hands firmly planted in deep coat pockets. They're making a beeline for the same alleyway.

As if drawn by intuition, the mystery figure glanced up, catching Marty's eye.

Charlie.

Her eyes glint at him. She smiles and winks before disappearing into the alleyway, sliding a chef's knife out of her pocket as she goes.

Like what you read?

Come and visit me at **clsutton.com** for special edition news, discounts, mailing list fun, and bundles.

Alternatively, drop me an email at hello@clsutton.com and I will endeavour to reply to you personally.

More books by C.L. Sutton

<u>Killing For Innocence</u>

Read for <u>FREE</u> at https://BookHip.com/ZRJFVTW

How far would you go to protect the innocent? Could you kill?

Michelle's life is on the brink of collapse, and she has never truly got over the abuse she experienced at the hands of her parents. Now, living in her friend's spare bedroom and relying on alcohol for comfort, she's not sure she'll ever end the spiral of self-destruction.

When successful and glamorous Pam recruits Michelle to work at her charity helping victims of child abuse, Michelle finally finds her calling.

But when Pam's requests take a dark turn, an inner darkness awakens in Michelle, throwing her into a world of secrets, pain, and murder. A life more exciting than Michelle dare admit.

It's only when seven-year-old Teddy, a child close to her heart, goes missing, does Michelle realise her quest is so much bigger than she imagined. And so much more brutal.

Killing for Innocence is a spectacular standalone psychological thriller by C.L Sutton that features dark themes, raw emotions, and superb plot twists.

NANA

I finally have it all - a devoted husband, a picture-perfect home, and the promise of a baby. But all good things must come to an end...

As I settle into my new life, the facade of normalcy begins to crumble. My once-loving husband is growing colder by the day, I can tell the neighbours are keeping secrets. Yet, it's Nana, the eccentric neighbour with a disturbing history and a penchant for violence, who casts the longest shadow over my existence.

Somehow, I've managed to find myself thrust into a harrowing descent of deceit, betrayal, and this ominous feeling of looming danger. I feel myself being swallowed whole by this relentless chaos consuming me, and I wonder if I can make it out ... or if escape will become increasingly elusive.

<u>The Therapist</u>

I've spent years helping others face their demons. Now mine are coming to collect.

As a therapist specialising in helping victims of domestic abuse, I've spent my career helping people confront their traumas. But now, my own are threatening to destroy everything I've built.

When Millie walks into my office, I'm captivated. She's vulnerable, beautiful, and in desperate need of saving. I know I can save her. But as our relationship deepens, the line between therapist and obsession blurs, leaving me exposed.

My perfect life starts to crumble. My wife grows suspicious, my daughter withdraws, and my domineering father's secrets threaten to tear our family apart. Then there's the bodies...

Am I losing my mind? I'm forced to question everything I thought I knew about myself and those closest to me.
To save my family and my sanity, I'll have to face my own darkness. But how can I trust my own mind when it might be my worst enemy?

Nothing is as it seems in this twisted psychological thriller that will keep you guessing until the last page.

Liar

Maisie has always craved attention. But when a desperate lie spirals out of control, she learns too late that crying wolf has deadly consequences.

After exposing a cheating scandal that wasn't hers to reveal, Maisie's relationship with her boyfriend, Caleb, is in ruins. Determined to win him back, she tells a small lie. A harmless one. And when it works, she tells another. But soon, the lies stack too high, and keeping her story straight becomes a dangerous game.

Because someone is watching. Someone who knows what she's done. And when the threats Maisie invented start happening for real, no one believes her. Not Caleb. Not her family. Not even her best friend.

Now, with nowhere to turn and the walls closing in, Maisie must uncover the truth before it's too late. But the deeper she digs, the more she begins to wonder... Was she ever in control at all?

Printed in Dunstable, United Kingdom